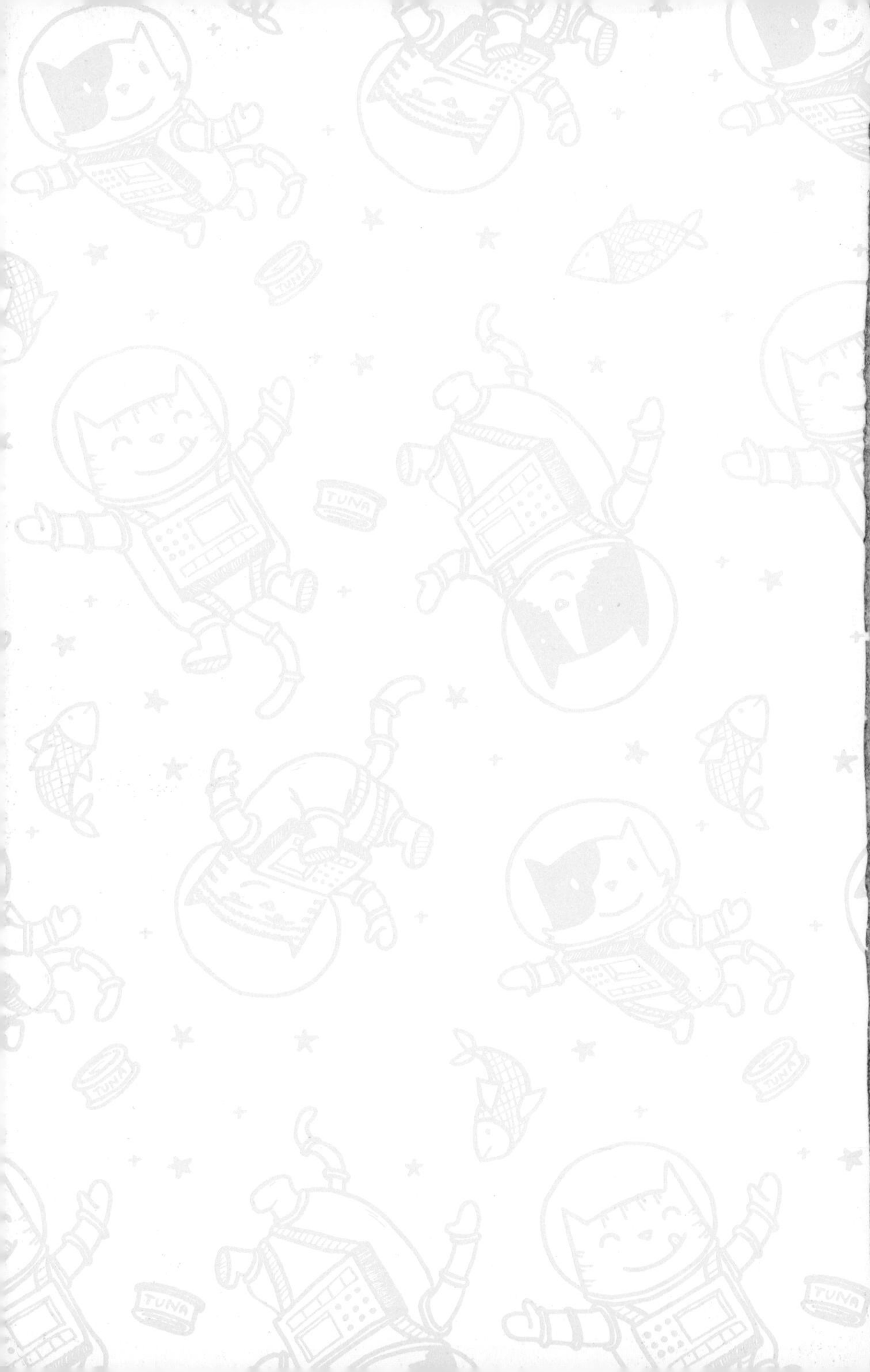
TUNA
TUNA
TUNA
TUNA
TUNA

CatStronauts

MISSION MOON

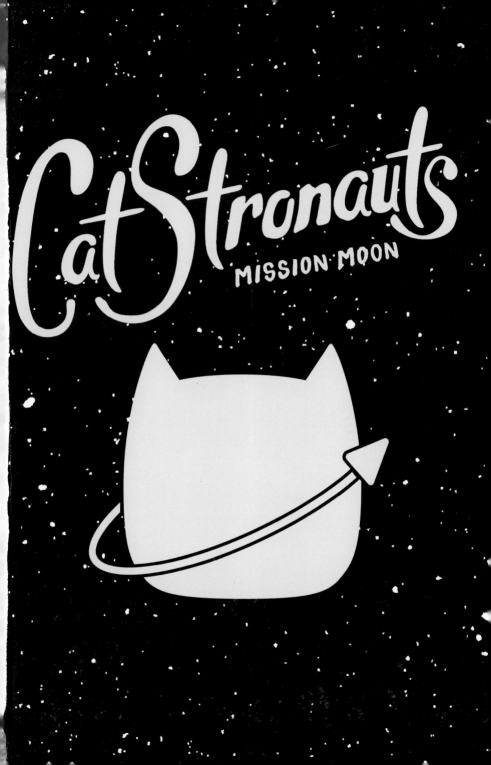

CatStronauts

MISSION MOON

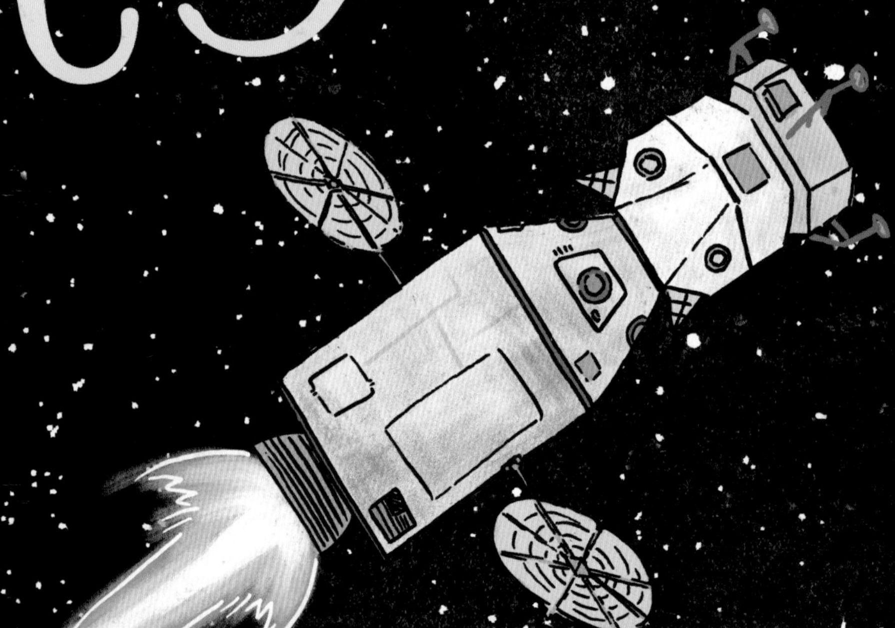

BY DREW BROCKINGTON

LB

Little, Brown and Company
New York Boston

Little, Brown and Company

Hachette Book Group
1290 Avenue of the Americas, New York, NY 10104
Visit us at lb-kids.com

Little, Brown and Company is a division of Hachette Book Group, Inc.
The Little, Brown name and logo are trademarks of Hachette Book Group, Inc.

The publisher is not responsible for websites (or their content) that are not owned by the publisher.

First Edition: April 2017

Library of Congress Cataloging-in-Publication Data
Names: Brockington, Drew.
Title: Cat-stronauts : Mission Moon / by Drew Brockington.
Description: First edition. | New York ; Boston : Little, Brown and Company, 2017. |
Summary: Alerted to a global energy crisis, the President consults with the World's Best Scientist, who suggests sending a special group of astronauts to turn the Moon into a solar power plant.
Identifiers: LCCN 2015039108| ISBN 9780316307475 (hardcover) | ISBN 9780316307451 (trade pbk.) | ISBN 9780316307468 (ebook)
Subjects: LCSH: Graphic novels. | CYAC: Graphic novels. | Astronauts—Fiction. | Space Flight to the moon—Fiction. | Presidents—Fiction. | Cats—Fiction.
Classification: LCC PZ7.7.B76 Cat 2017 | DDC 741.5/973—dc23
LC record available at http://lccn.loc.gov/2015039108

10 9 8 7 6 5 4 3 2 1

1010

Printed in China

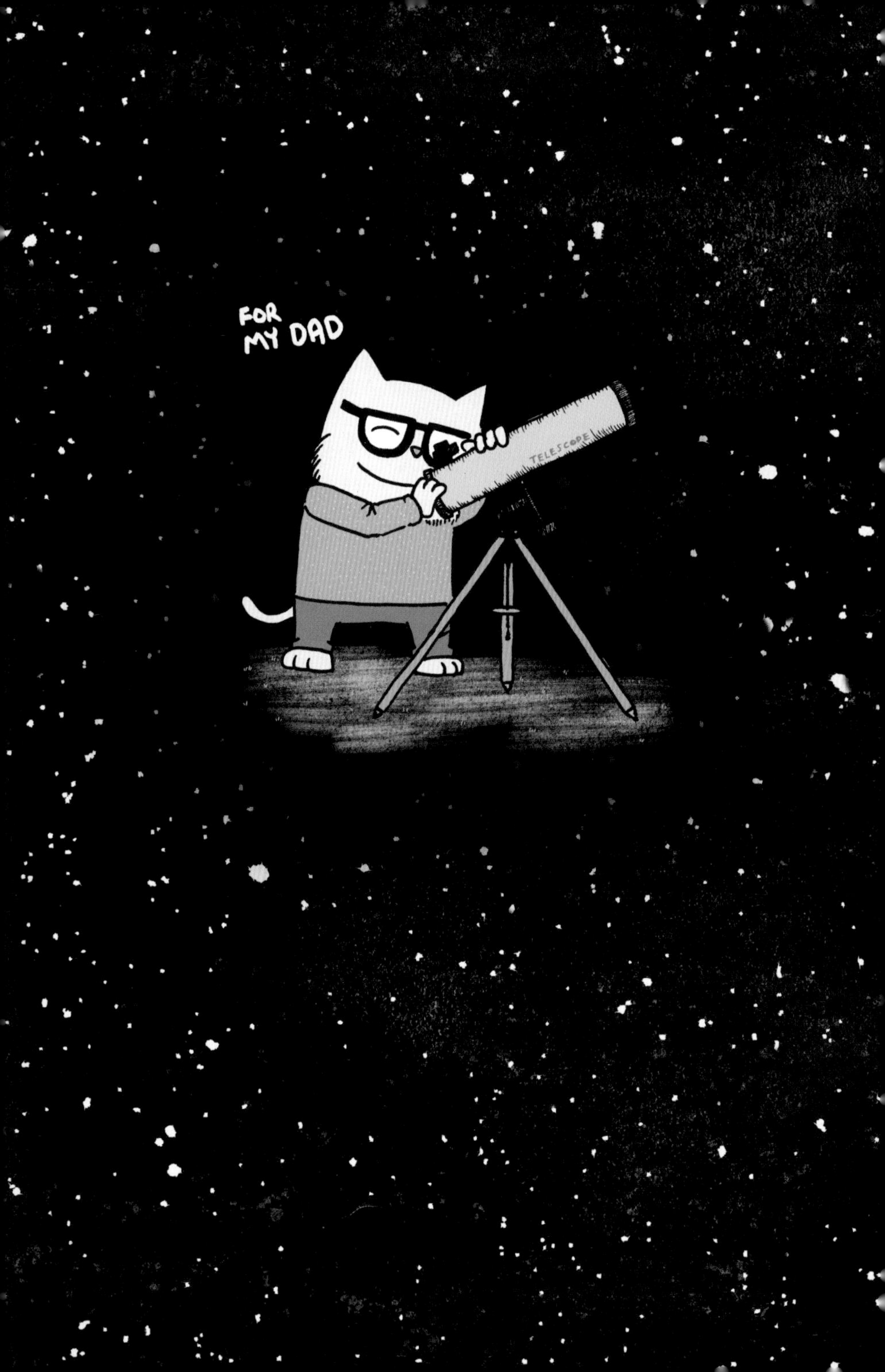
FOR
MY DAD
TELESCOPE

CatStronauts

MISSION MOON

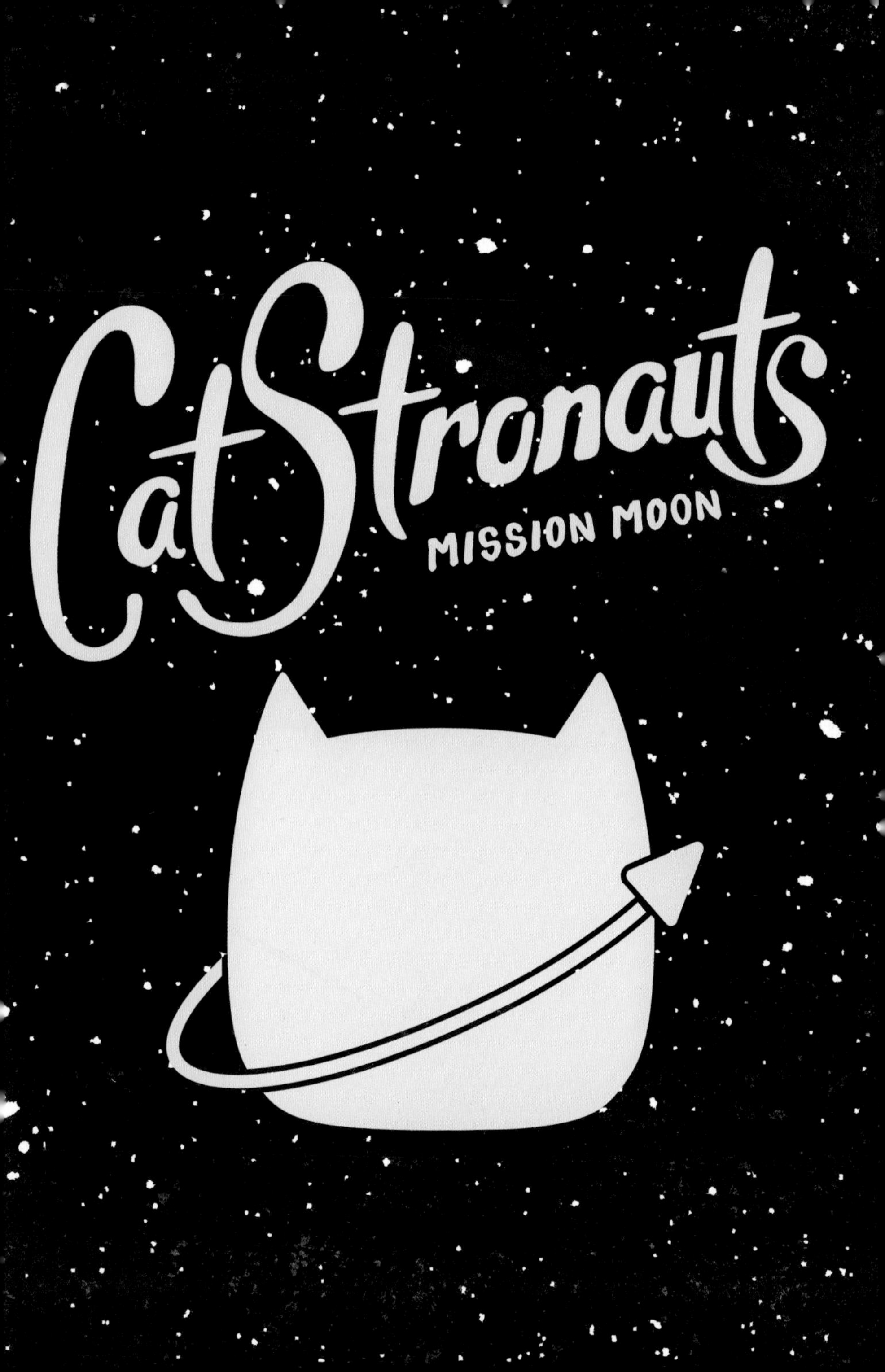

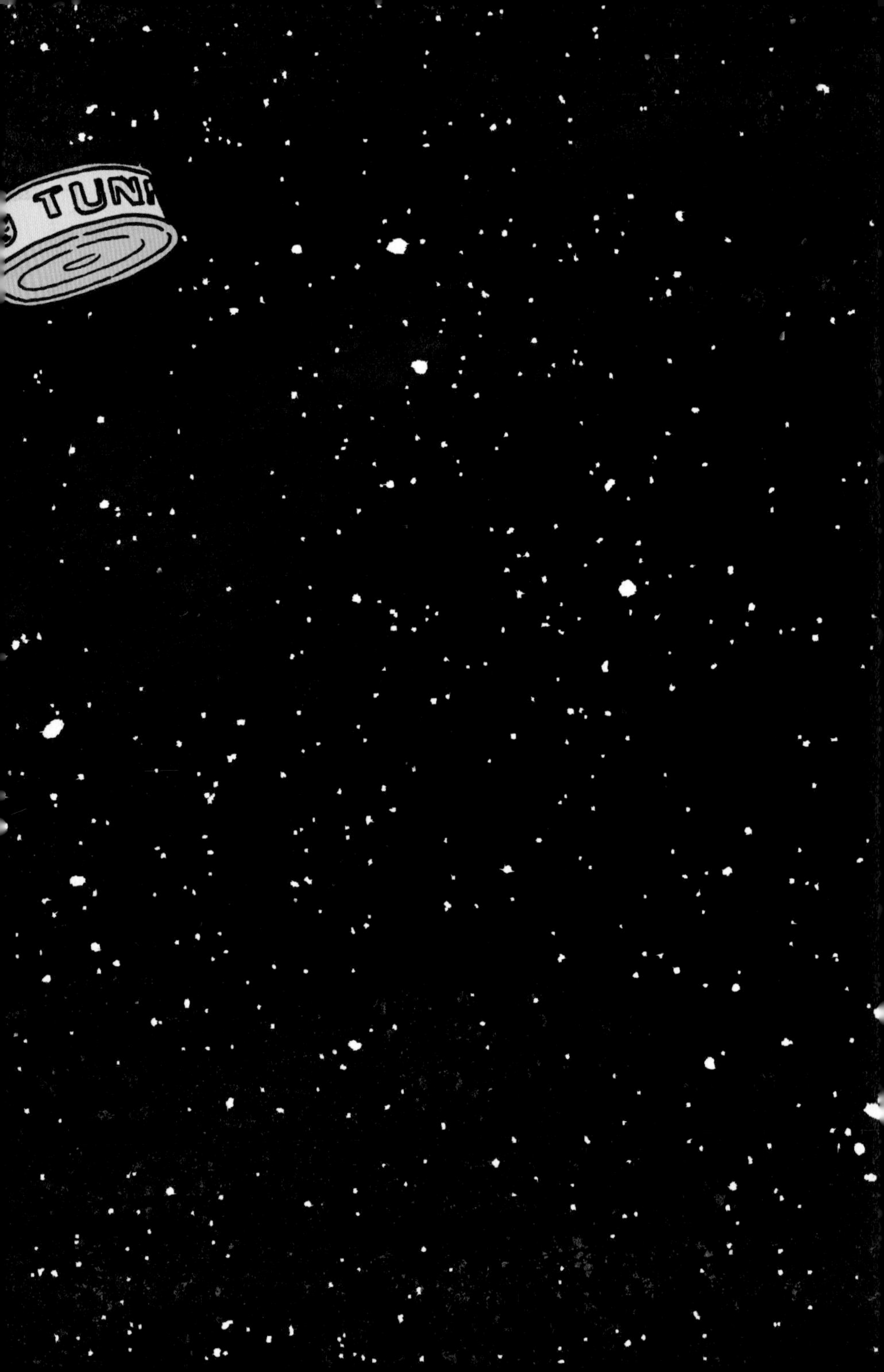

CHAPTER 1

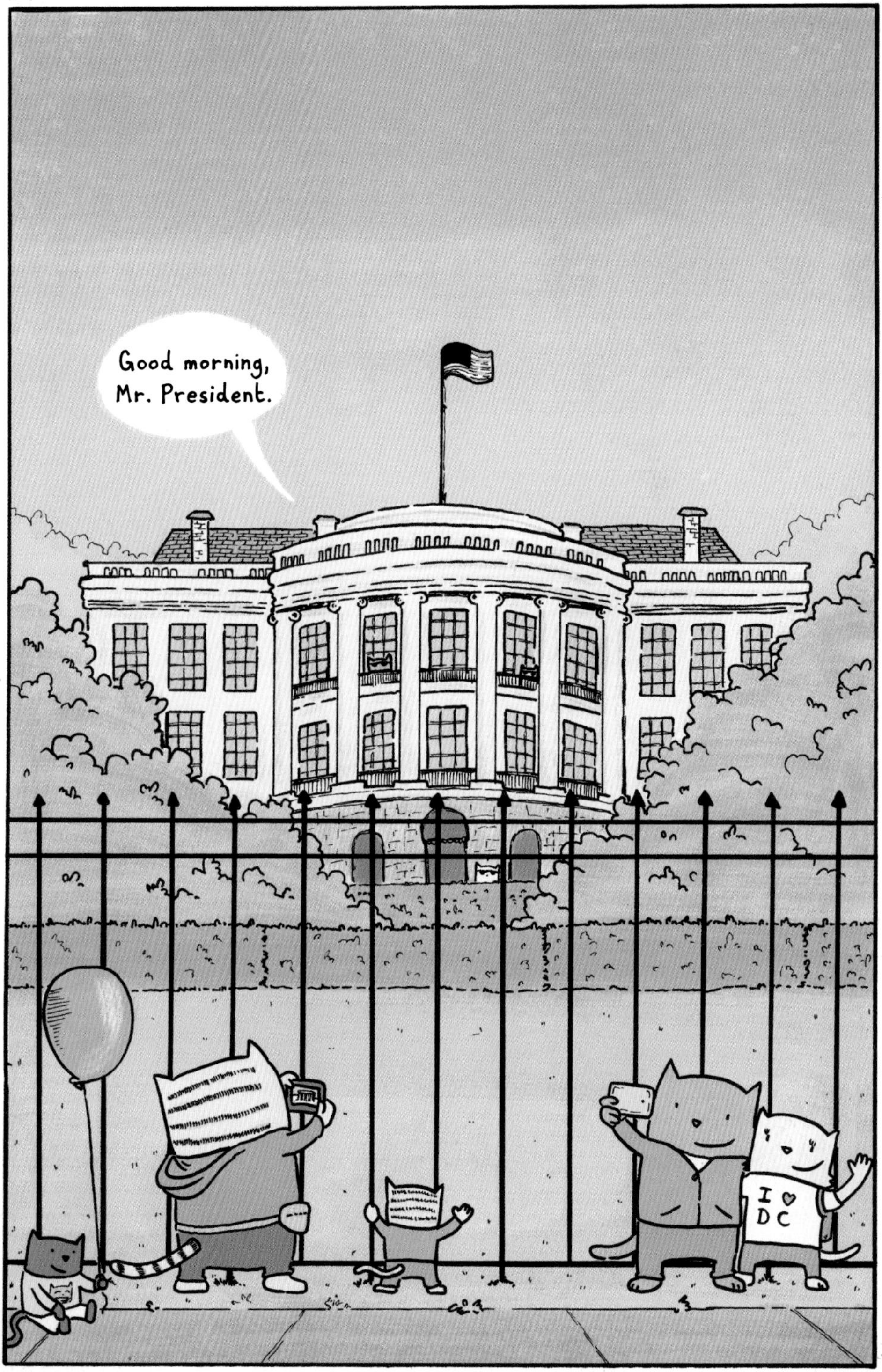
Good morning, Mr. President.
I ♥ DC

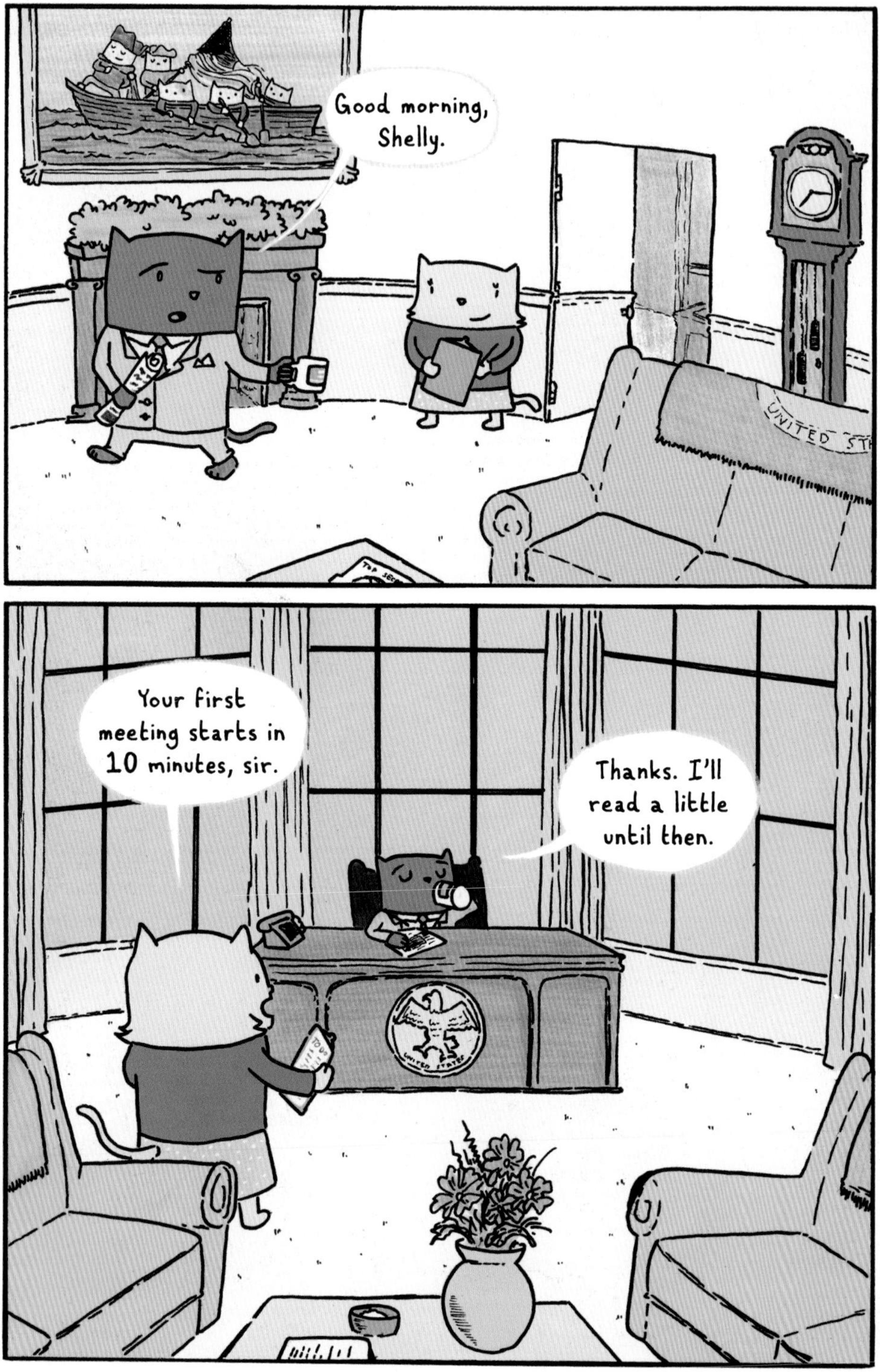
Good morning, Shelly.
UNITED ST
TOP SECRET
Your first meeting starts in 10 minutes, sir.
Thanks. I'll read a little until then.

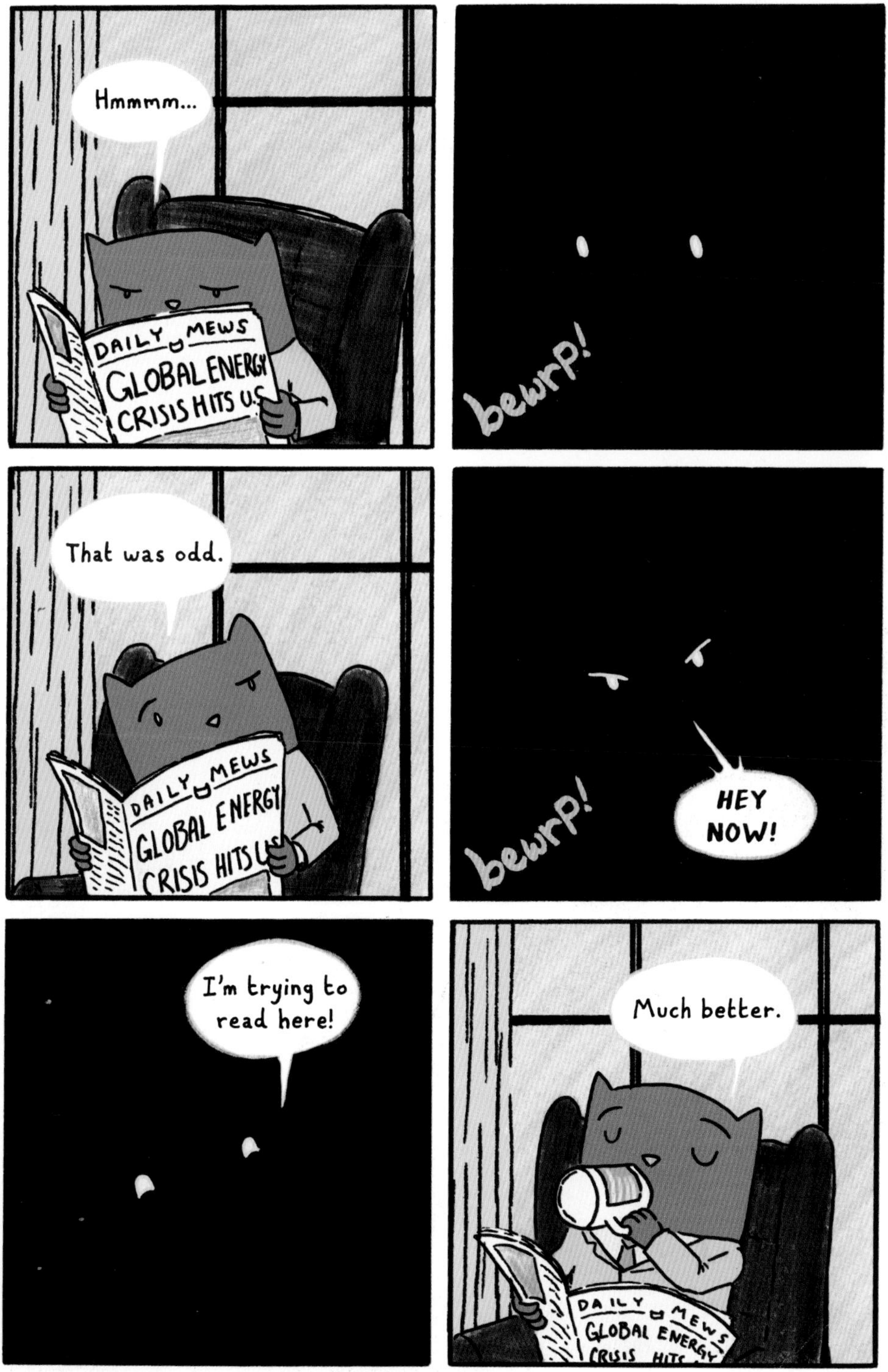
Hmmmm...
DAILY MEWS
GLOBAL ENERGY CRISIS HITS U.S.
bewrp!
That was odd.
DAILY MEWS
GLOBAL ENERGY CRISIS HITS U.S.
bewrp!
HEY NOW!
I'm trying to read here!
Much better.
DAILY MEWS
GLOBAL ENERGY

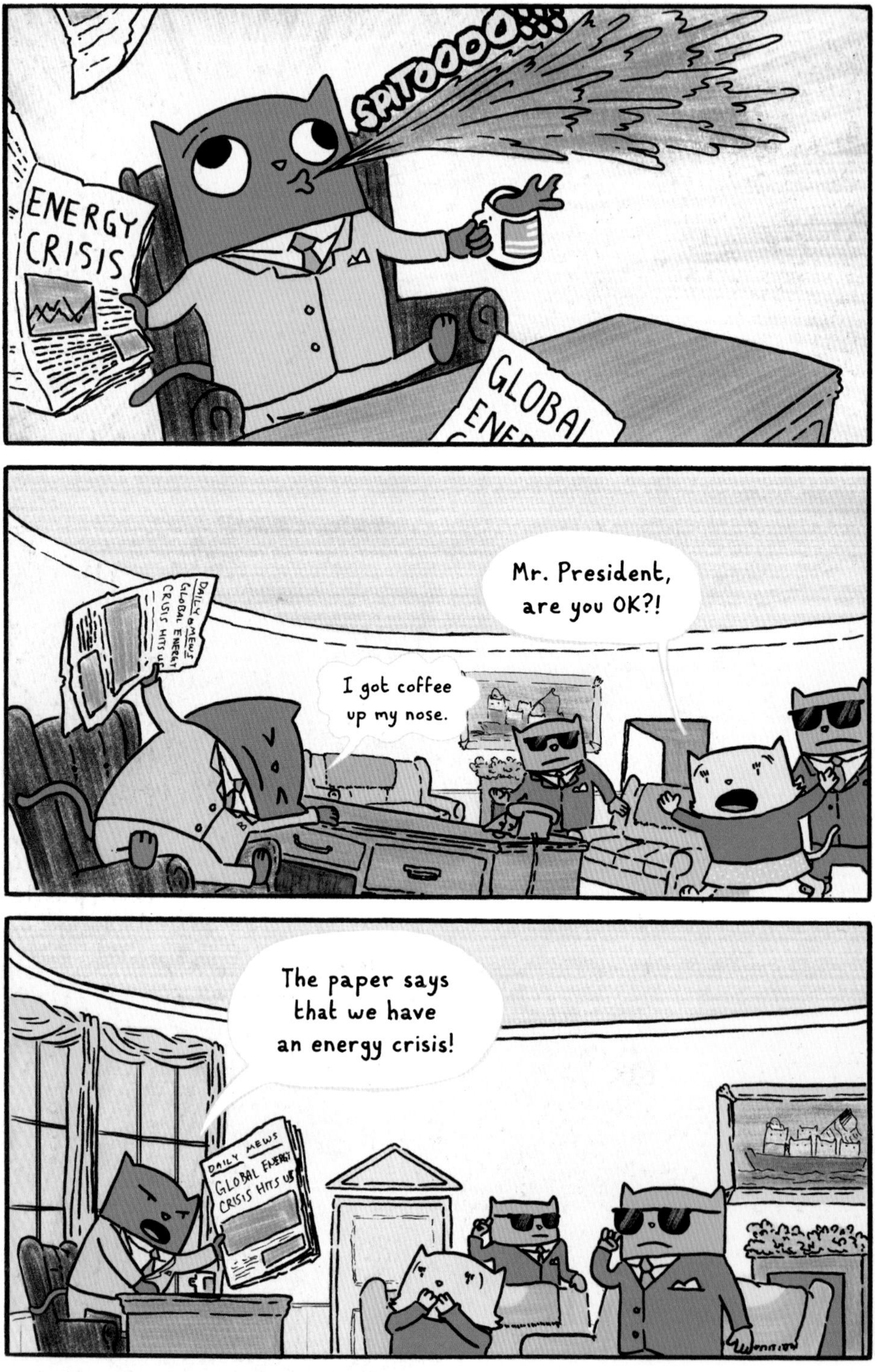
SPITOOOO!!!
ENERGY CRISIS
GLOBAL ENER
DAILY MEWS GLOBAL ENERGY CRISIS HITS US
Mr. President, are you OK?!
I got coffee up my nose.
The paper says that we have an energy crisis!
DAILY MEWS GLOBAL ENERGY CRISIS HITS US

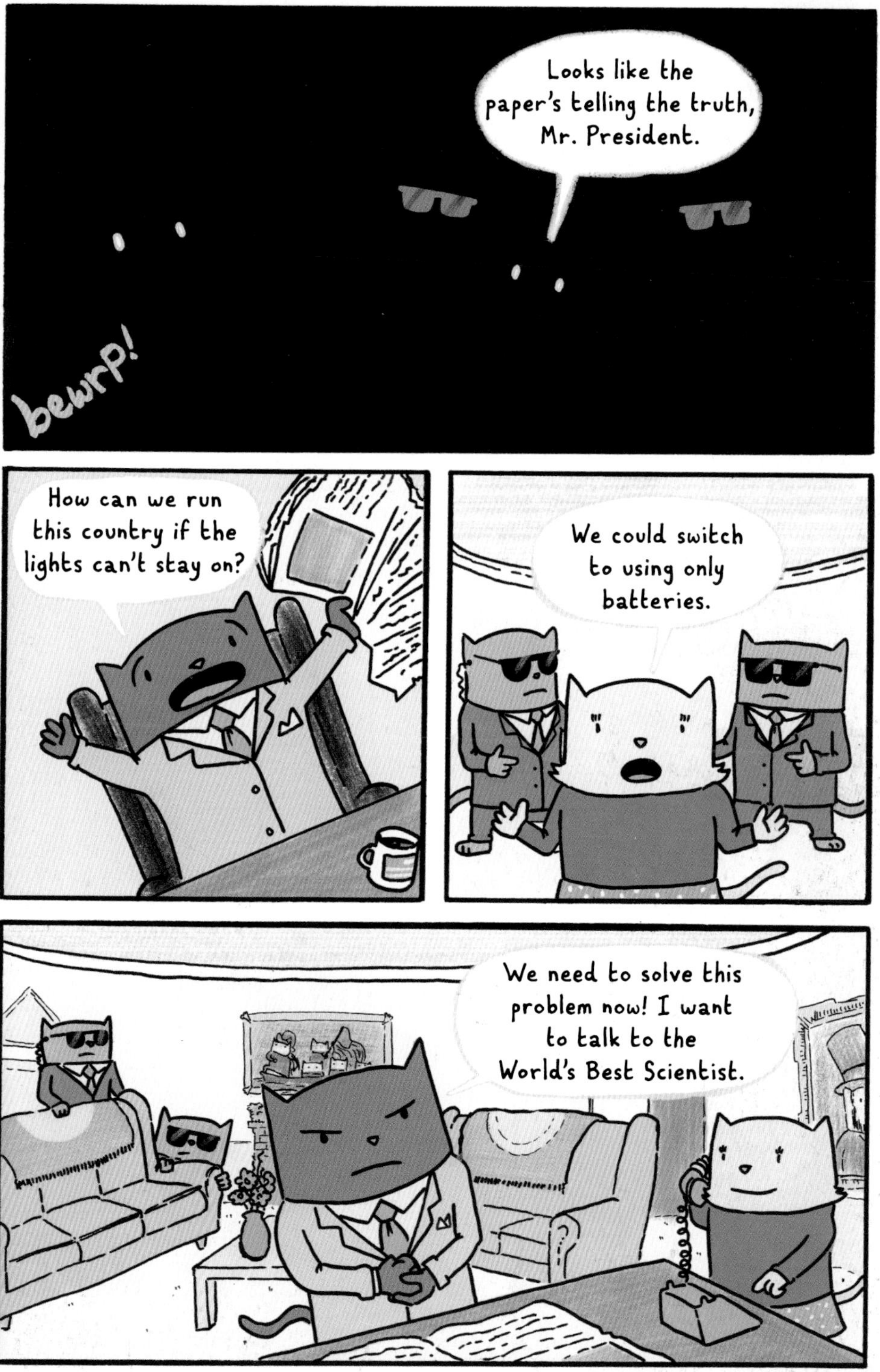
Looks like the paper's telling the truth, Mr. President.
bewrp!
How can we run this country if the lights can't stay on?
We could switch to using only batteries.
We need to solve this problem now! I want to talk to the World's Best Scientist.

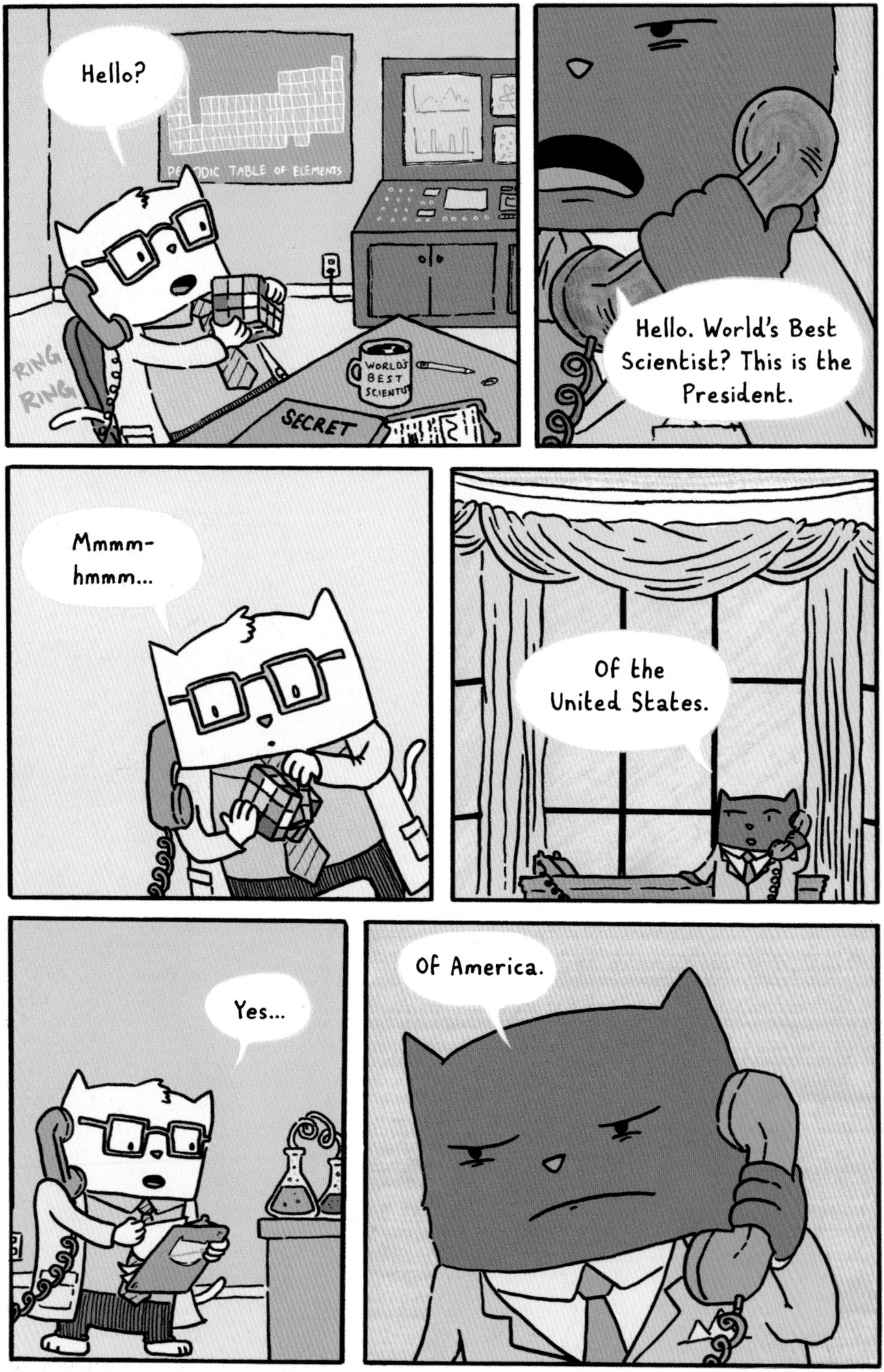
Hello?
RING
RING
SECRET
Hello. World's Best Scientist? This is the President.
Mmmm-hmmm...
Of the United States.
Yes...
Of America.

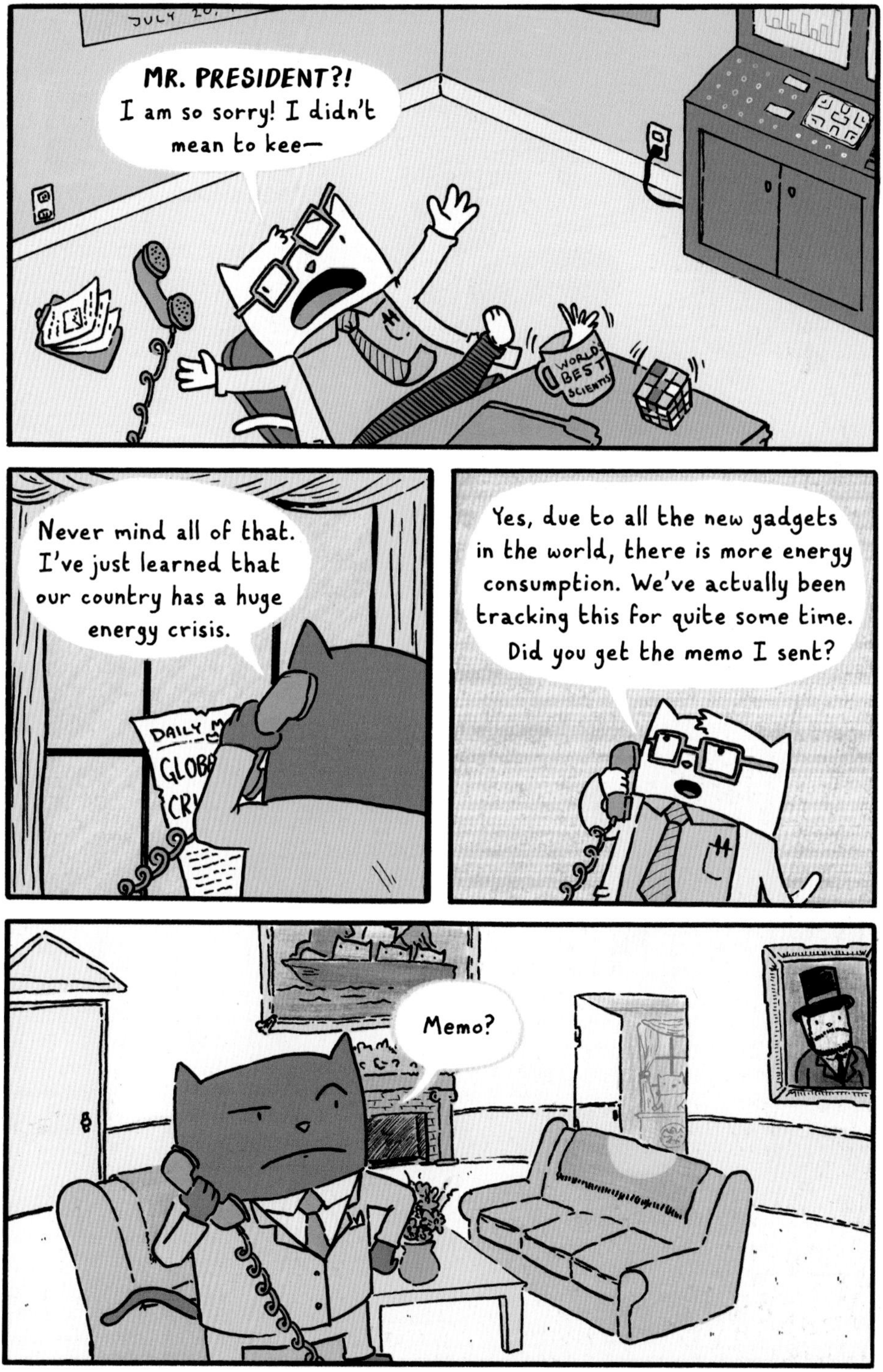
JULY 20,
MR. PRESIDENT?! I am so sorry! I didn't mean to kee—
WORLD'S BEST SCIENTIST
Never mind all of that. I've just learned that our country has a huge energy crisis.
DAILY M
GLOB
CR
Yes, due to all the new gadgets in the world, there is more energy consumption. We've actually been tracking this for quite some time. Did you get the memo I sent?
Memo?

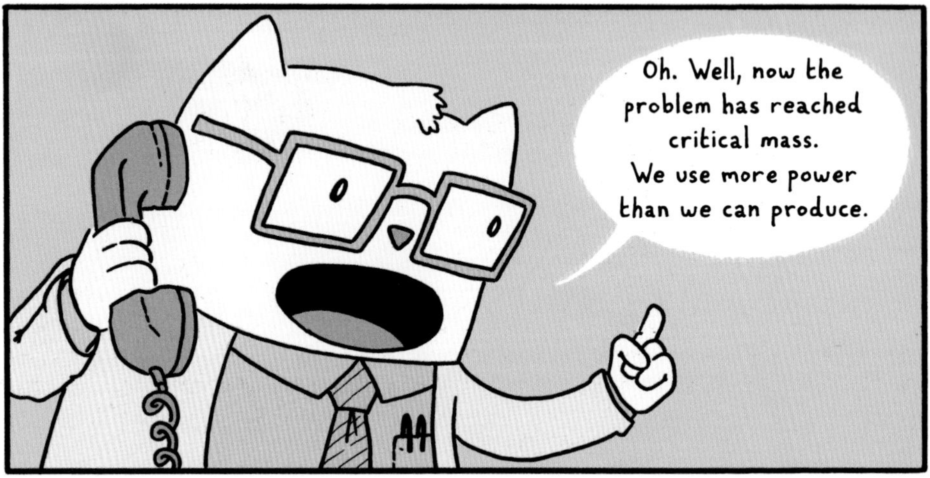
Oh. Well, now the problem has reached critical mass. We use more power than we can produce.

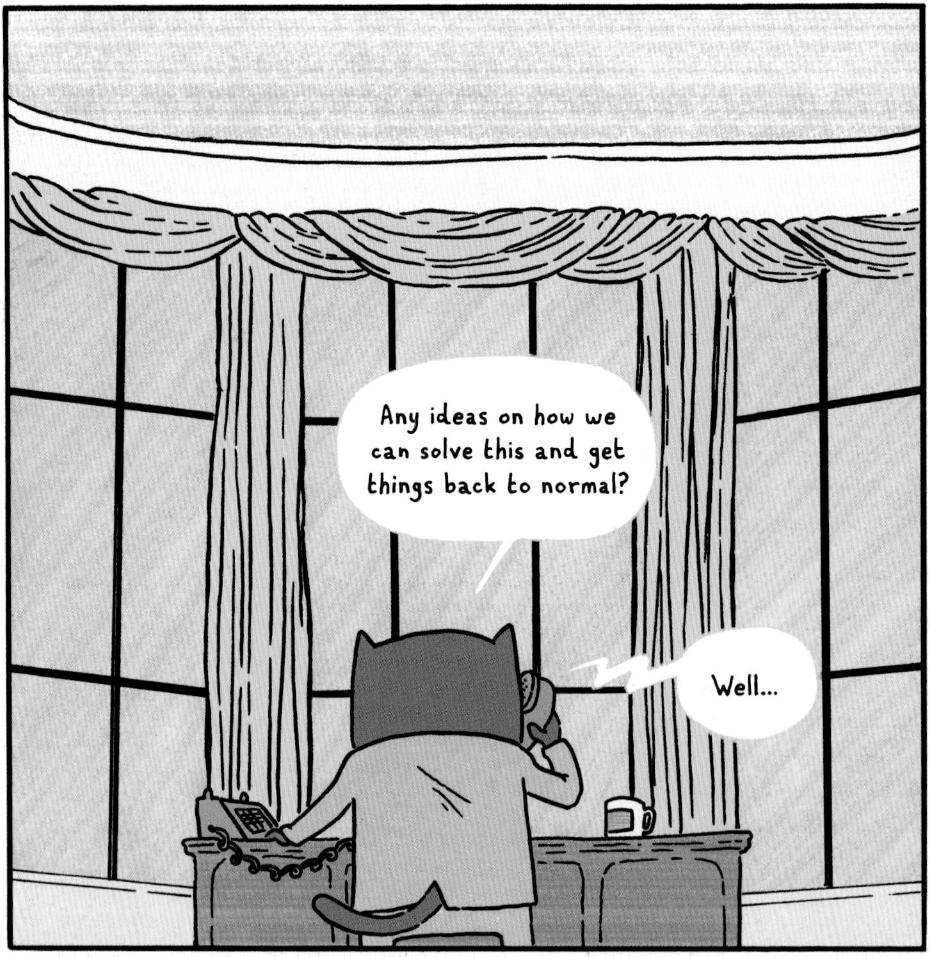
Any ideas on how we can solve this and get things back to normal?
Well...

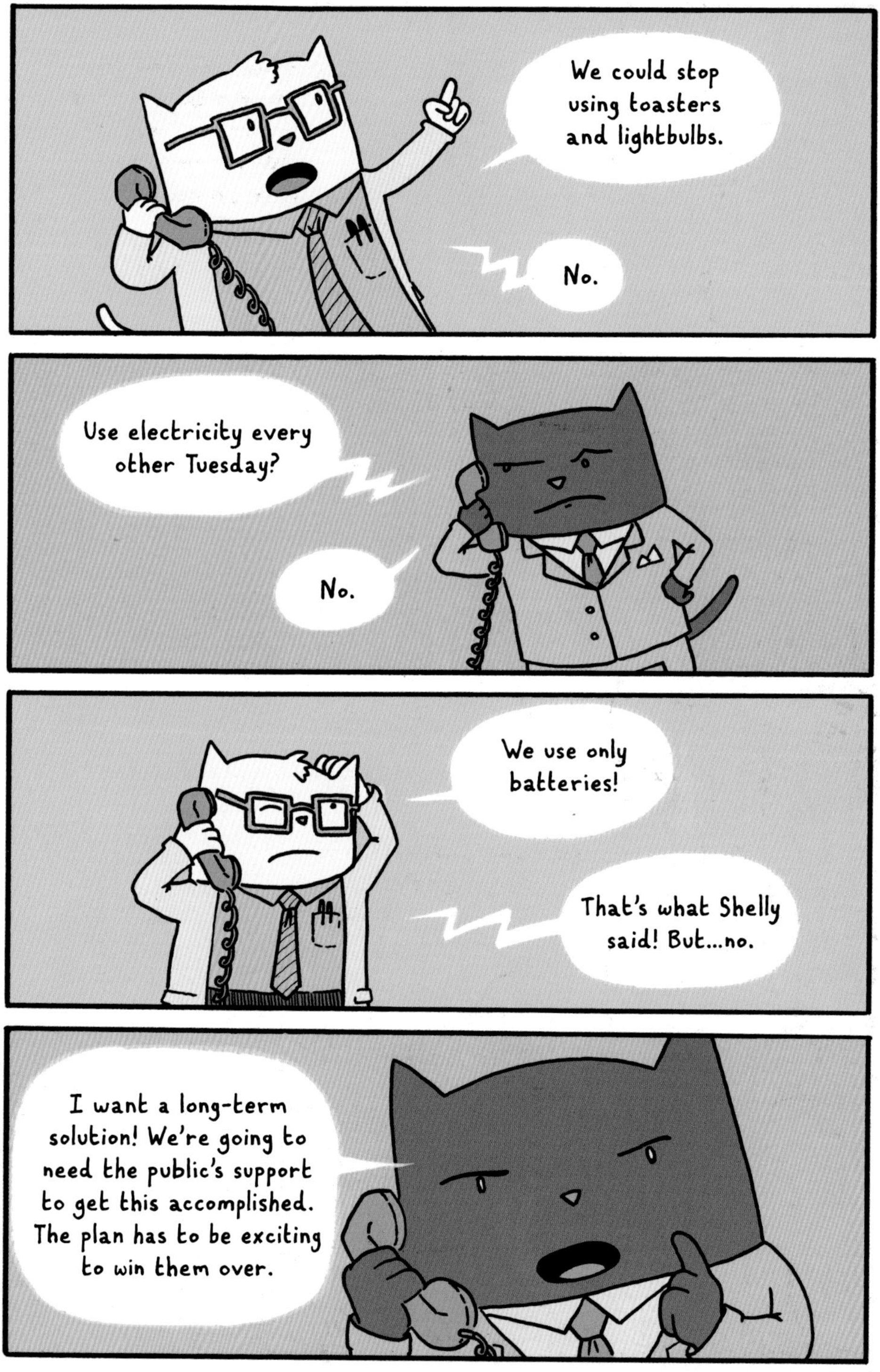
We could stop using toasters and lightbulbs.
No.
Use electricity every other Tuesday?
No.
We use only batteries!
That's what Shelly said! But...no.
I want a long-term solution! We're going to need the public's support to get this accomplished. The plan has to be exciting to win them over.

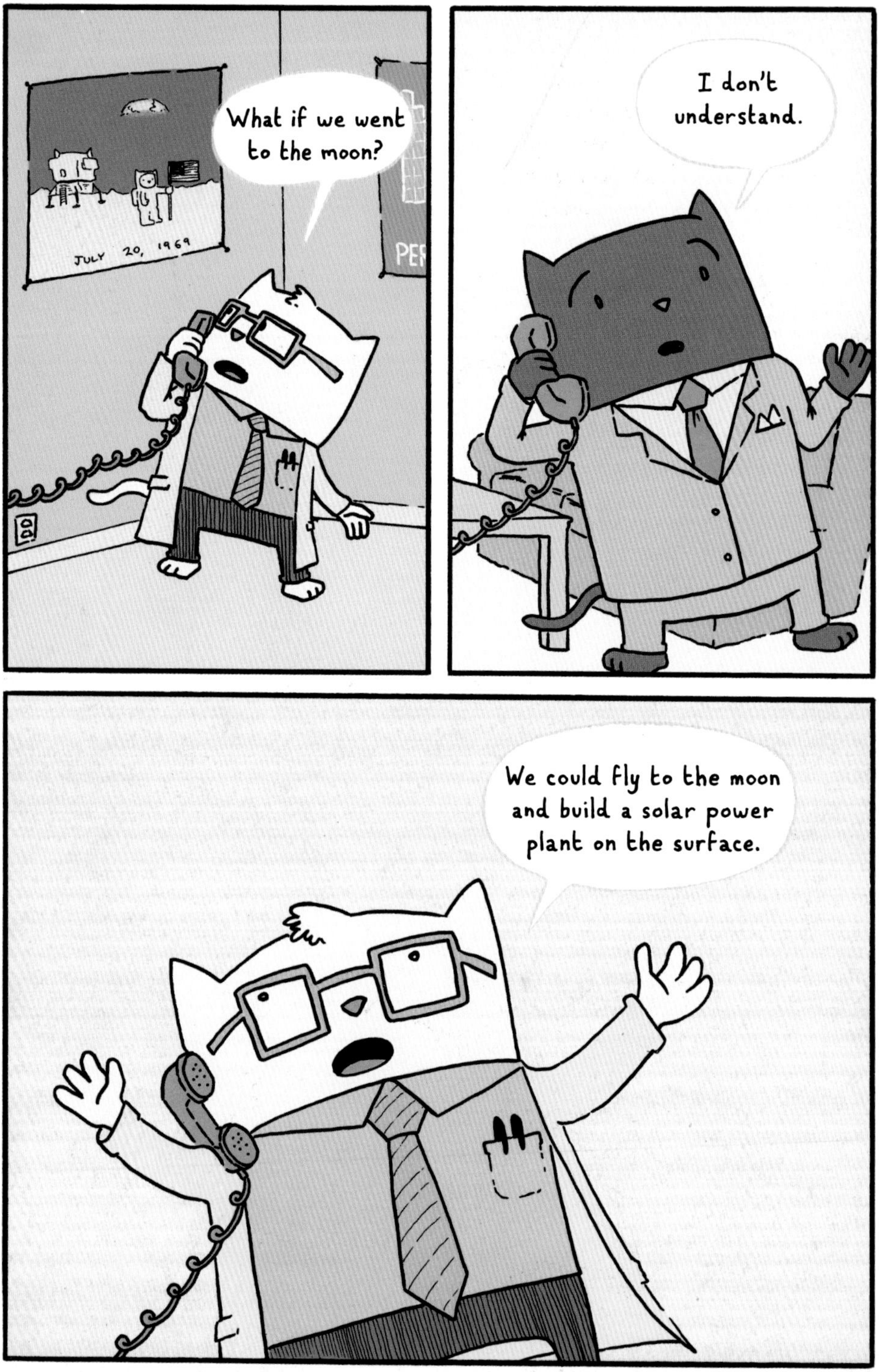
JULY 20, 1969
What if we went to the moon?
I don't understand.
We could fly to the moon and build a solar power plant on the surface.

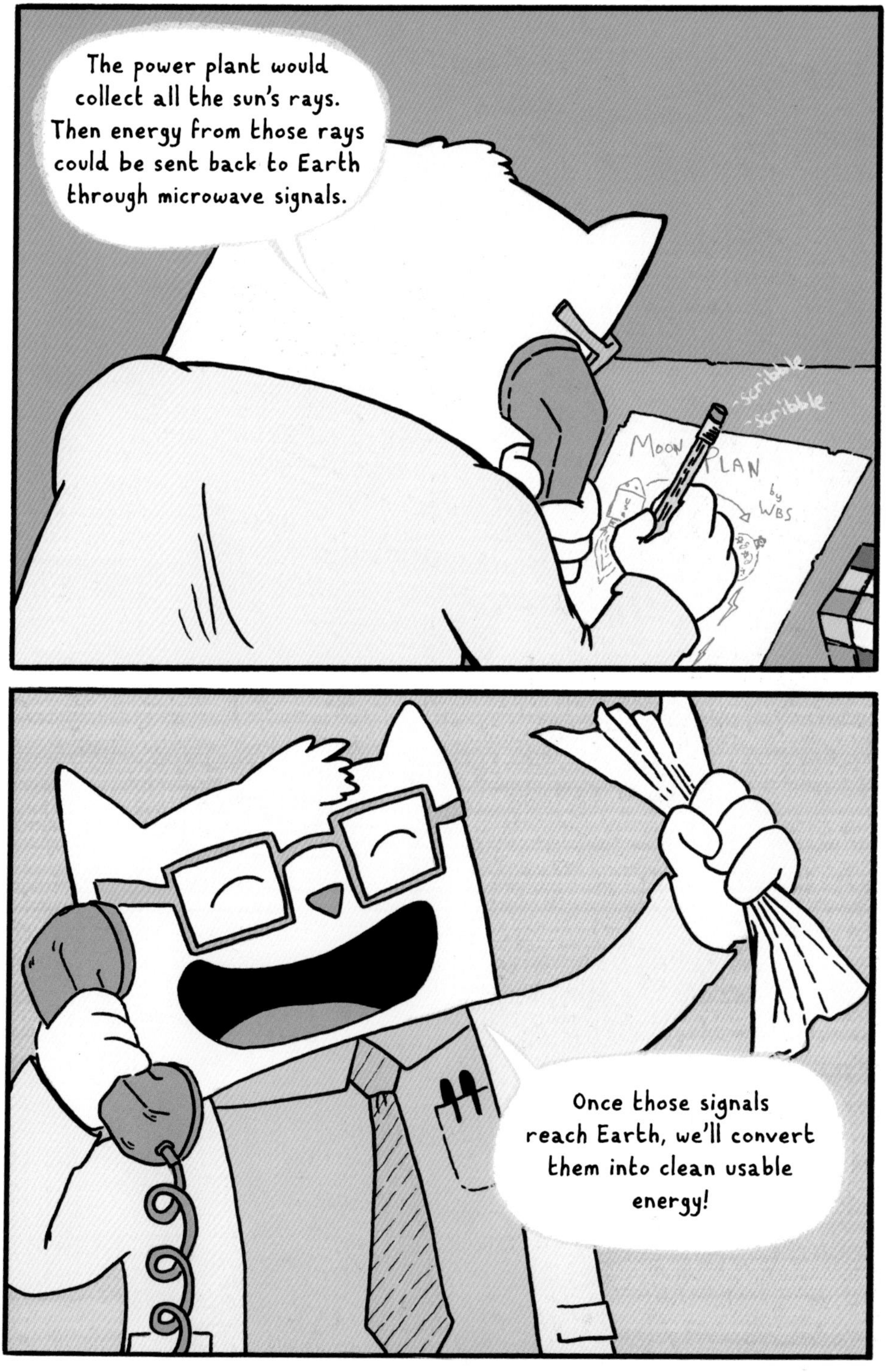
The power plant would collect all the sun's rays. Then energy from those rays could be sent back to Earth through microwave signals.
-scribble
-scribble
MOON PLAN
by WBS
Once those signals reach Earth, we'll convert them into clean usable energy!

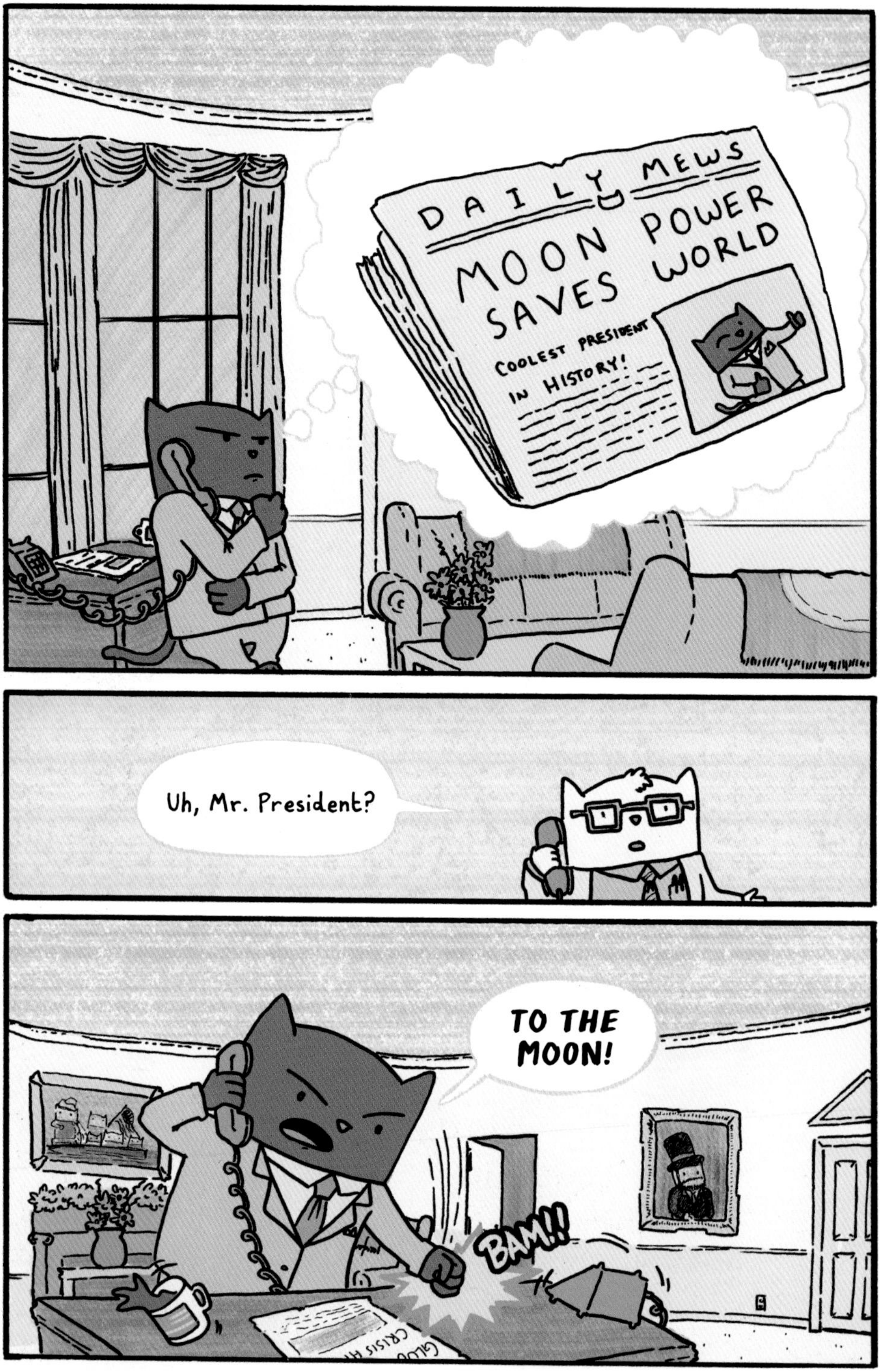
DAILY MEWS
MOON POWER SAVES WORLD
COOLEST PRESIDENT IN HISTORY!
Uh, Mr. President?
TO THE MOON!
BAM!!

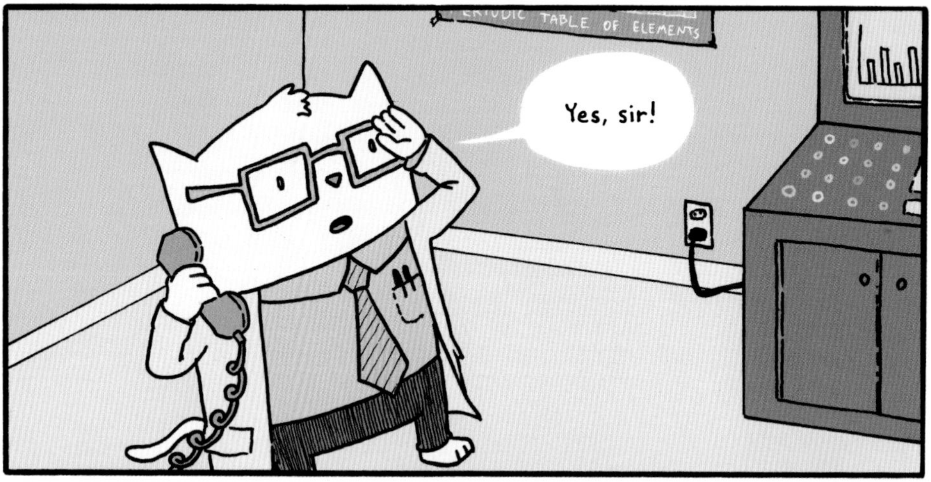
TABLE OF ELEMENTS
Yes, sir!

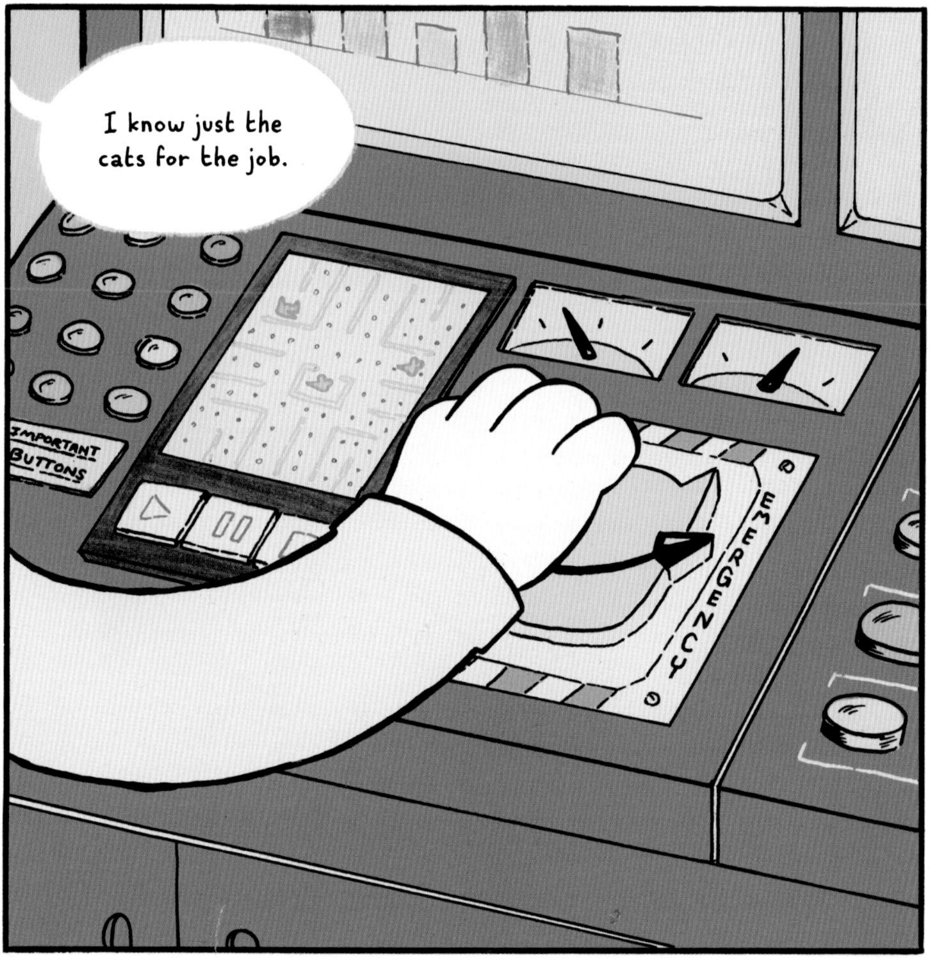
I know just the cats for the job.
IMPORTANT BUTTONS
EMERGENCY

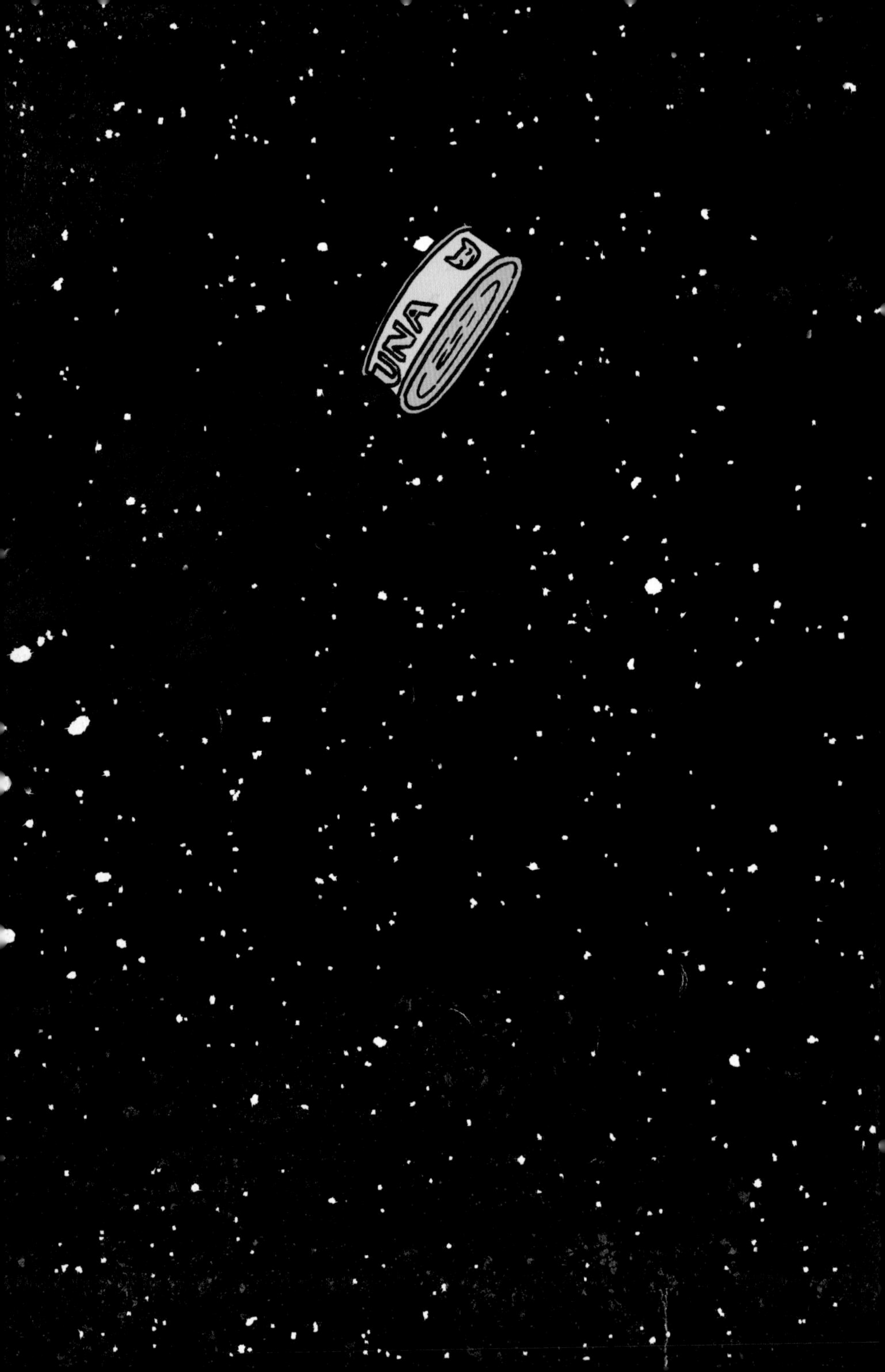
UNA

CHAPTER 2

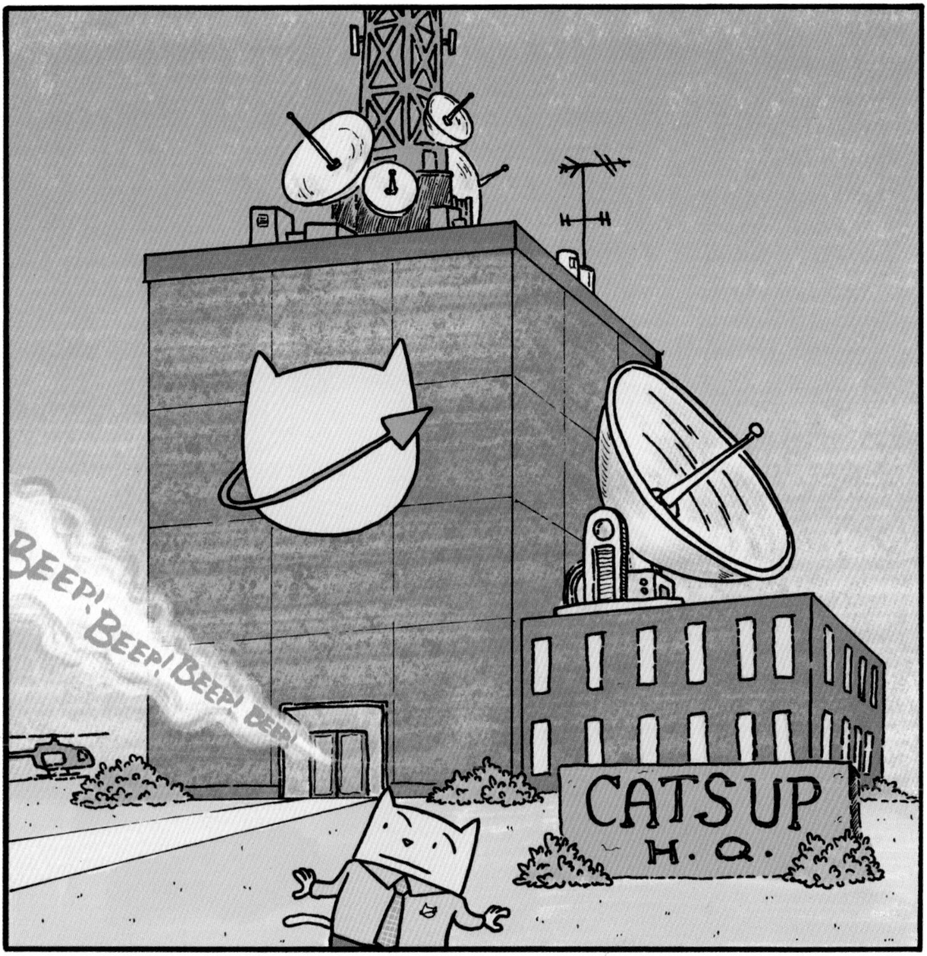
BEEP! BEEP! BEEP! BEEP!
CATSUP H.Q.

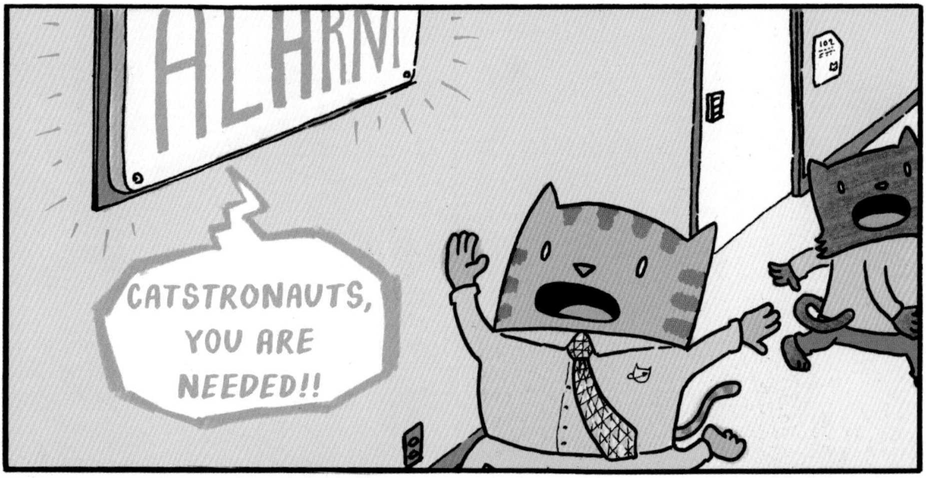
ALARM
CATSTRONAUTS, YOU ARE NEEDED!!

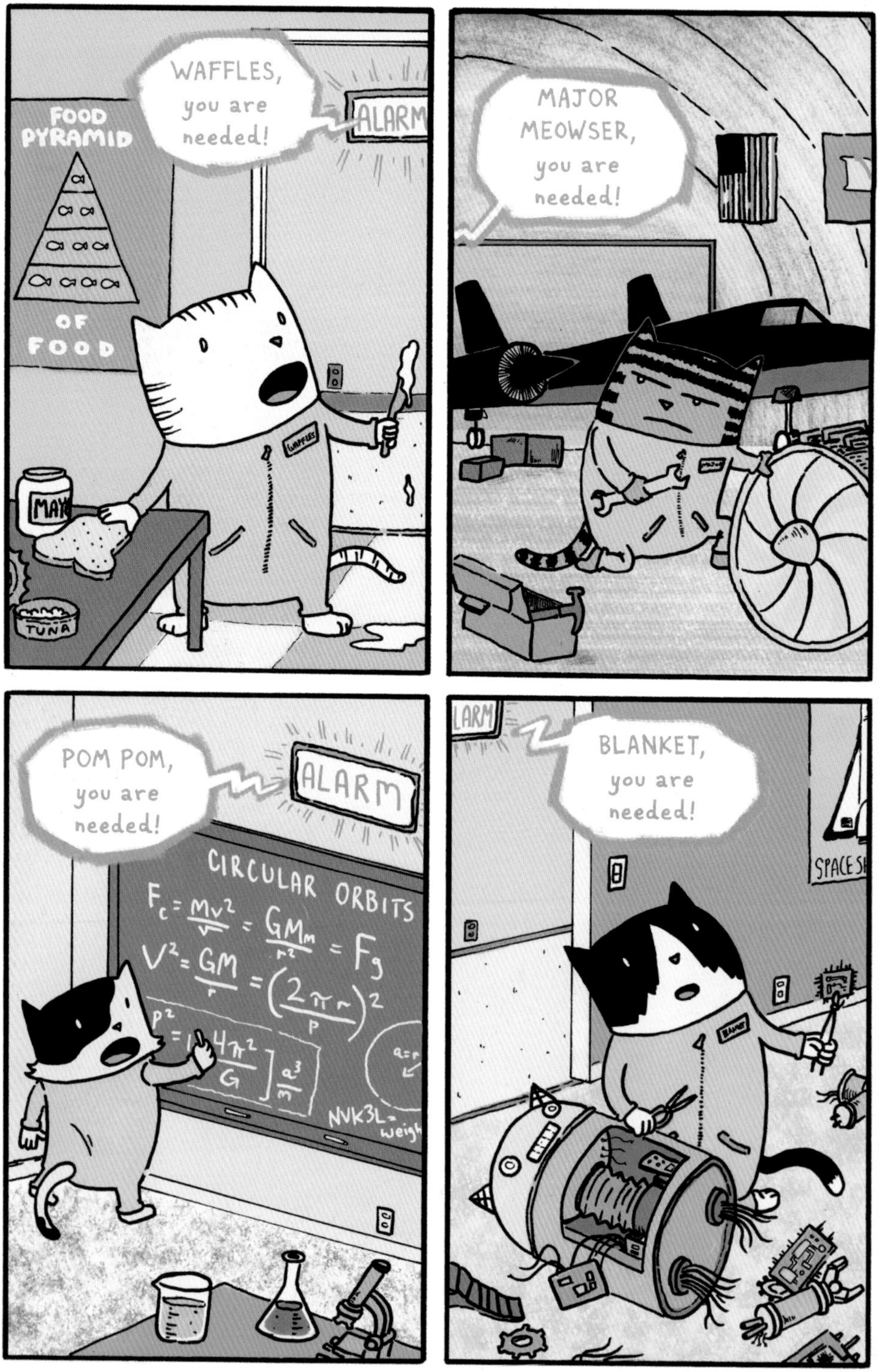
WAFFLES, you are needed!
ALARM
FOOD PYRAMID OF FOOD
MAYO
TUNA
MAJOR MEOWSER, you are needed!
POM POM, you are needed!
ALARM
CIRCULAR ORBITS
BLANKET, you are needed!

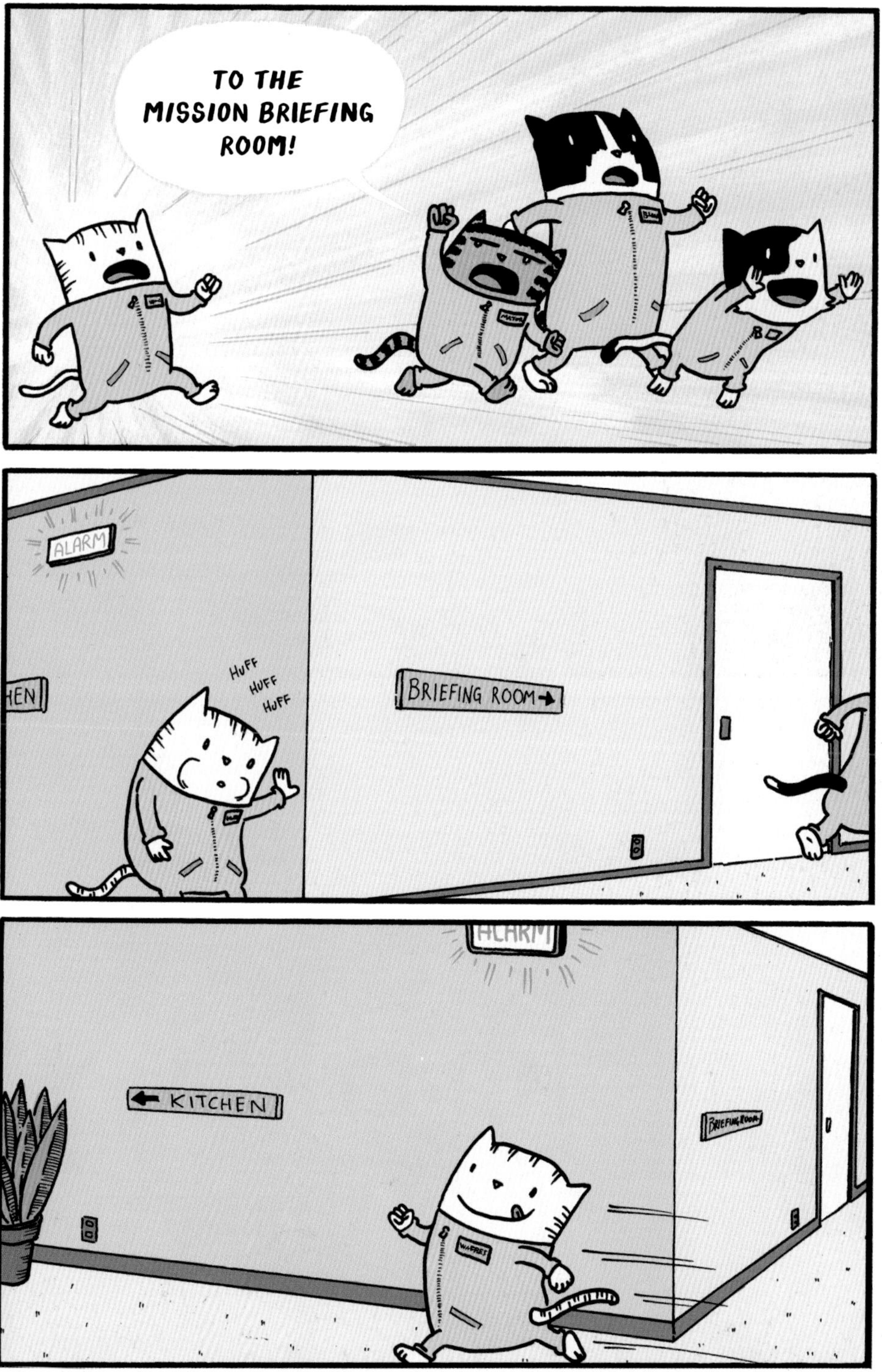
TO THE MISSION BRIEFING ROOM!
ALARM
HUFF
HUFF
HUFF
BRIEFING ROOM
ALARM
KITCHEN
BRIEFING ROOM

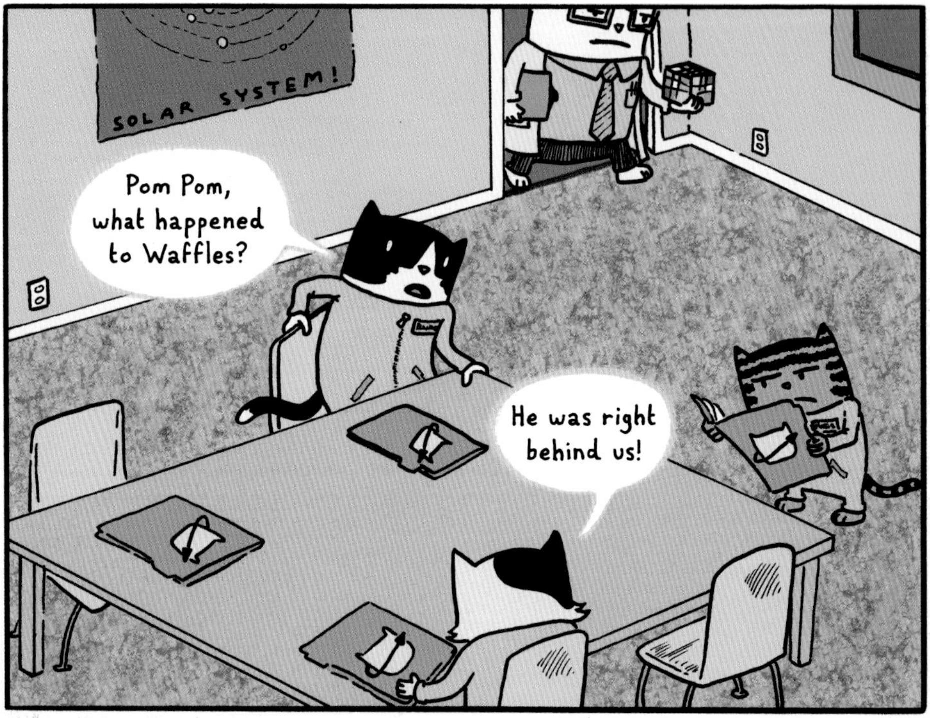
SOLAR SYSTEM!
Pom Pom, what happened to Waffles?
He was right behind us!

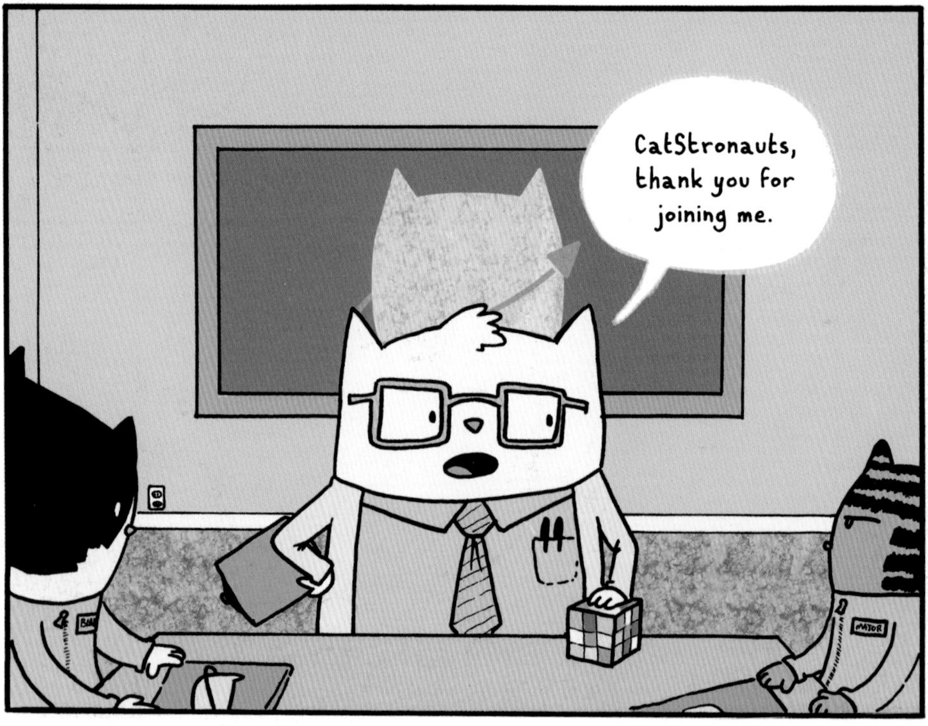
CatStronauts, thank you for joining me.

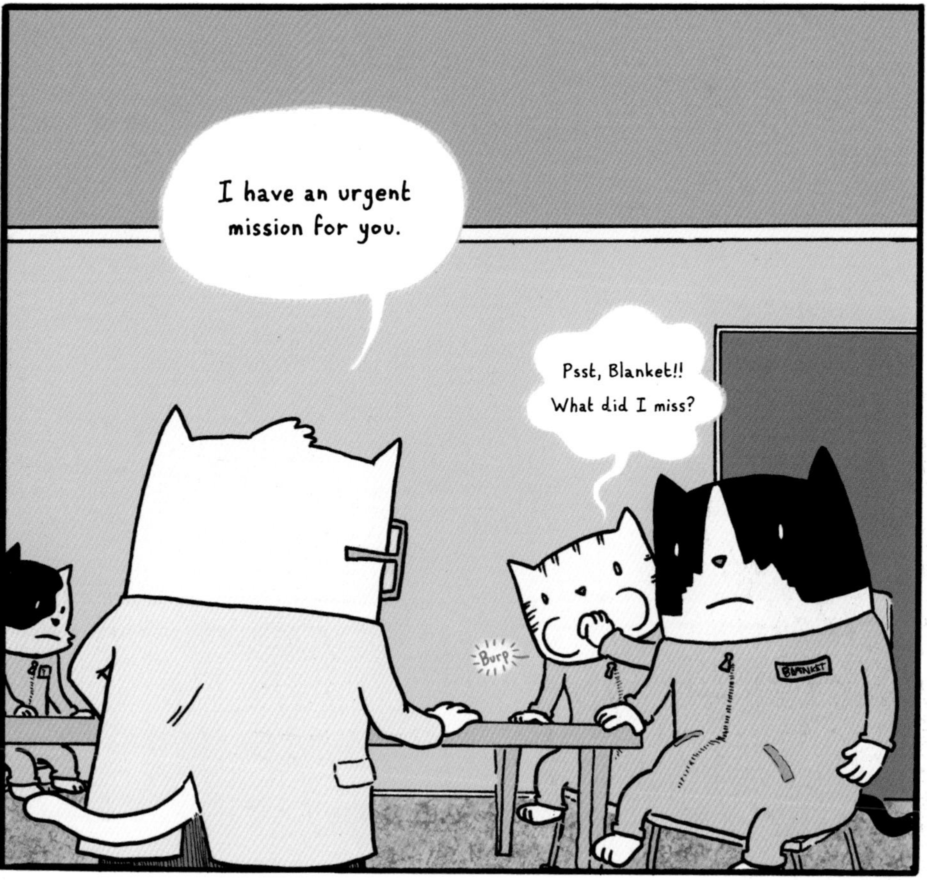
I have an urgent mission for you.
Psst, Blanket!! What did I miss?
Burp
BLANKET

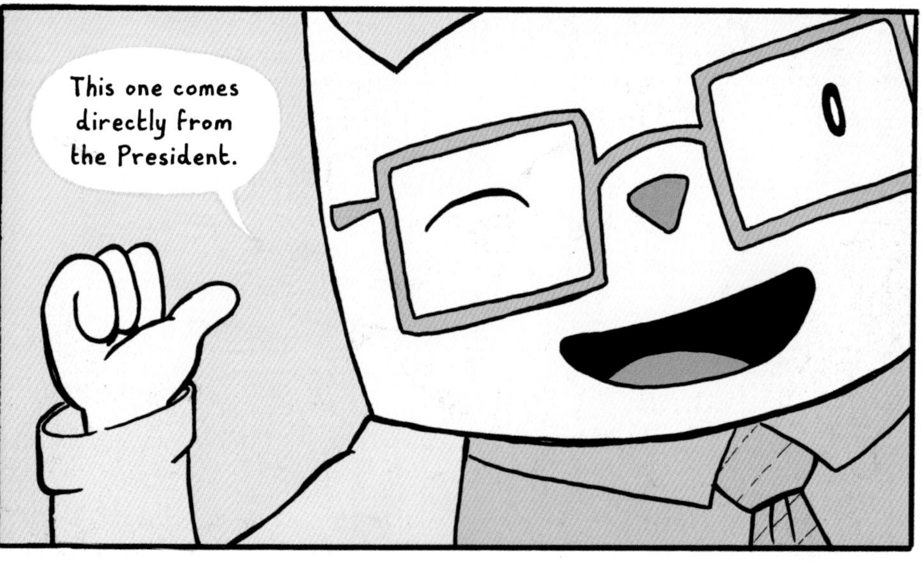
This one comes directly from the President.

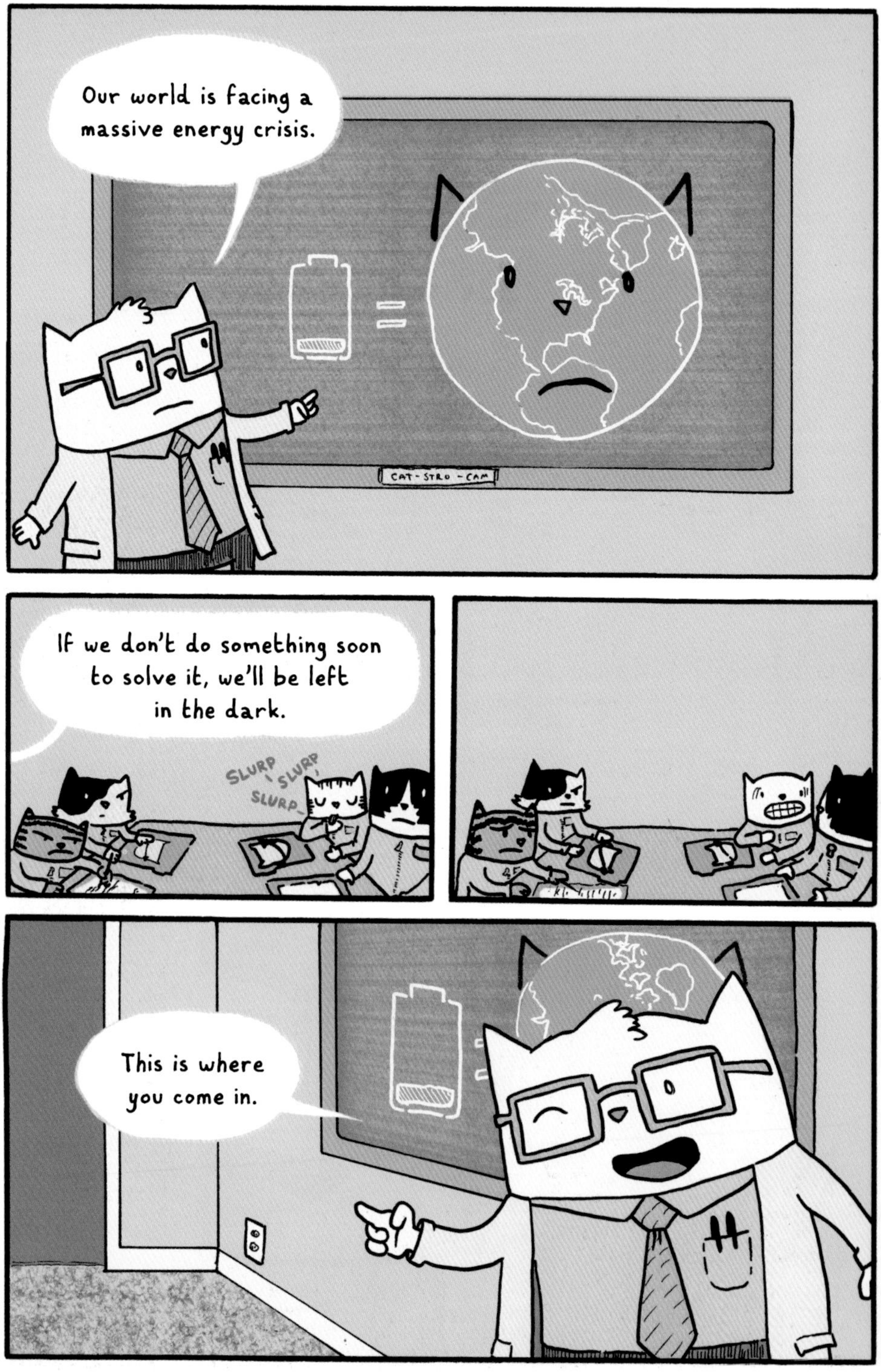
Our world is facing a massive energy crisis.
CAT-STRO-CAM
If we don't do something soon to solve it, we'll be left in the dark.
SLURP SLURP SLURP
This is where you come in.

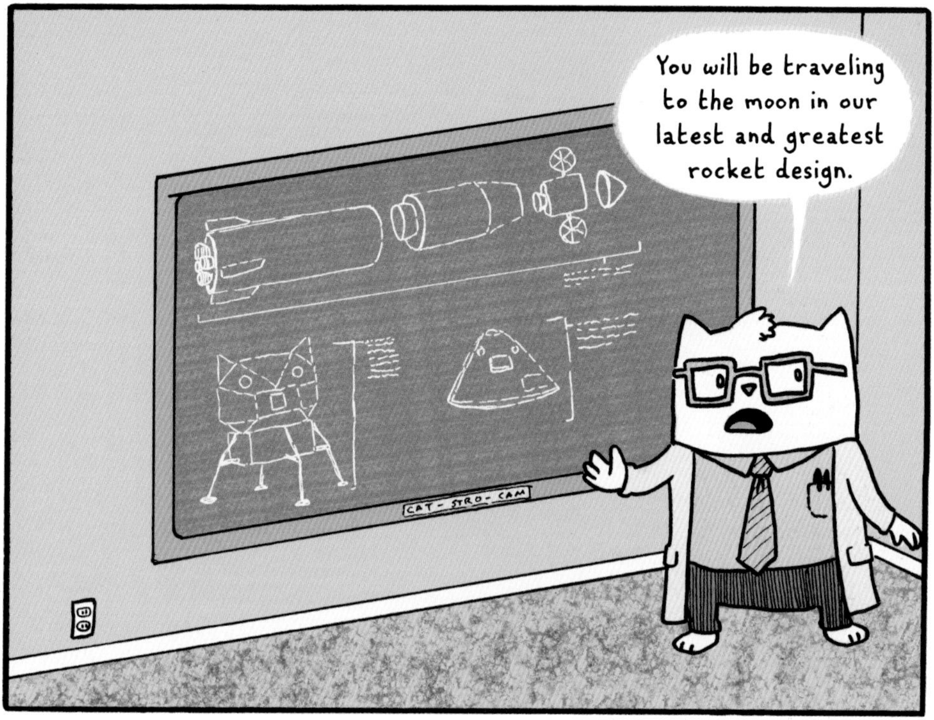
You will be traveling to the moon in our latest and greatest rocket design.
CAT-STRO-CAM

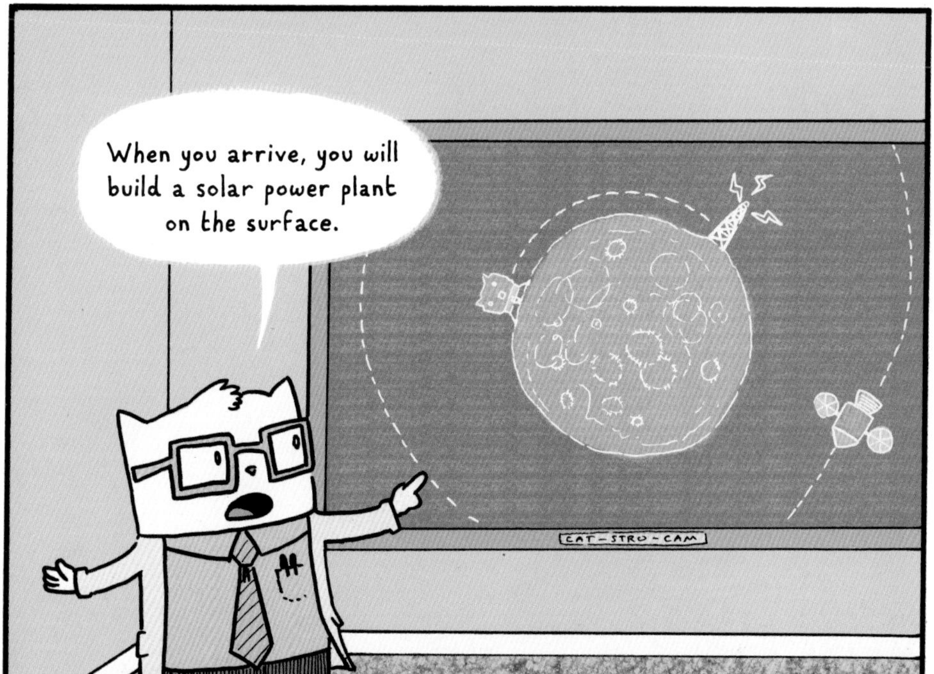
When you arrive, you will build a solar power plant on the surface.
CAT-STRO-CAM

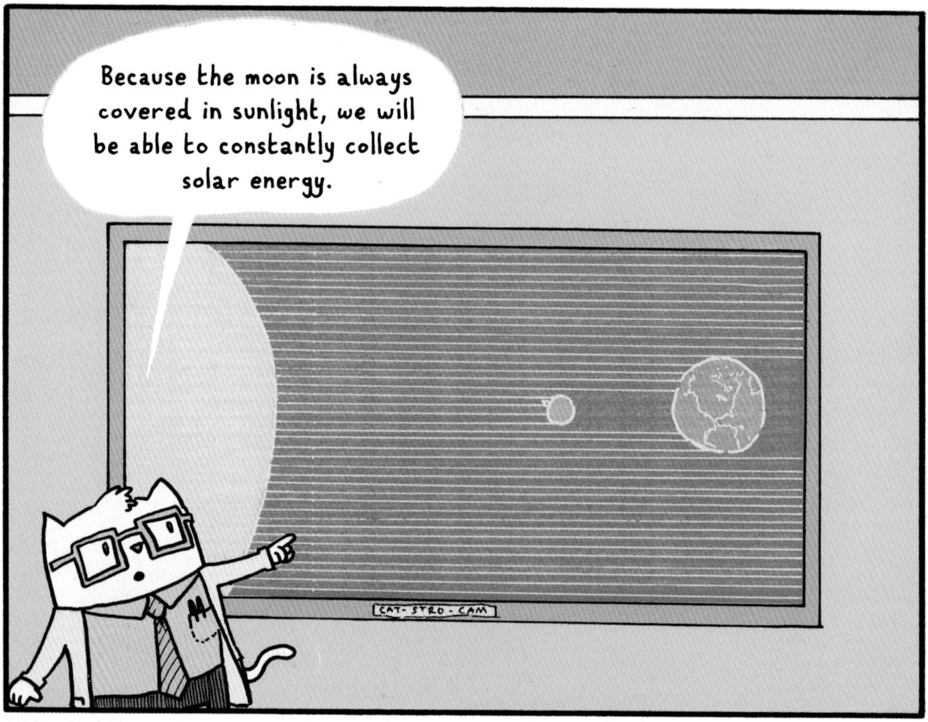
Because the moon is always covered in sunlight, we will be able to constantly collect solar energy.
CAT-STRO-CAM

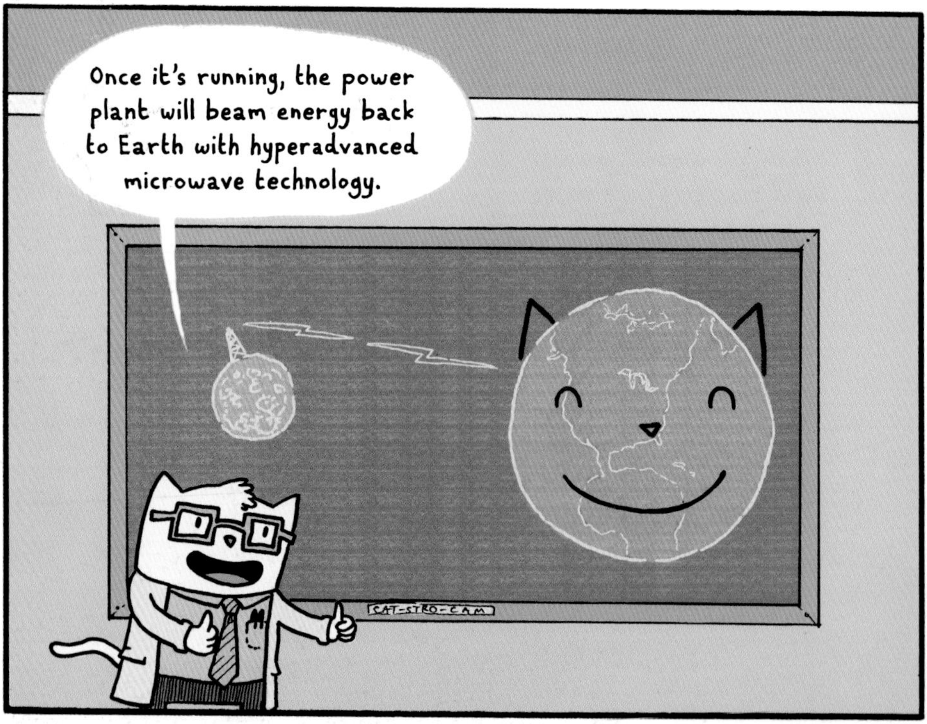
Once it's running, the power plant will beam energy back to Earth with hyperadvanced microwave technology.
CAT-STRO-CAM

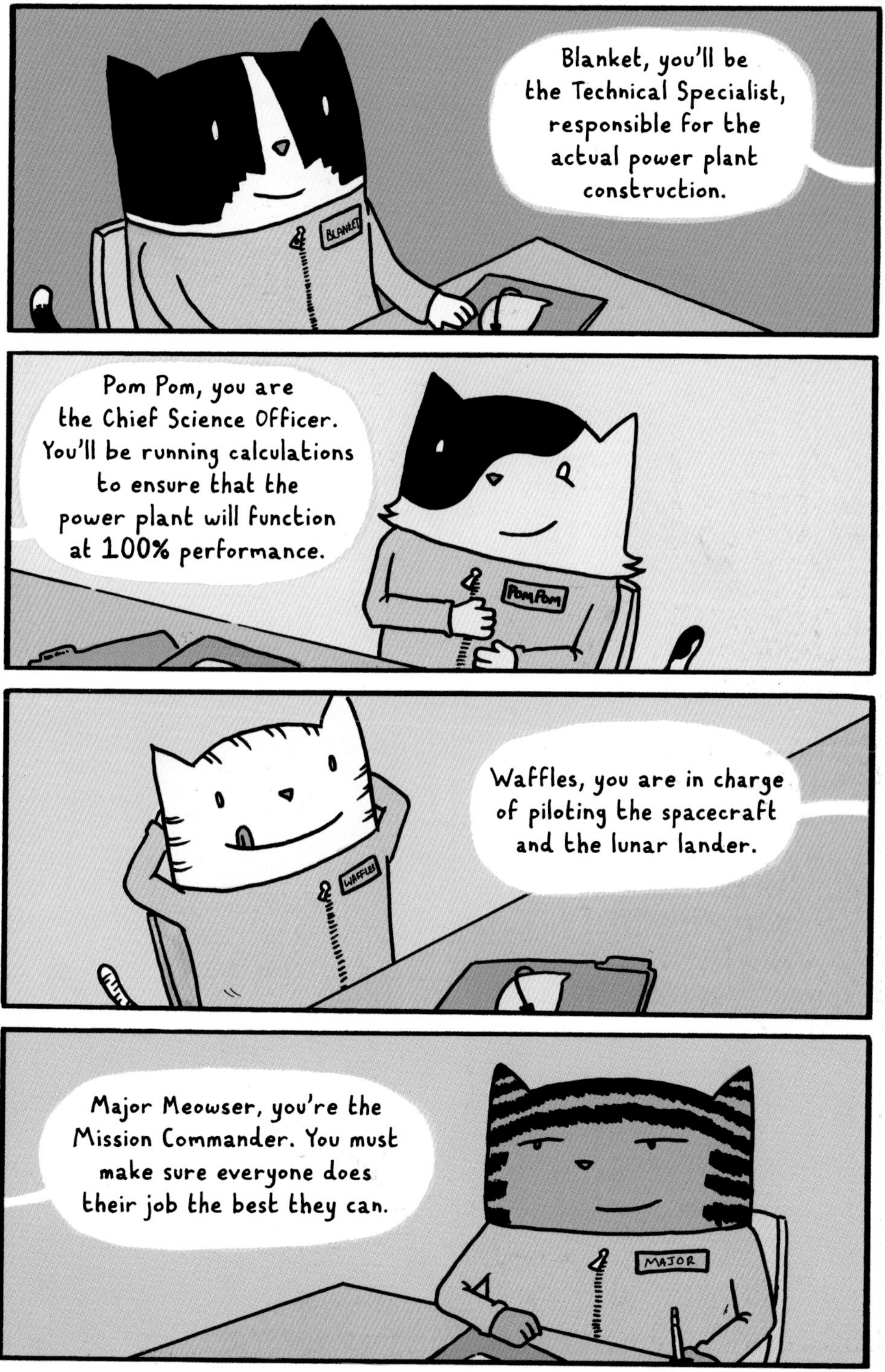

Blanket, you'll be the Technical Specialist, responsible for the actual power plant construction.
BLANKET
Pom Pom, you are the Chief Science Officer. You'll be running calculations to ensure that the power plant will function at 100% performance.
POM POM
Waffles, you are in charge of piloting the spacecraft and the lunar lander.
WAFFLES
Major Meowser, you're the Mission Commander. You must make sure everyone does their job the best they can.
MAJOR

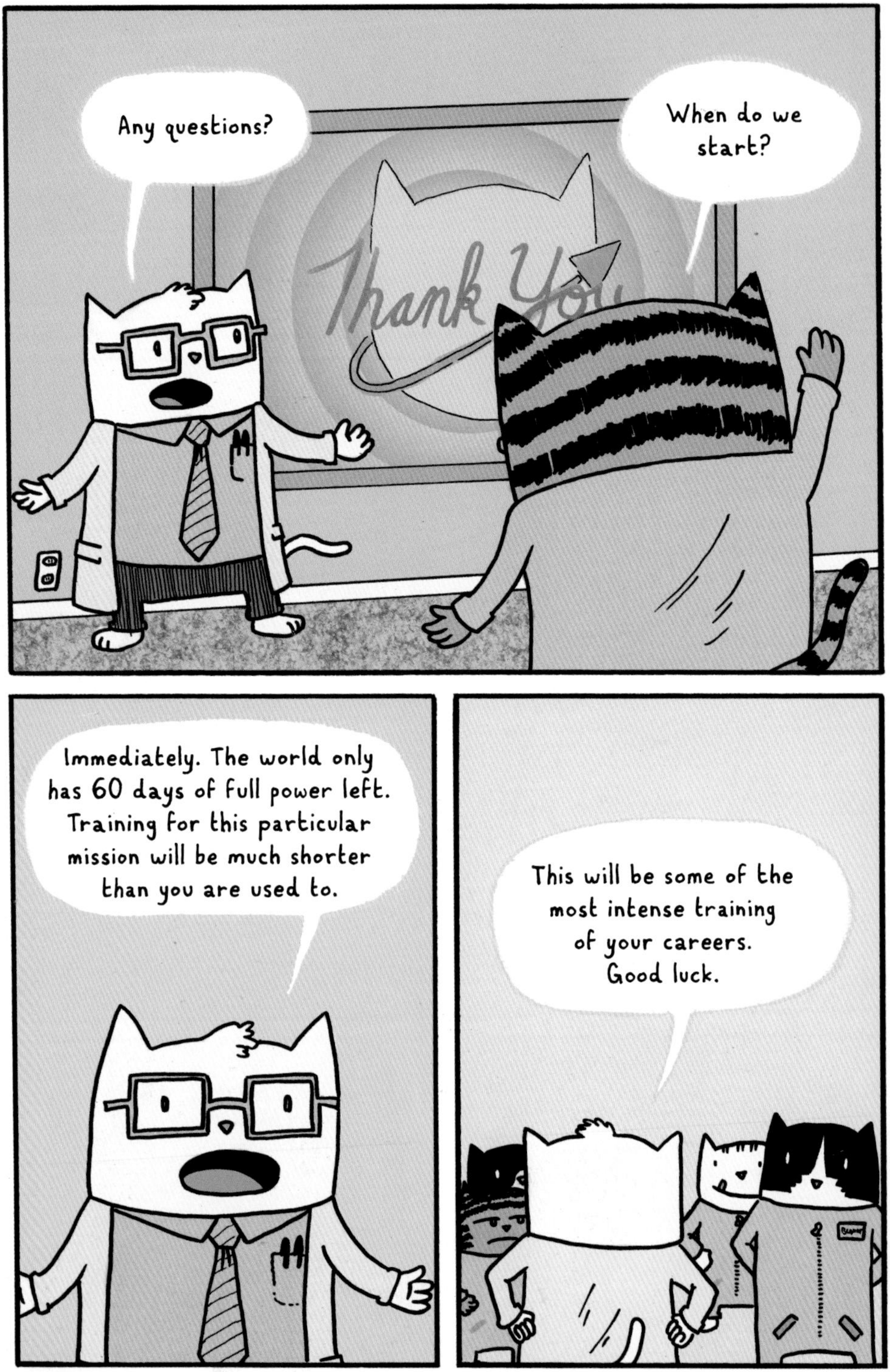
Any questions?
Thank You
When do we start?
Immediately. The world only has 60 days of full power left. Training for this particular mission will be much shorter than you are used to.
This will be some of the most intense training of your careers. Good luck.

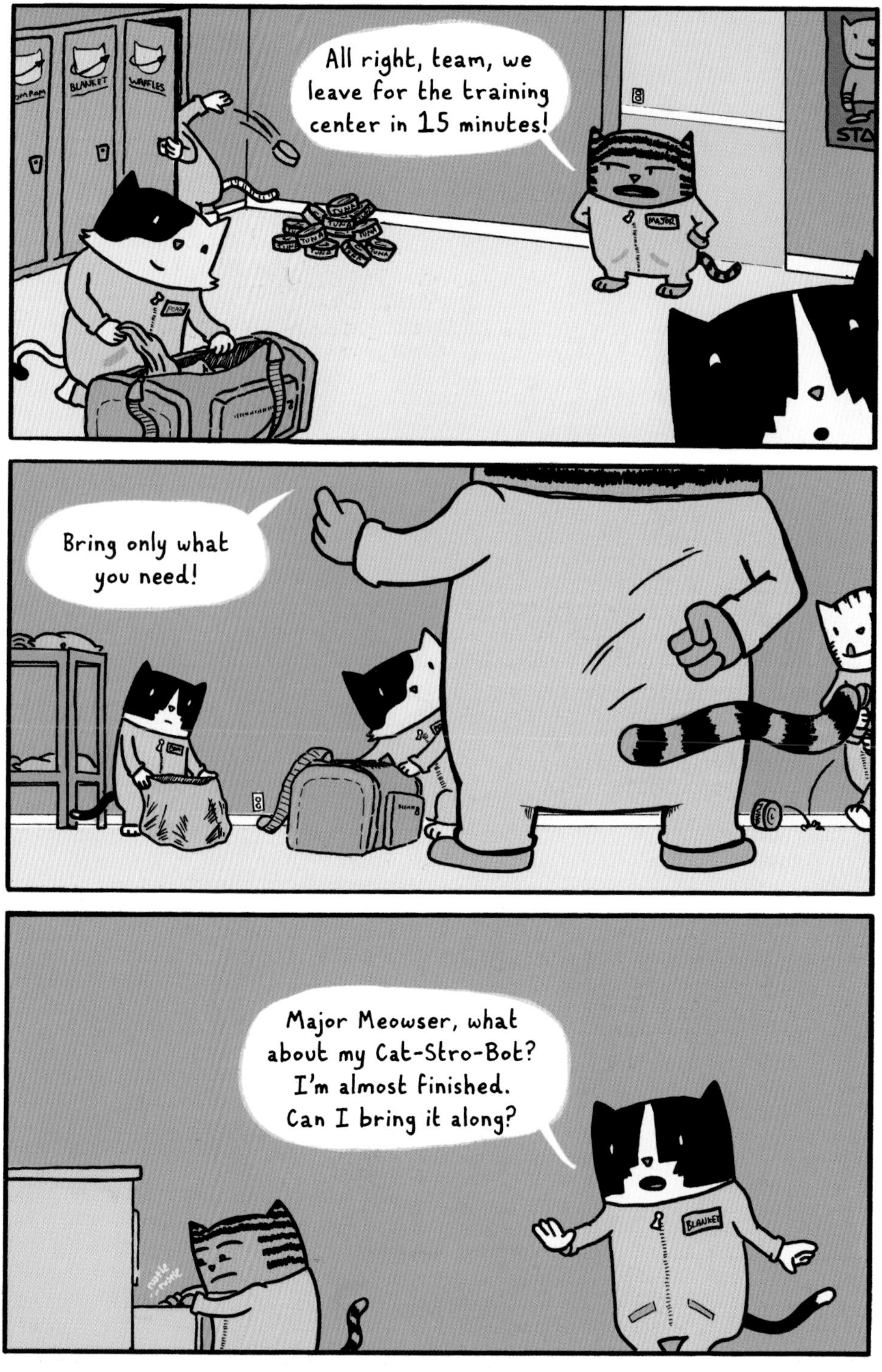
BLANKET
WAFFLES
All right, team, we leave for the training center in 15 minutes!
TUNA
MAJOR
Bring only what you need!
Major Meowser, what about my Cat-Stro-Bot? I'm almost finished. Can I bring it along?
BLANKET

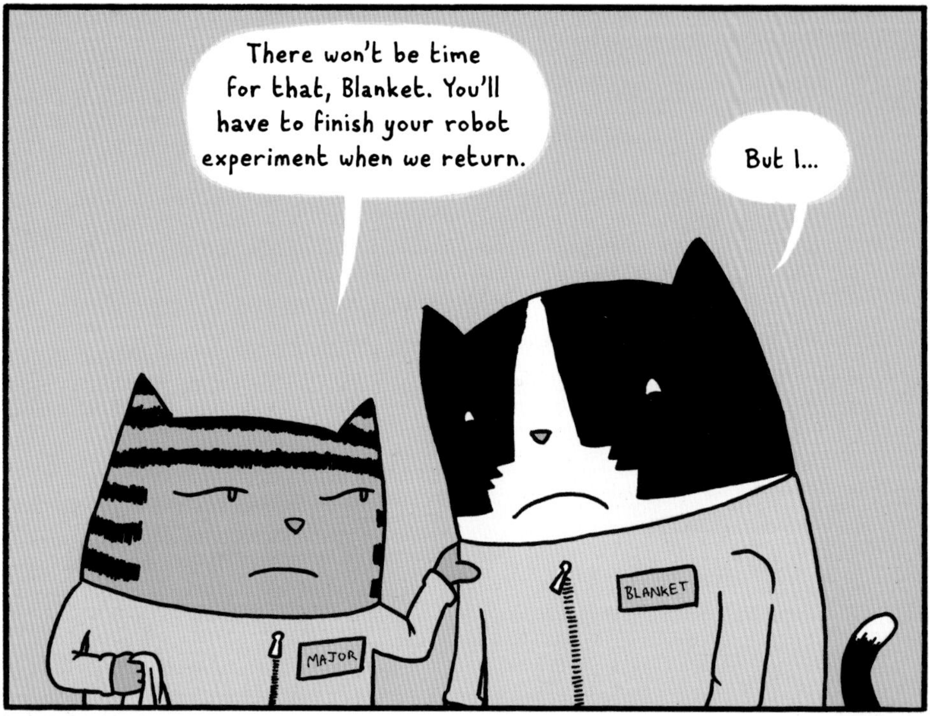
There won't be time for that, Blanket. You'll have to finish your robot experiment when we return.
But I...
MAJOR
BLANKET

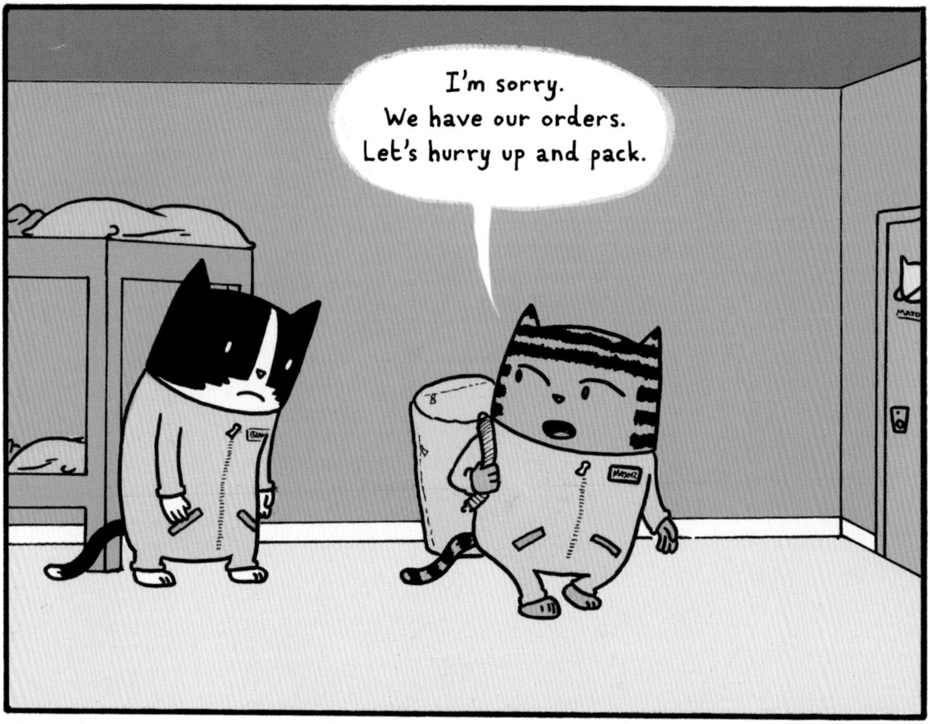
I'm sorry. We have our orders. Let's hurry up and pack.
MAJOR

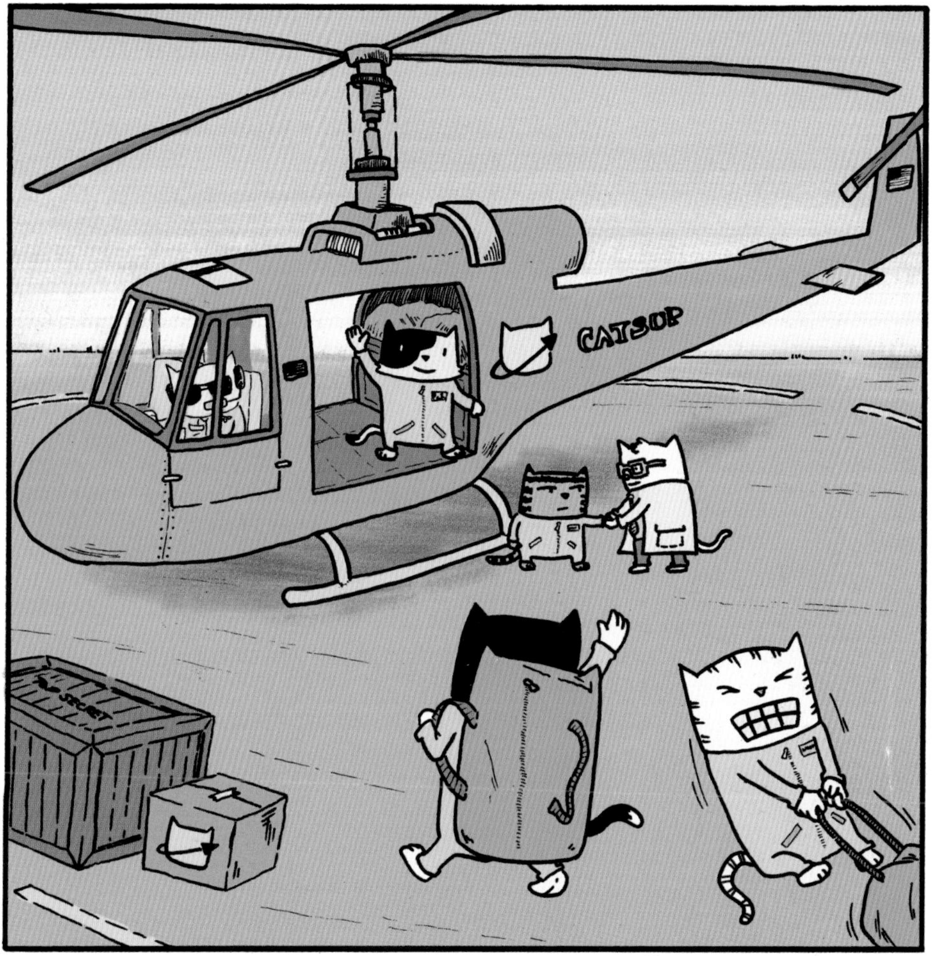
CATSUP

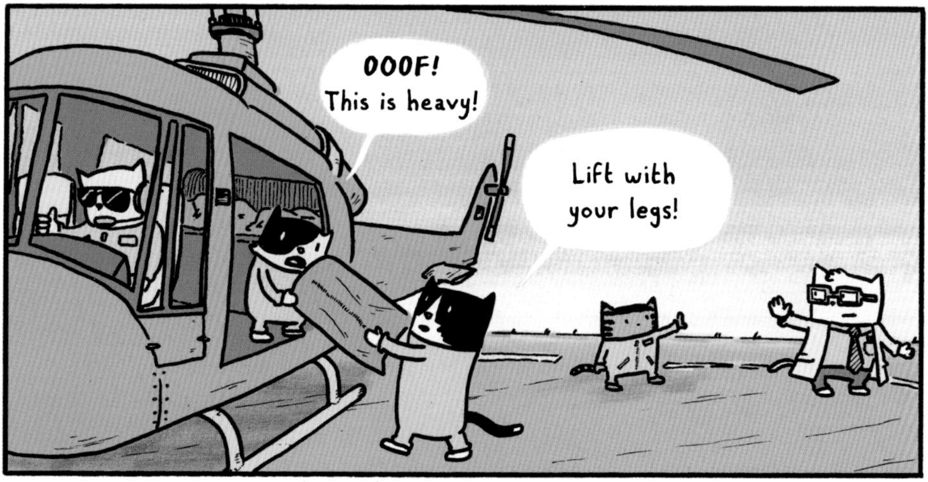
OOOF!
This is heavy!
Lift with
your legs!

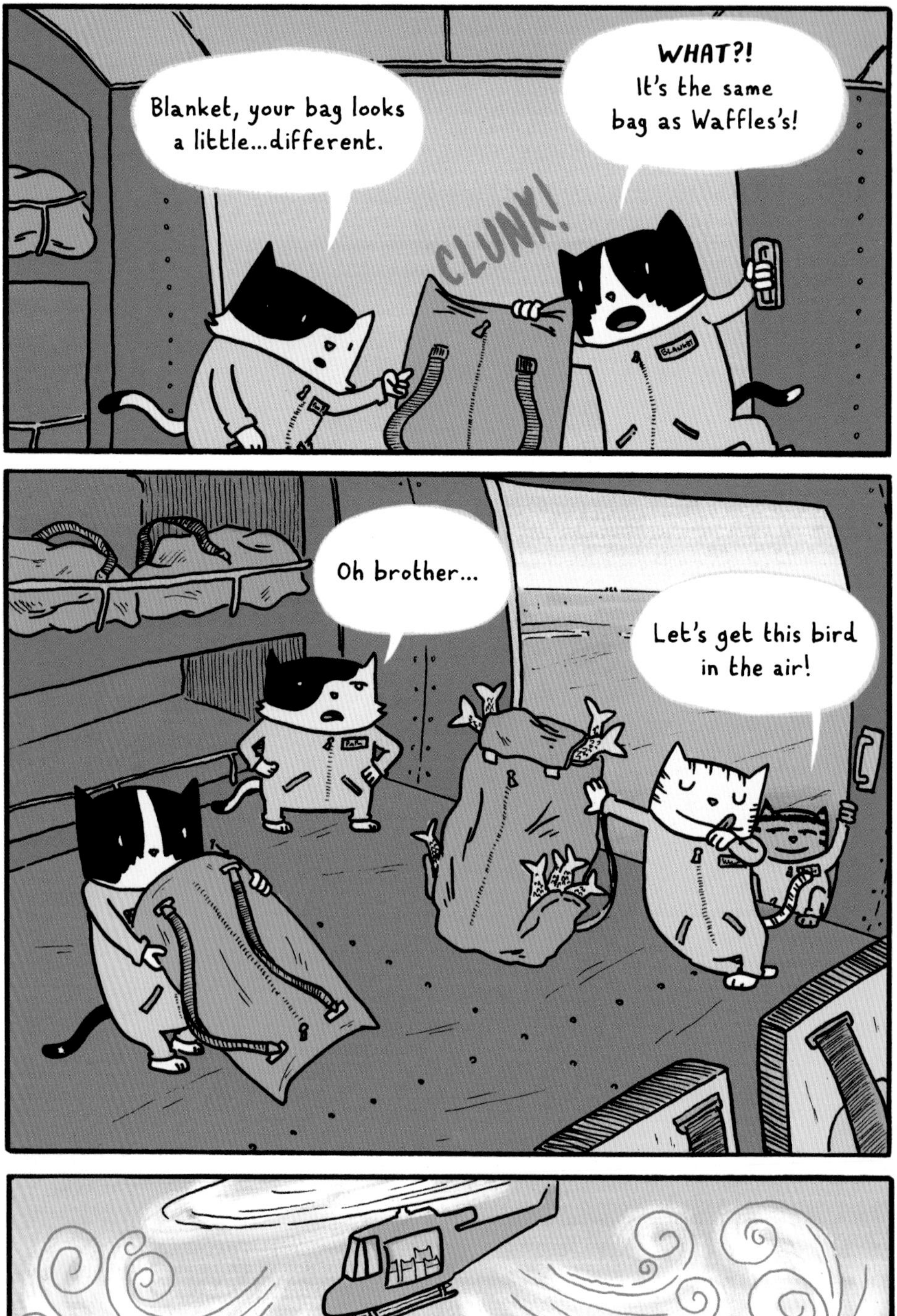
Blanket, your bag looks a little...different.
CLUNK!
WHAT?! It's the same bag as Waffles's!
Oh brother...
Let's get this bird in the air!

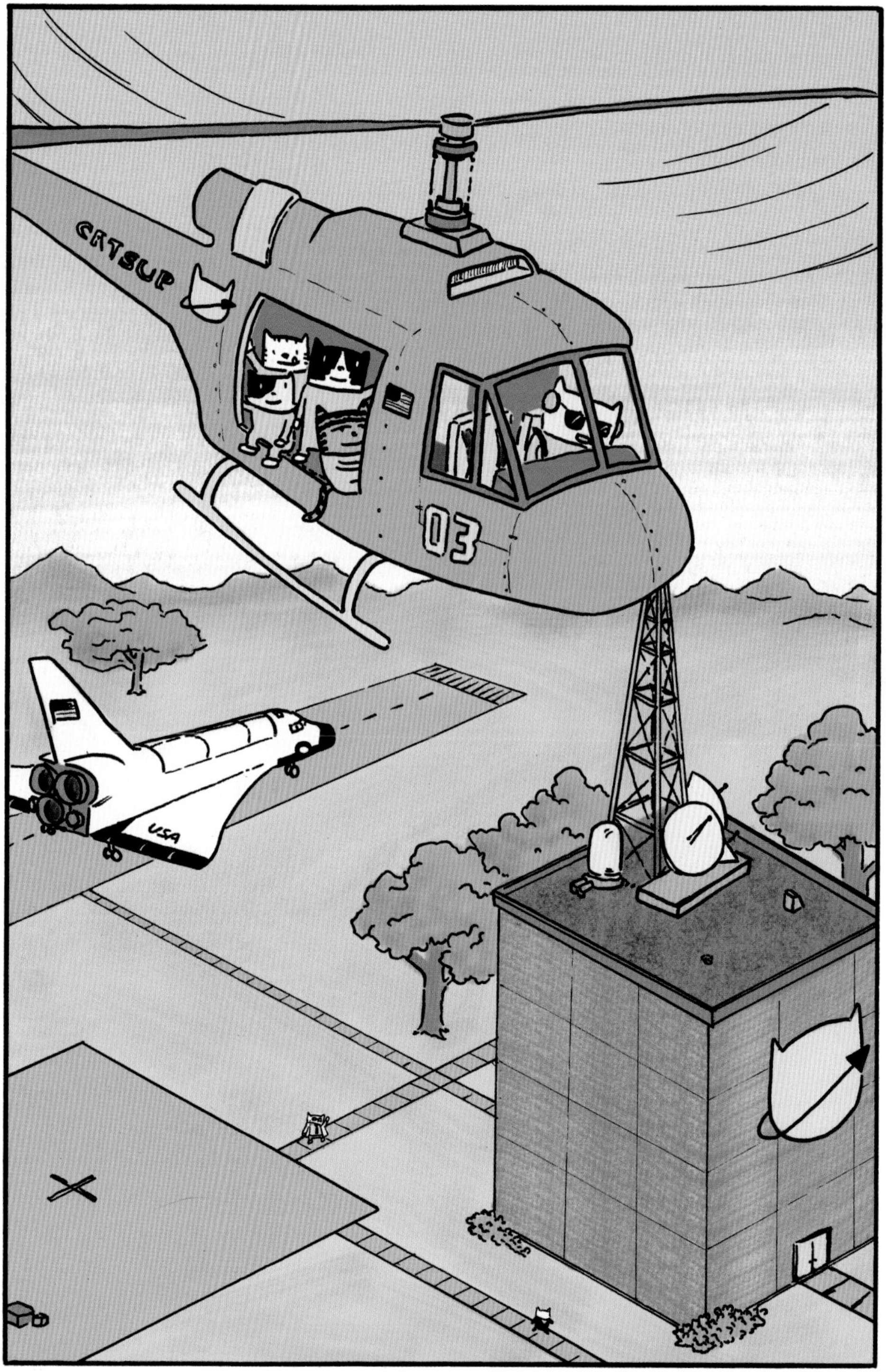
CATSUP
03
USA

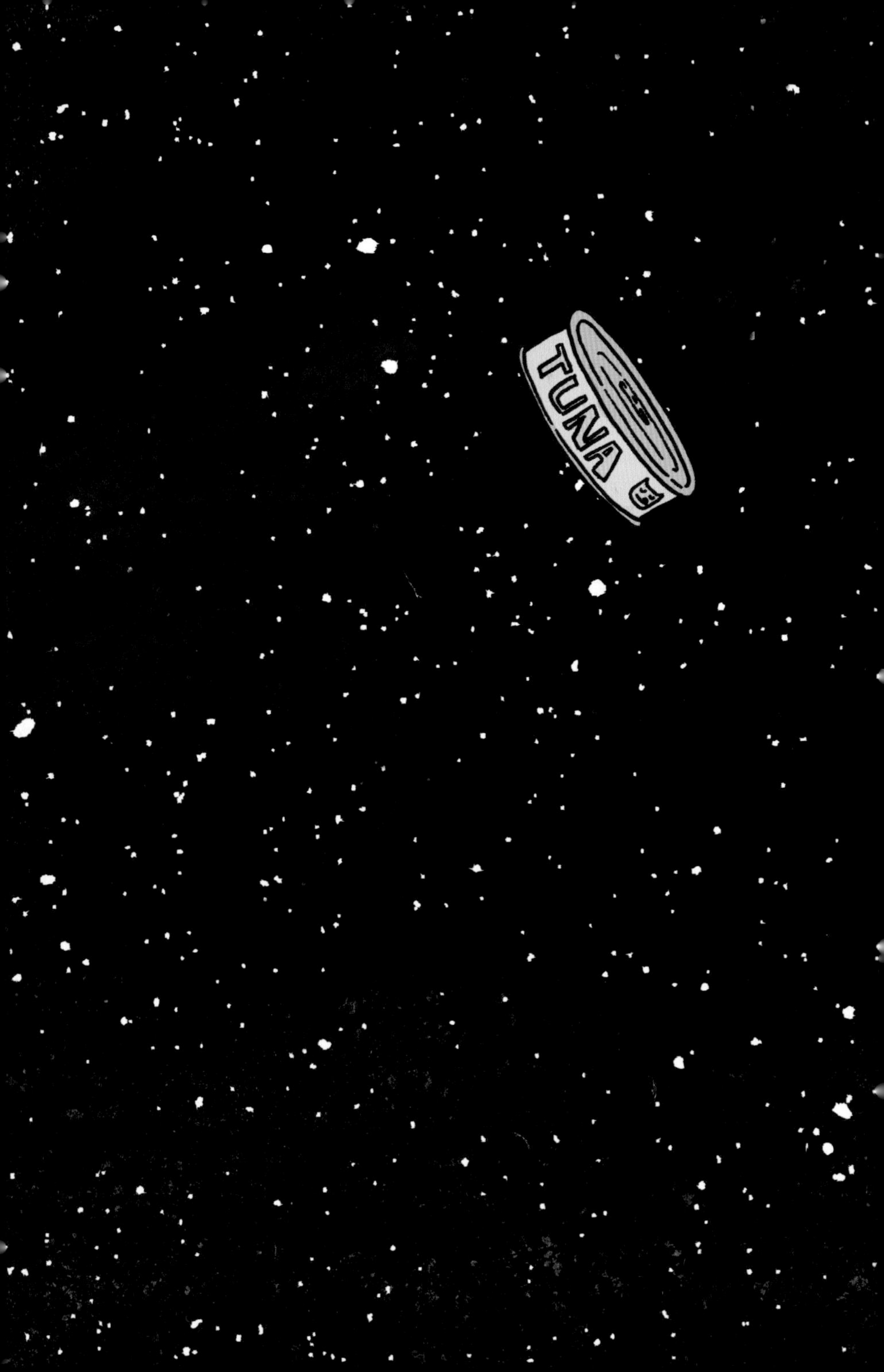
TUNA

CHAPTER 3

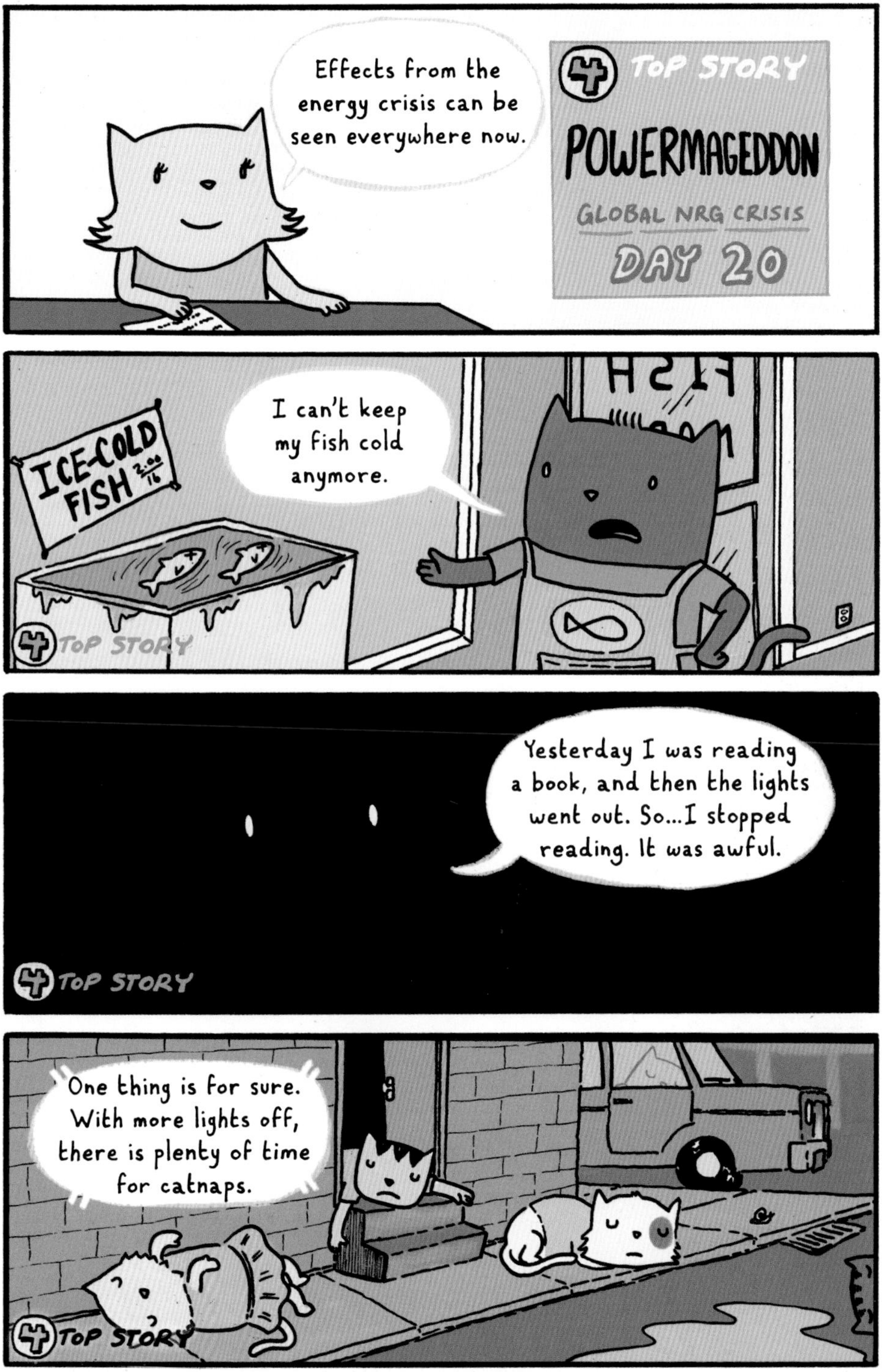
Effects from the energy crisis can be seen everywhere now.
TOP STORY
POWERMAGEDDON
GLOBAL NRG CRISIS
DAY 20
ICE-COLD FISH 2.00/16
I can't keep my fish cold anymore.
TOP STORY
Yesterday I was reading a book, and then the lights went out. So...I stopped reading. It was awful.
TOP STORY
One thing is for sure. With more lights off, there is plenty of time for catnaps.
TOP STORY

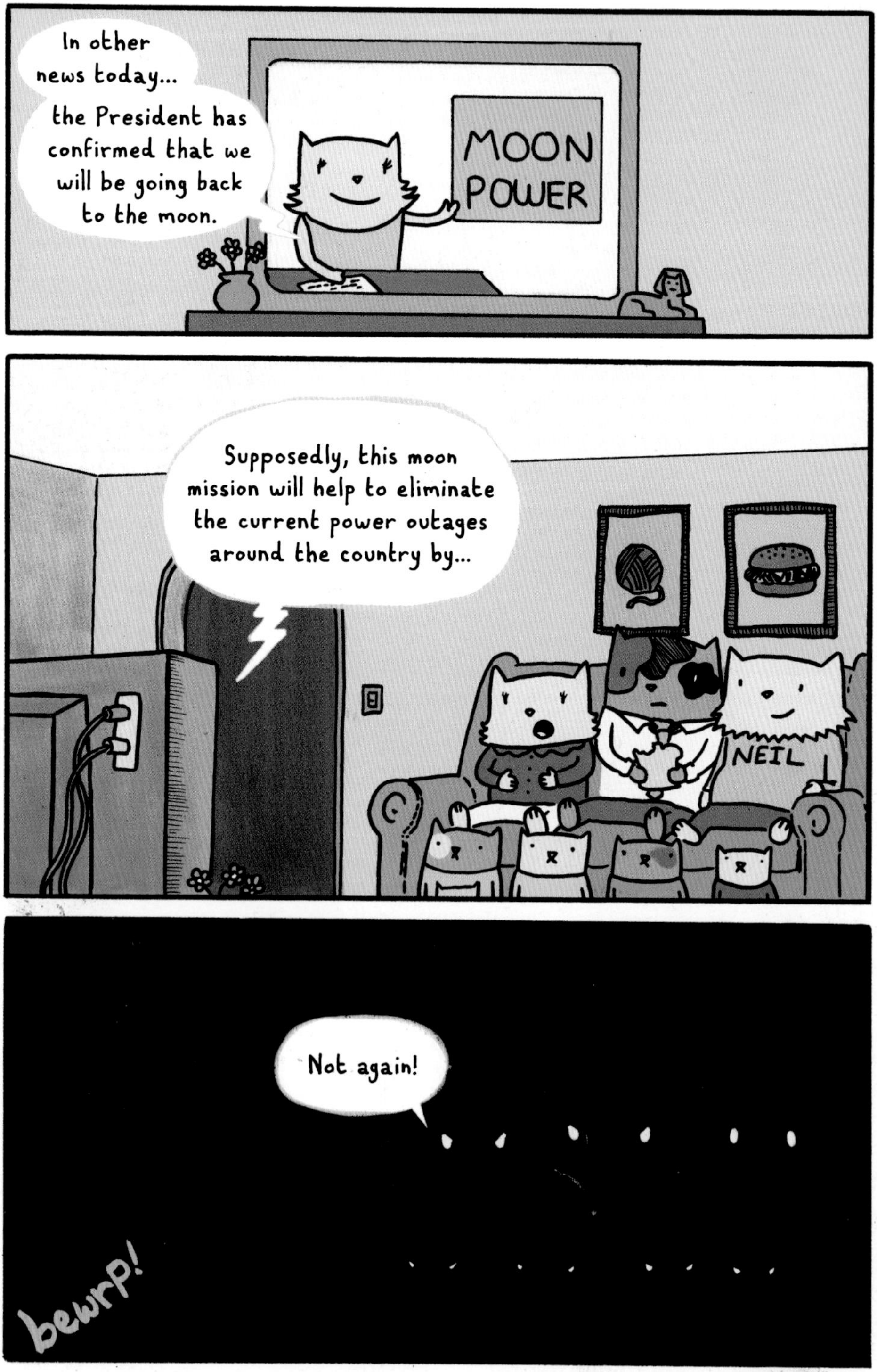
In other news today...
the President has confirmed that we will be going back to the moon.
MOON POWER
Supposedly, this moon mission will help to eliminate the current power outages around the country by...
NEIL
Not again!
bewrp!

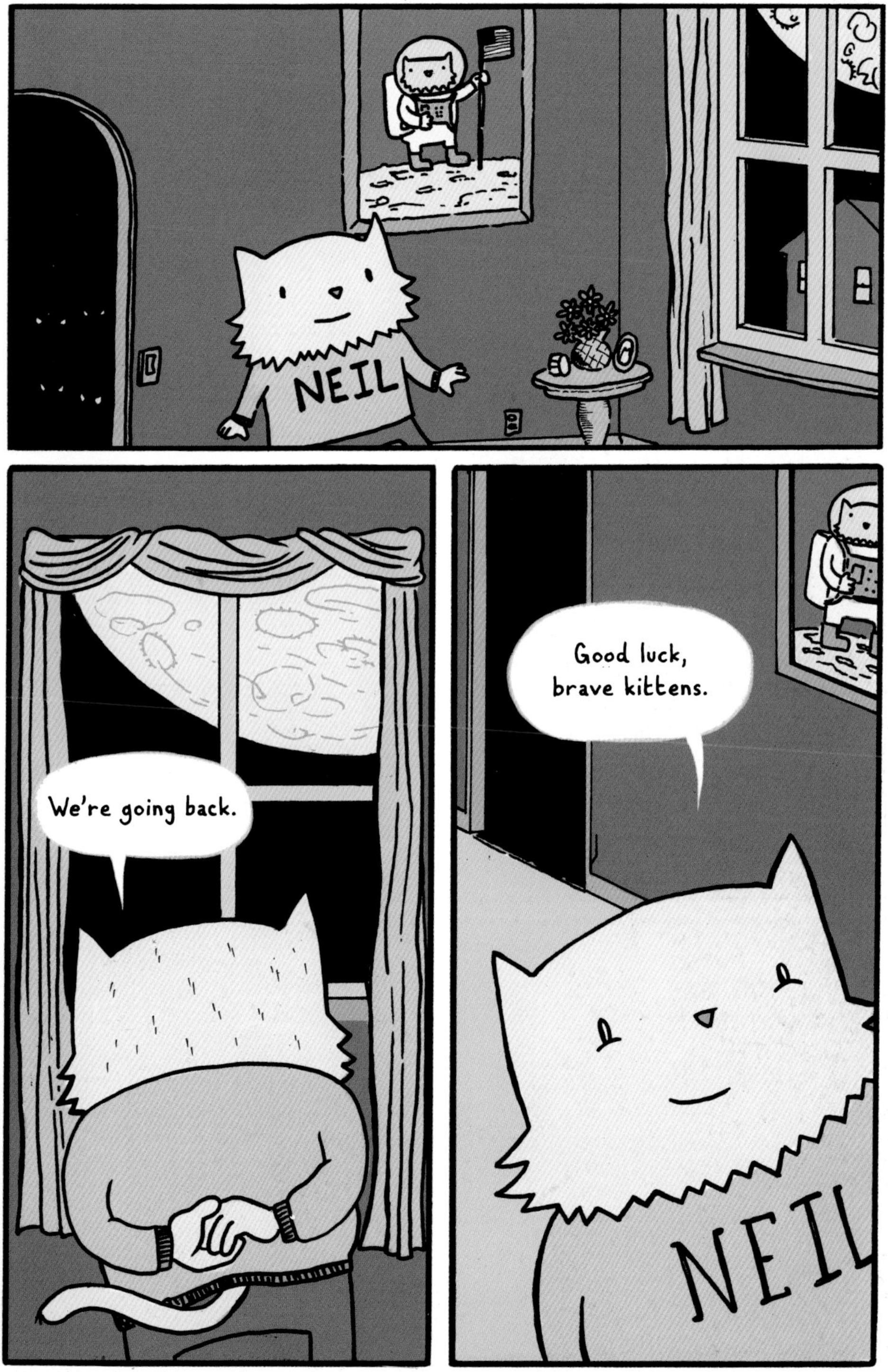
NEIL
We're going back.
Good luck,
brave kittens.
NEIL

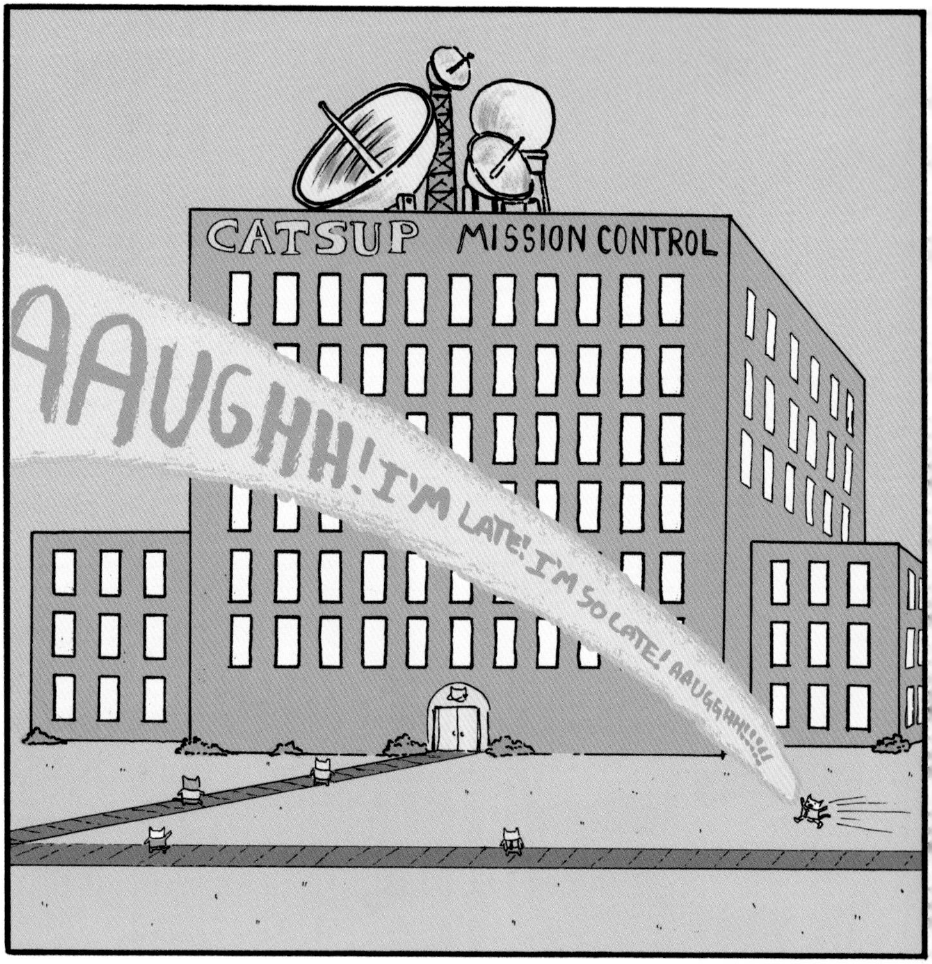
CATSUP MISSION CONTROL
AAUGHH! I'M LATE! I'M SO LATE! AAUGHH!!!!!

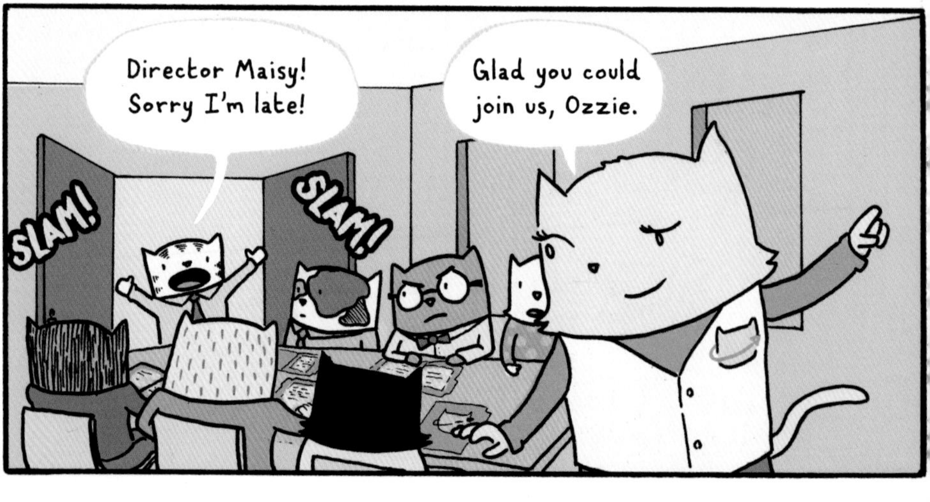
SLAM!
SLAM!
Director Maisy! Sorry I'm late!
Glad you could join us, Ozzie.

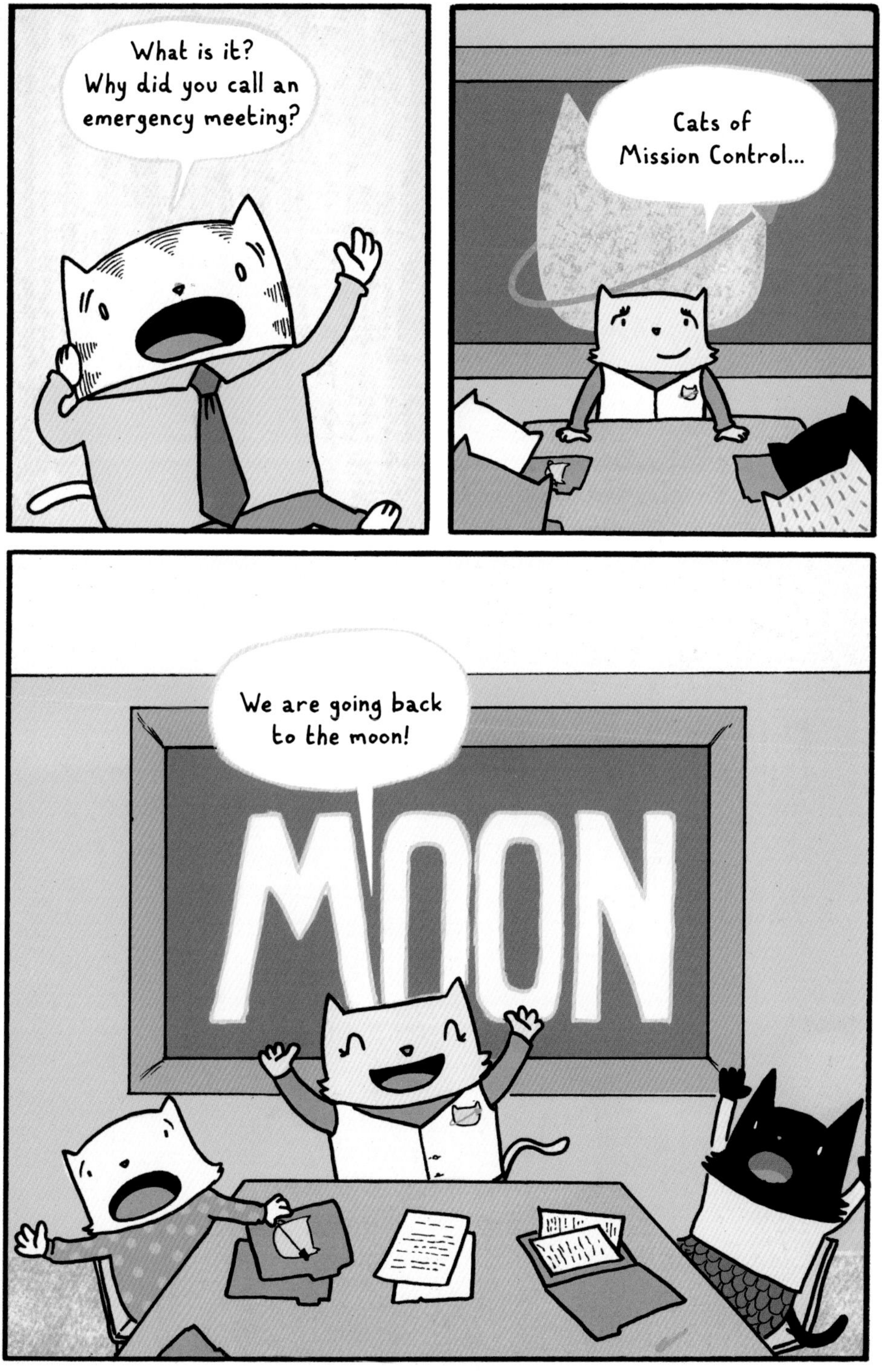
What is it?
Why did you call an emergency meeting?
Cats of Mission Control...
We are going back to the moon!
MOON

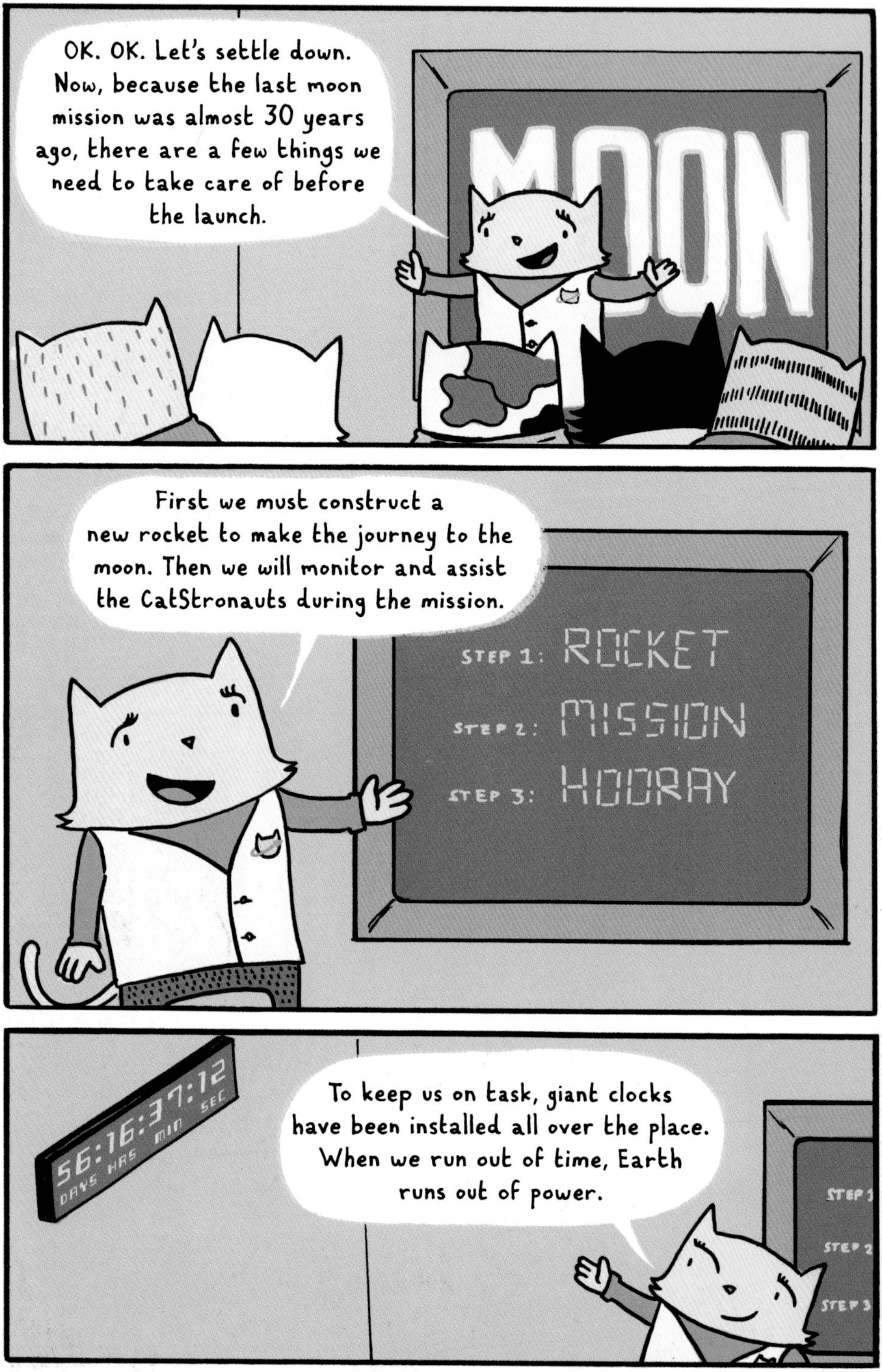
OK. OK. Let's settle down. Now, because the last moon mission was almost 30 years ago, there are a few things we need to take care of before the launch.
MOON
First we must construct a new rocket to make the journey to the moon. Then we will monitor and assist the CatStronauts during the mission.
STEP 1: ROCKET
STEP 2: MISSION
STEP 3: HOORAY
56:16:37:12
DAYS HRS MIN SEC
To keep us on task, giant clocks have been installed all over the place. When we run out of time, Earth runs out of power.

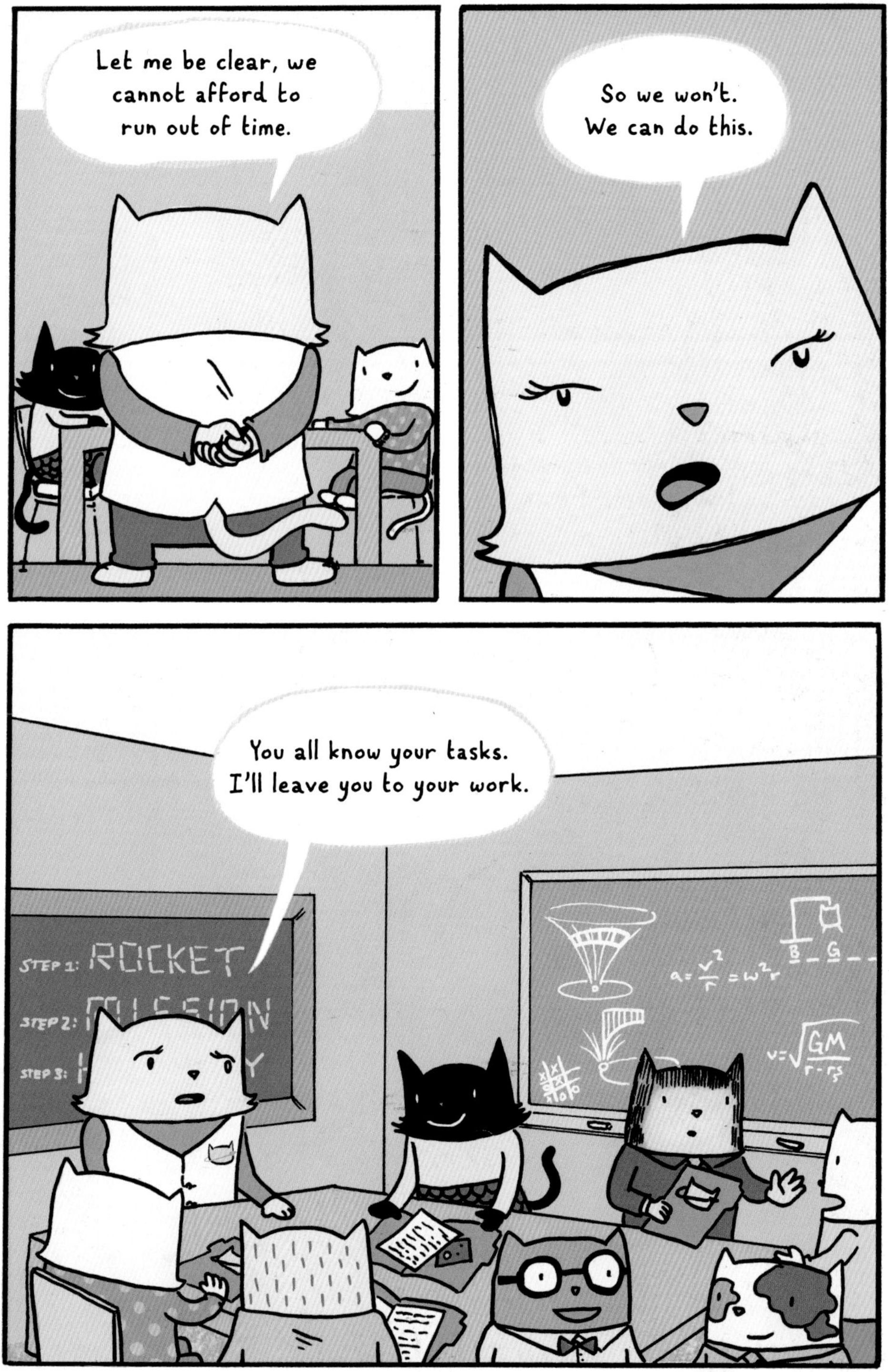
Let me be clear, we cannot afford to run out of time.
So we won't. We can do this.
You all know your tasks. I'll leave you to your work.
STEP 1: ROCKET
STEP 2:
STEP 3:

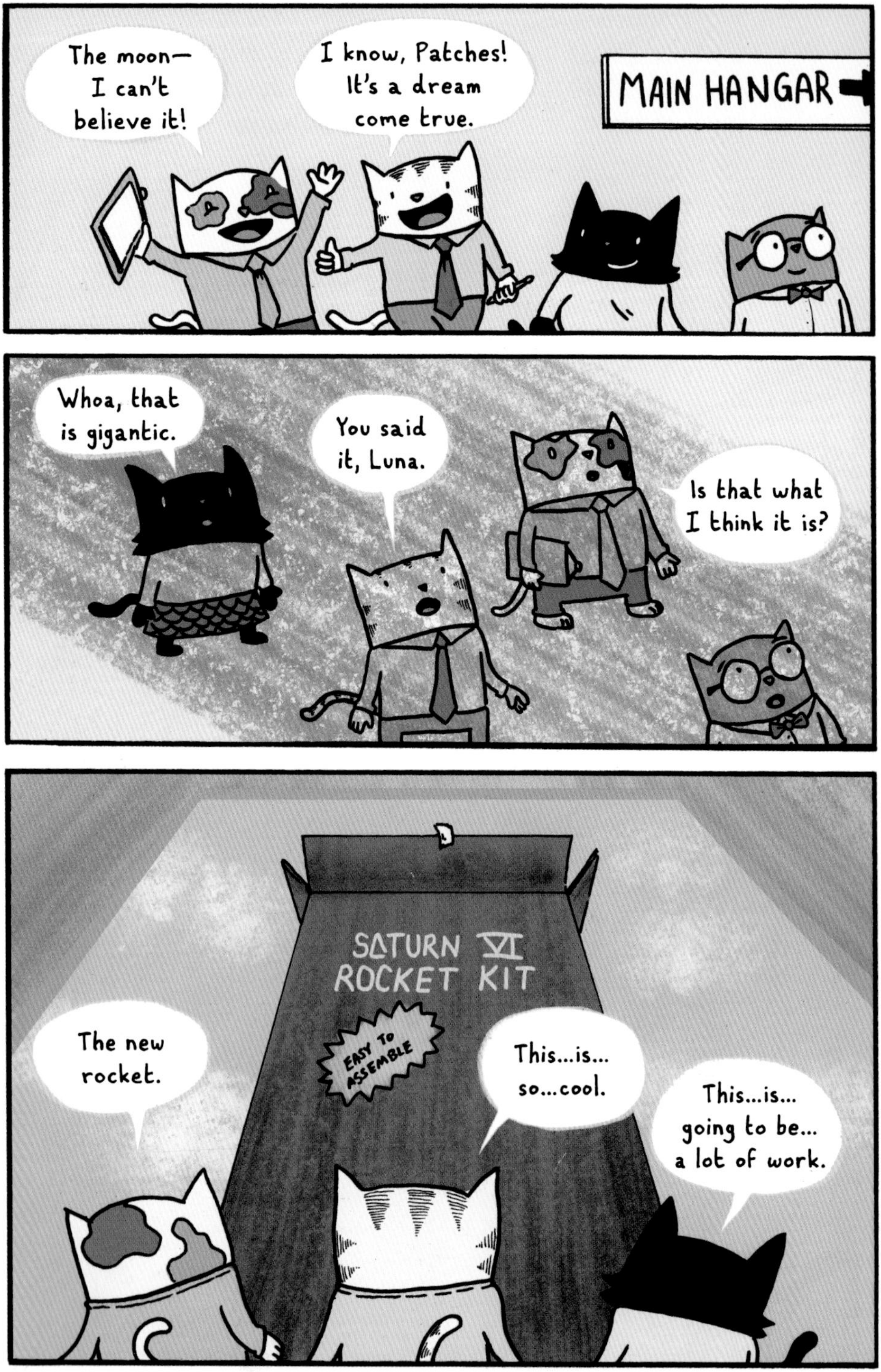
The moon— I can't believe it!
I know, Patches! It's a dream come true.
MAIN HANGAR
Whoa, that is gigantic.
You said it, Luna.
Is that what I think it is?
SATURN VI ROCKET KIT
EASY TO ASSEMBLE
The new rocket.
This...is... so...cool.
This...is... going to be... a lot of work.

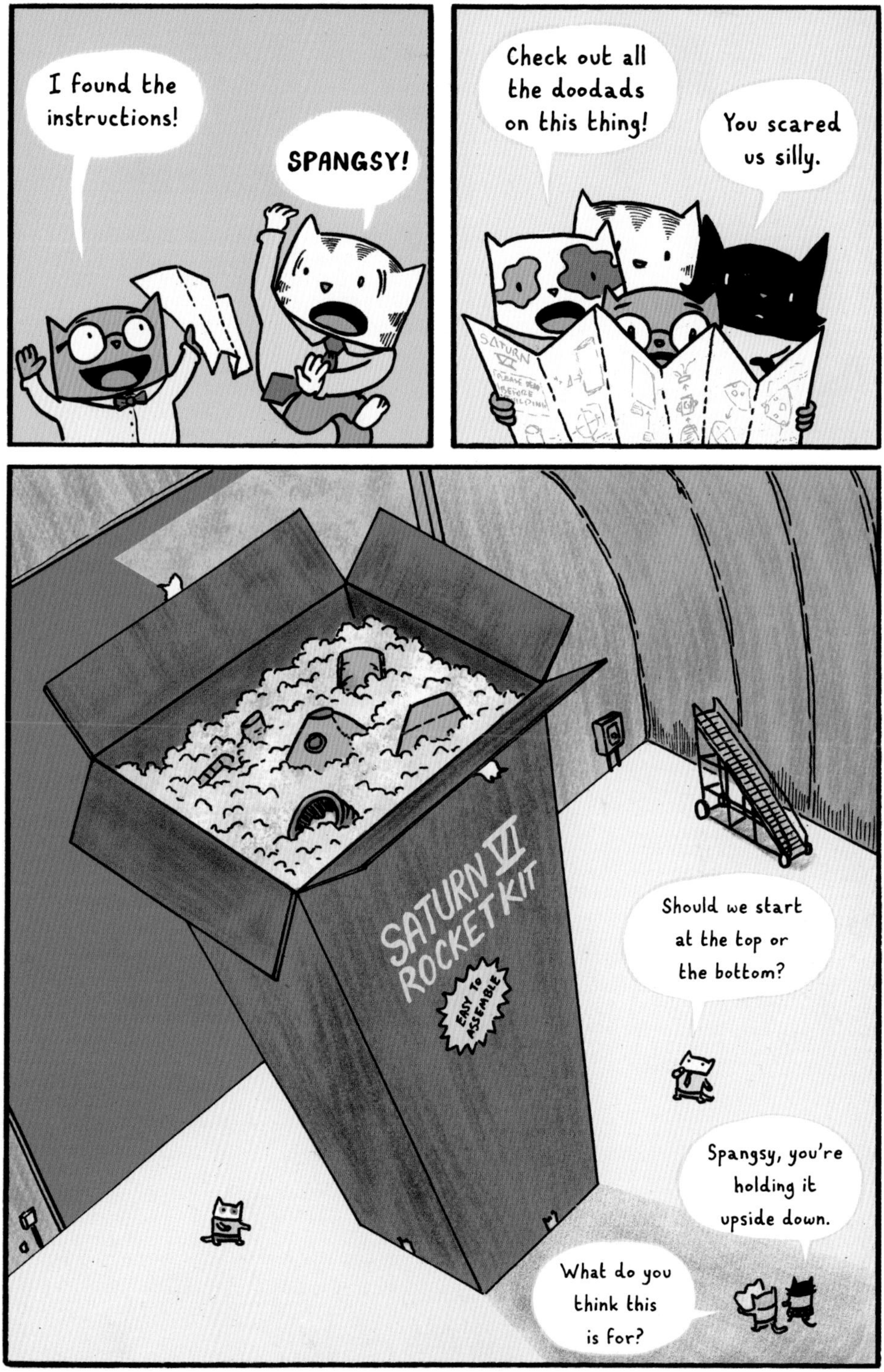
I found the instructions!
SPANGSY!
Check out all the doodads on this thing!
You scared us silly.
SATURN VI ROCKET KIT
EASY TO ASSEMBLE
Should we start at the top or the bottom?
Spangsy, you're holding it upside down.
What do you think this is for?

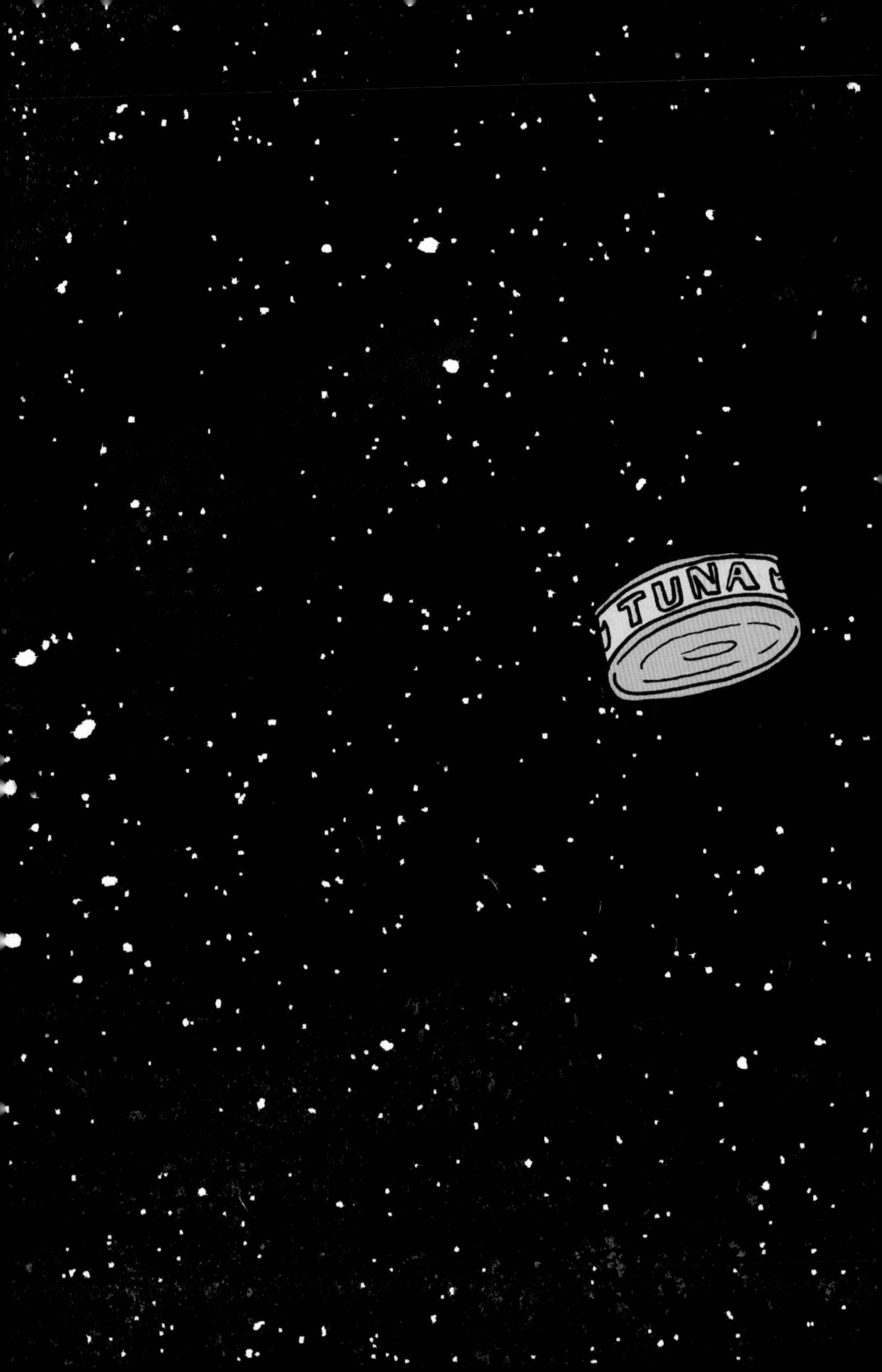
TUNA

CHAPTER 4

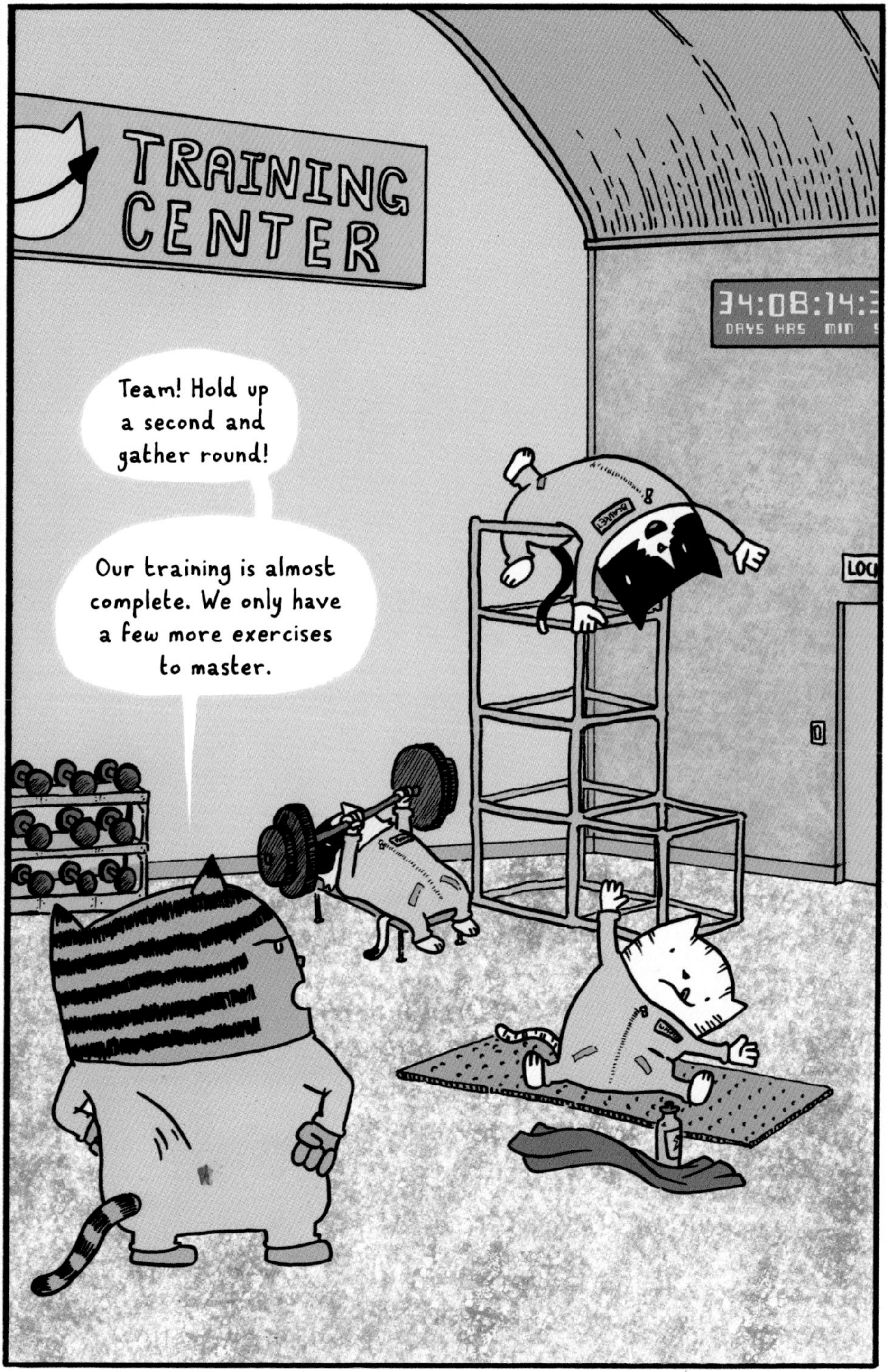
TRAINING CENTER
34:08:14:3
DAYS HRS MIN
Team! Hold up a second and gather round!
Our training is almost complete. We only have a few more exercises to master.

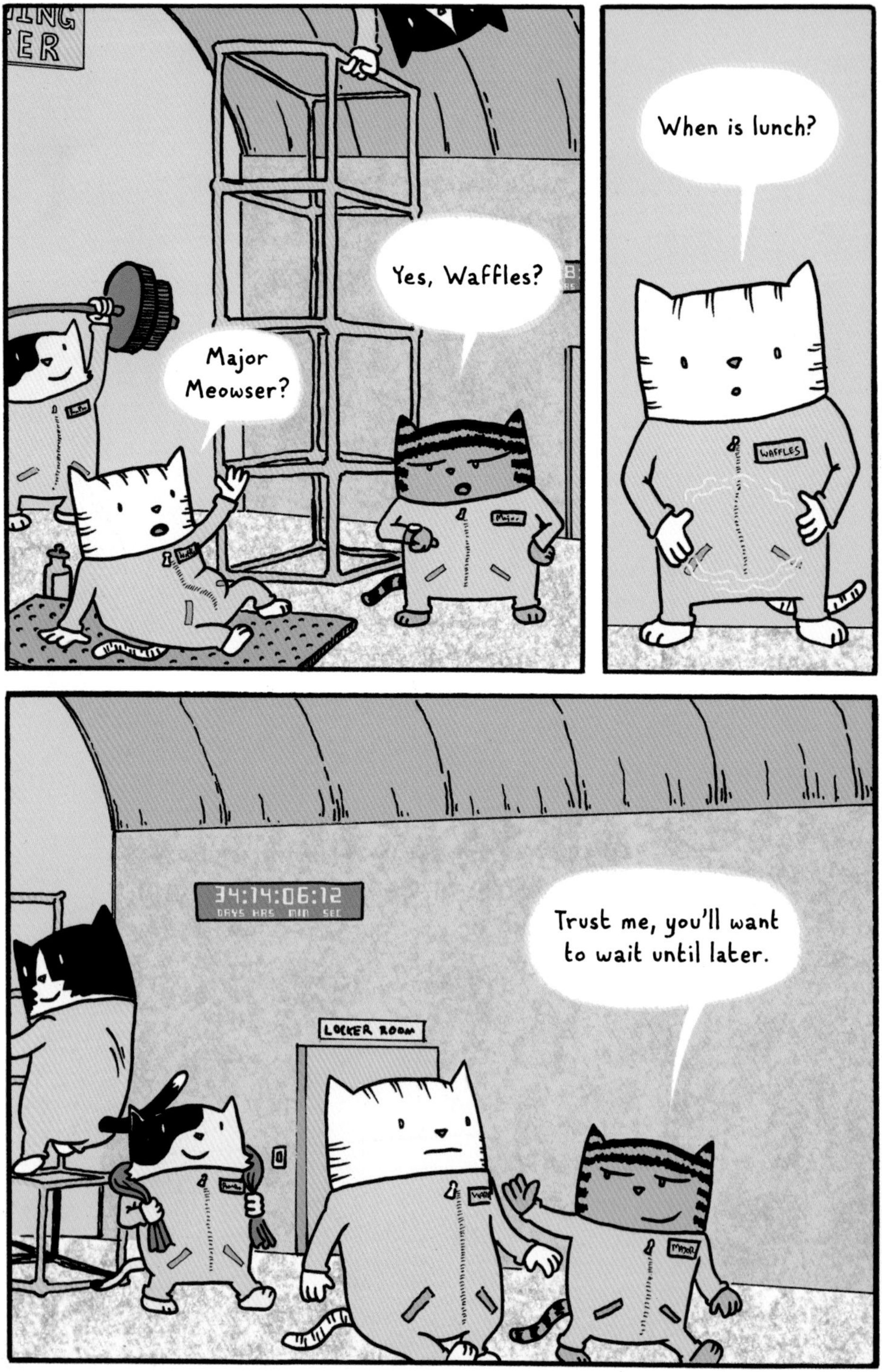
Major Meowser?
Yes, Waffles?
When is lunch?
WAFFLES
34:14:06:12
DAYS HRS MIN SEC
LOCKER ROOM
Trust me, you'll want to wait until later.

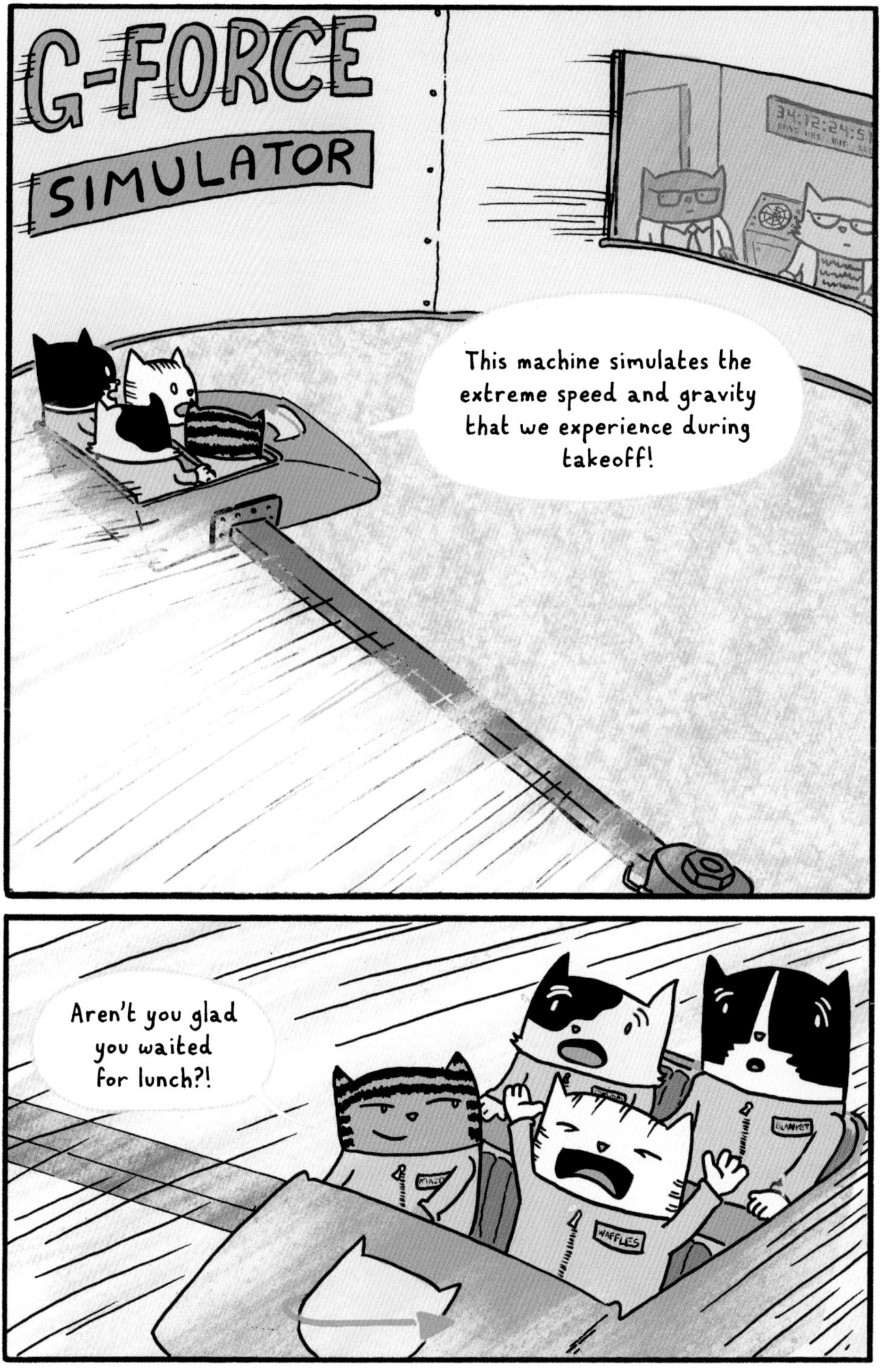
G-FORCE
SIMULATOR
This machine simulates the extreme speed and gravity that we experience during takeoff!
Aren't you glad you waited for lunch?!
BLANKET
WAFFLES

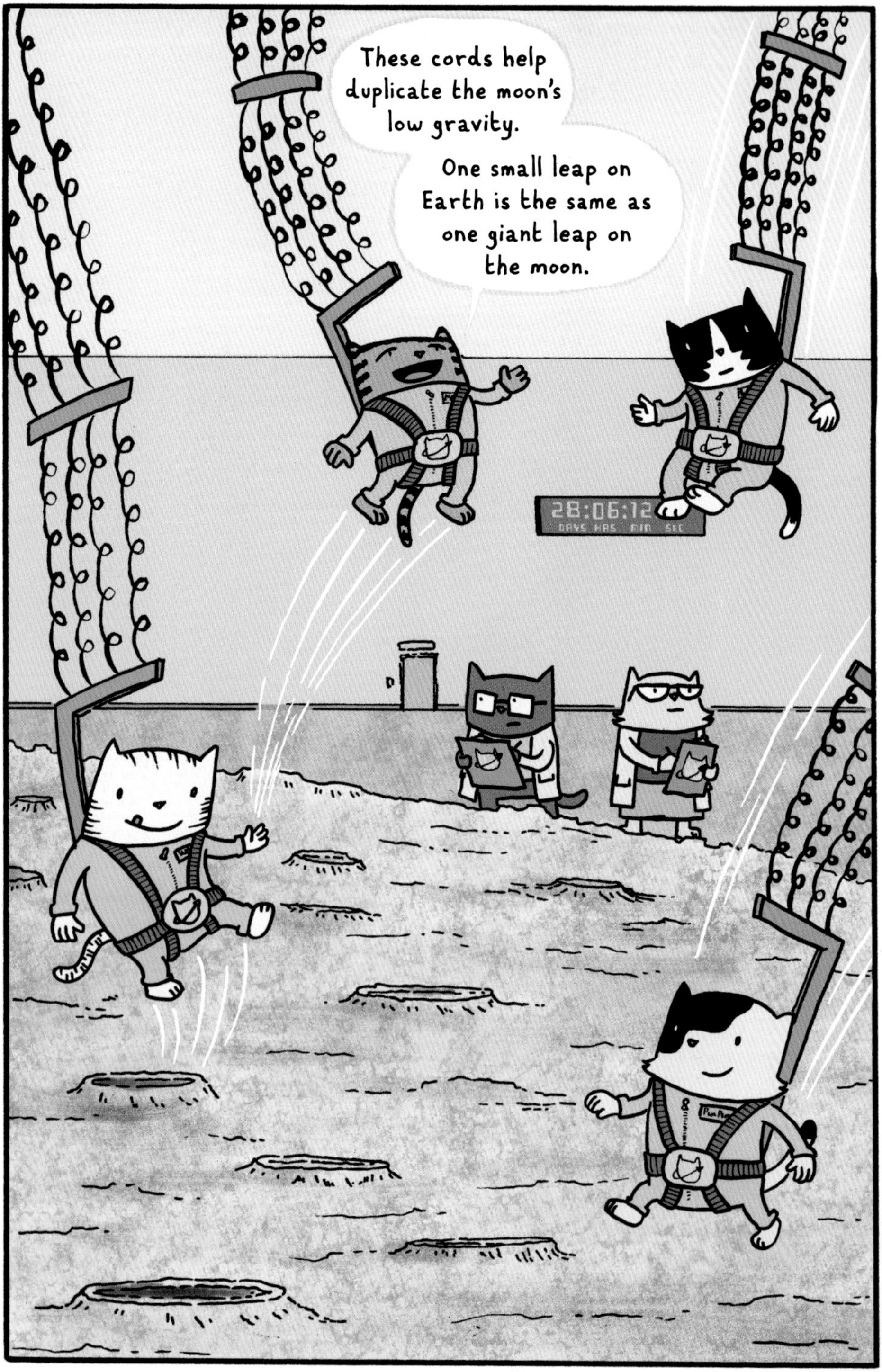
These cords help duplicate the moon's low gravity.
One small leap on Earth is the same as one giant leap on the moon.
28:06:12
DAYS HRS MIN SEC

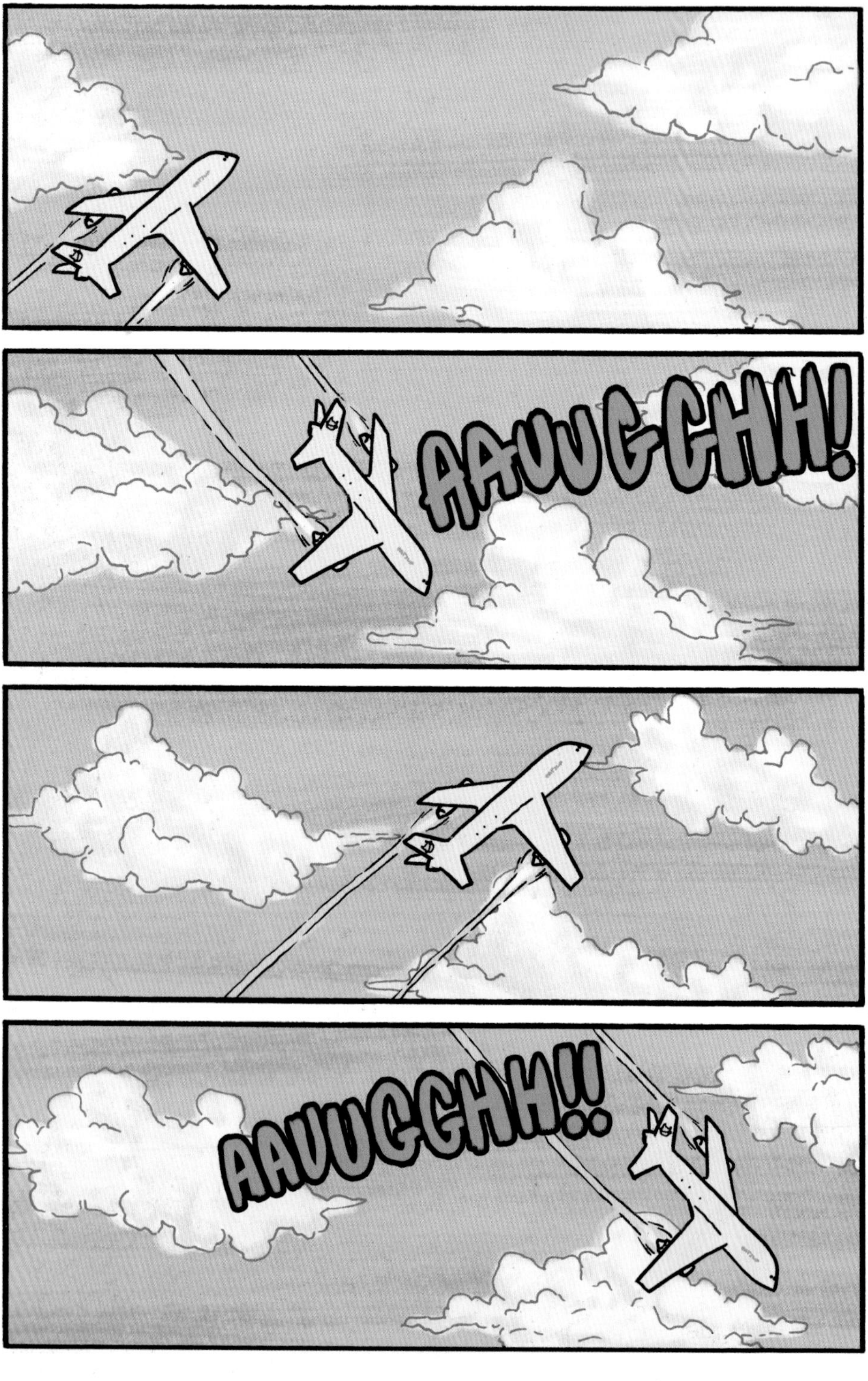
AAUUGCHH!
AAUUGGHH!!

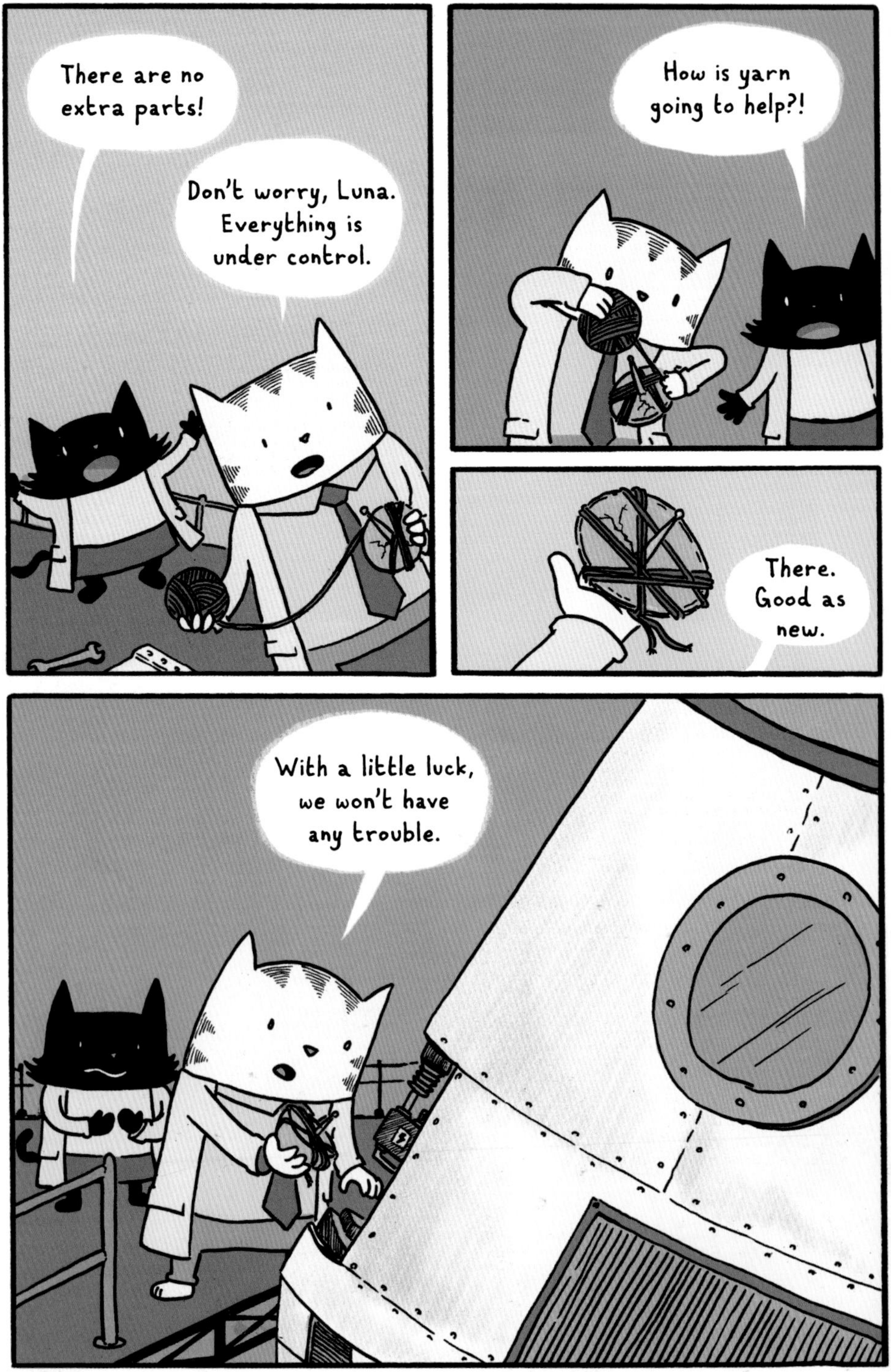
There are no extra parts!
Don't worry, Luna. Everything is under control.
How is yarn going to help?!
There. Good as new.
With a little luck, we won't have any trouble.

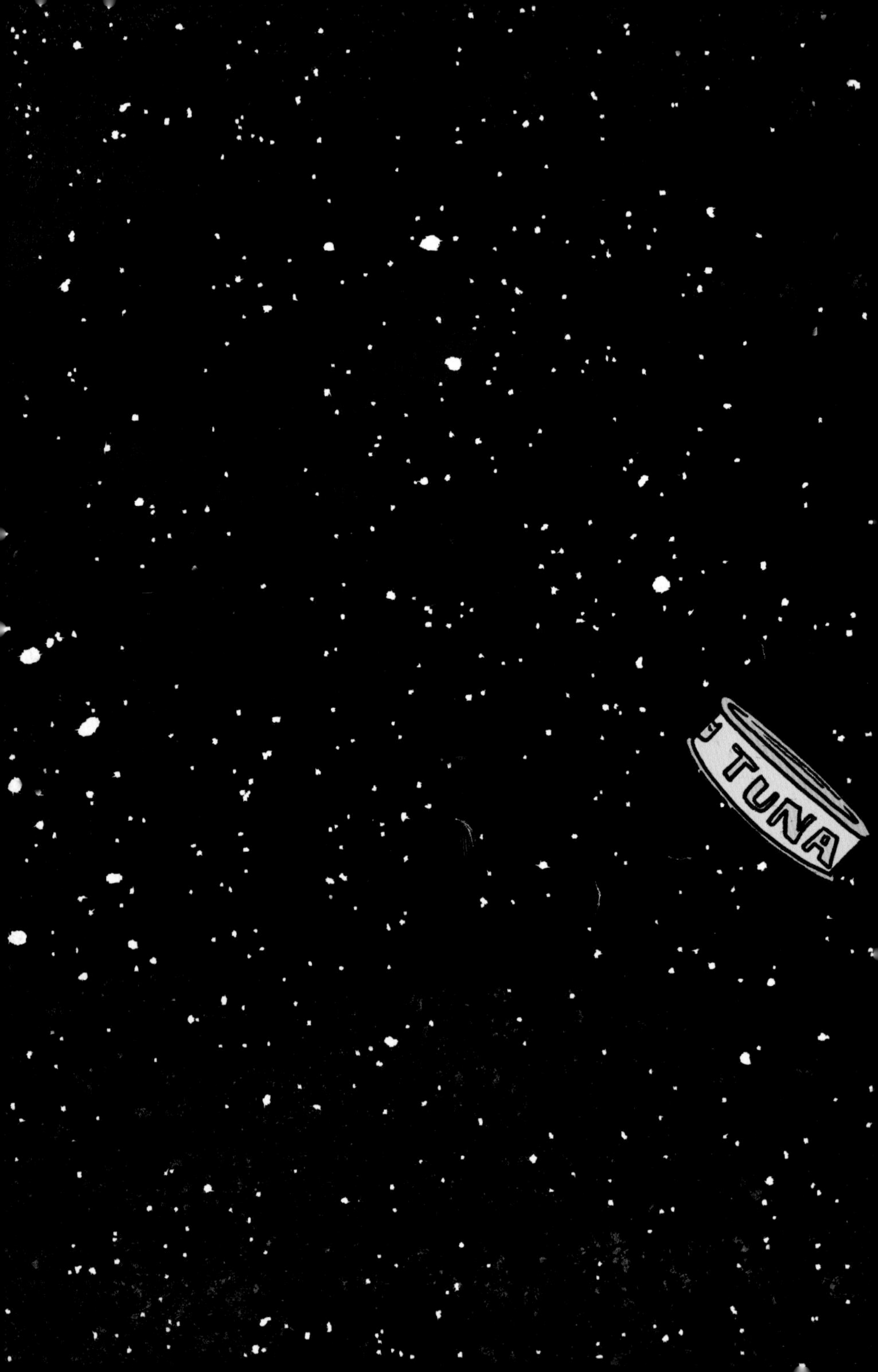
TUNA

CHAPTER 5

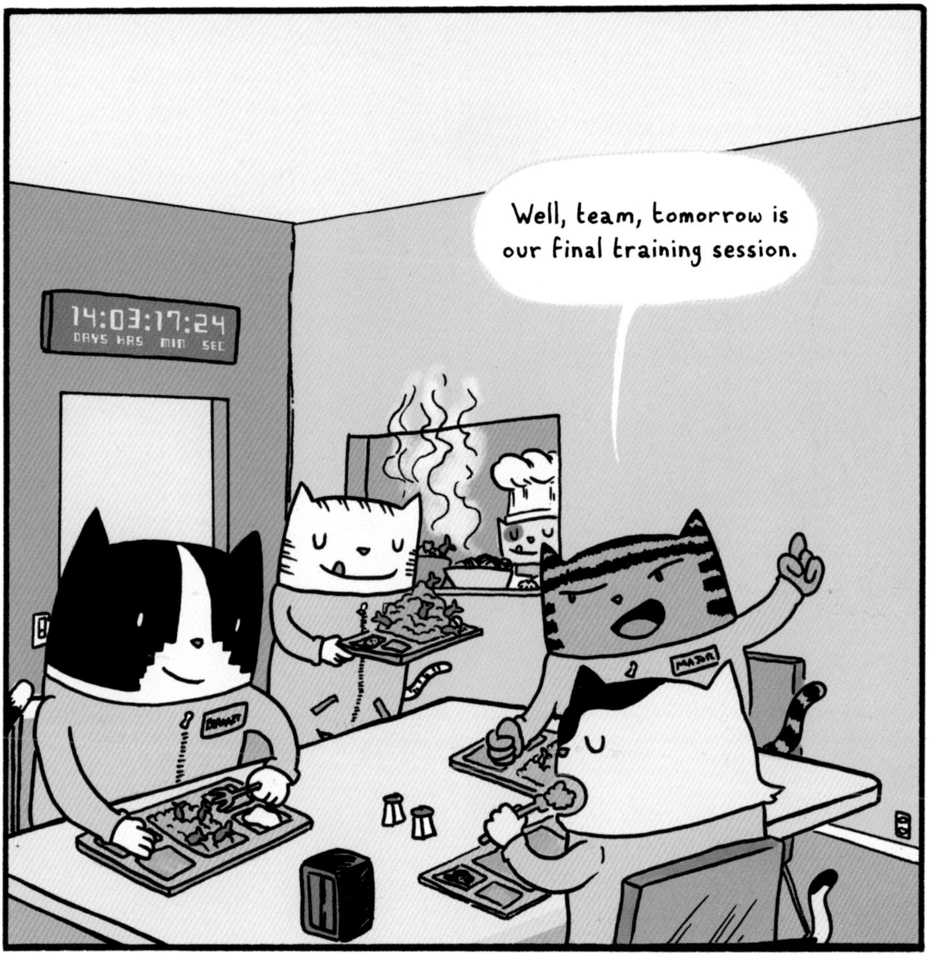
14:03:17:24
DAYS HRS MIN SEC
Well, team, tomorrow is our final training session.

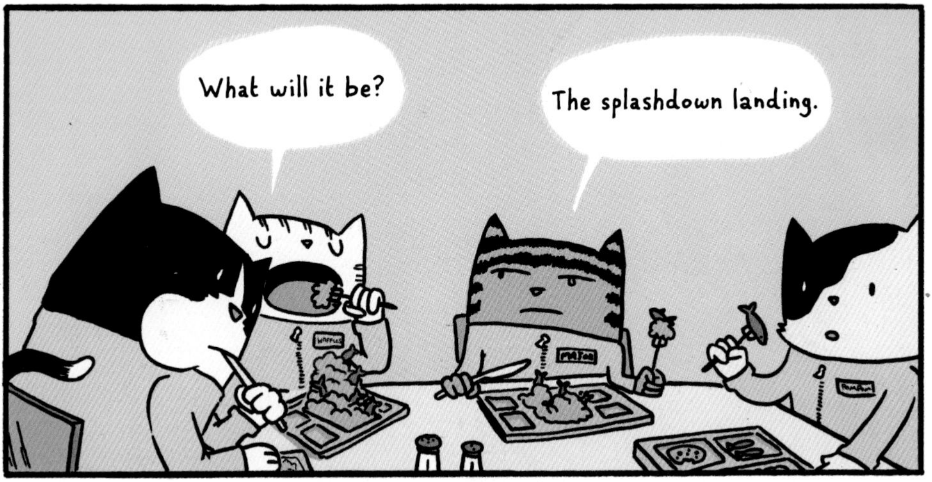
What will it be?
The splashdown landing.

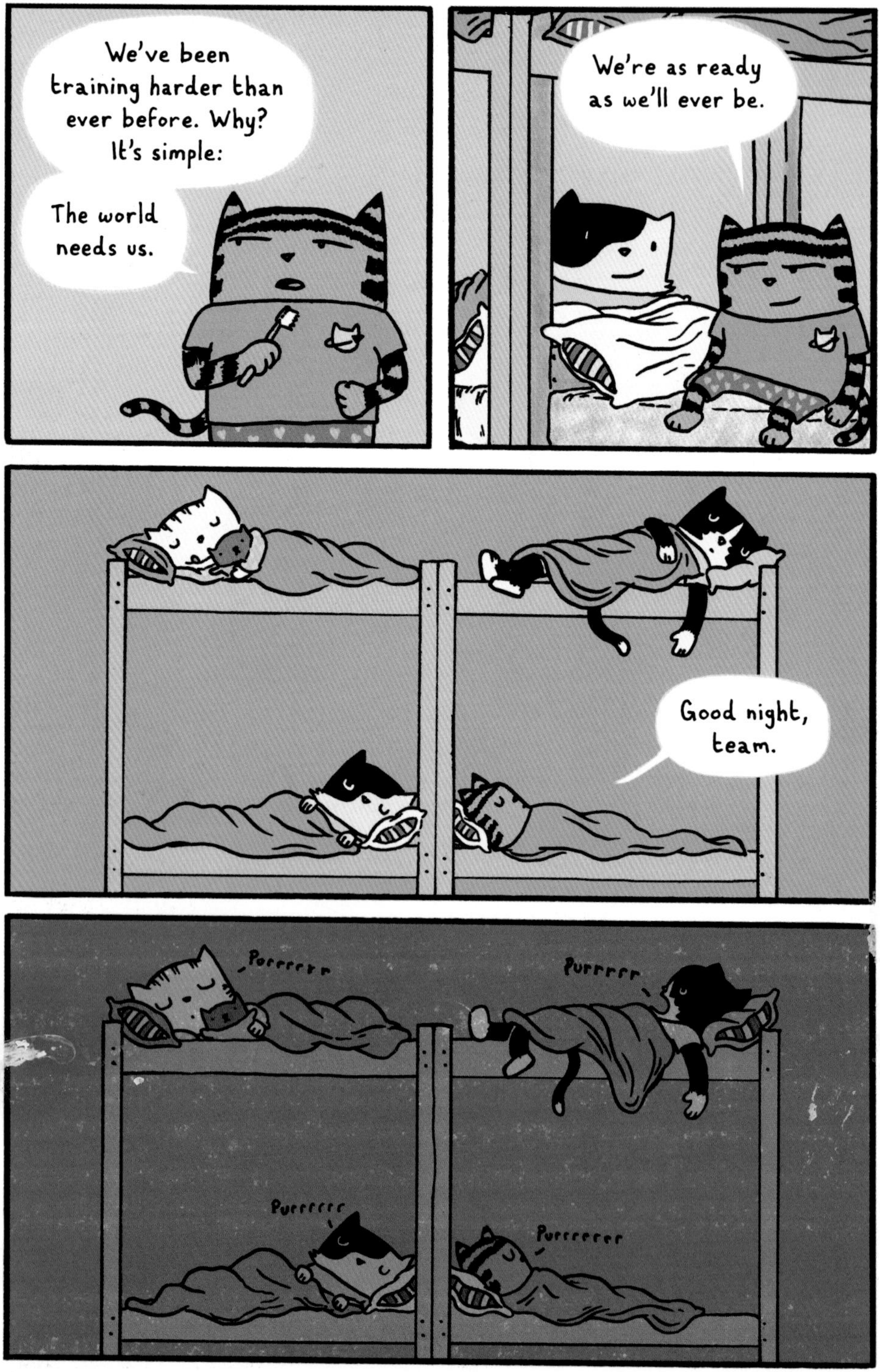
We've been training harder than ever before. Why? It's simple:
The world needs us.
We're as ready as we'll ever be.
Good night, team.
Purrrrrr
Purrrrrr
Purrrrrr
Purrrrrrr

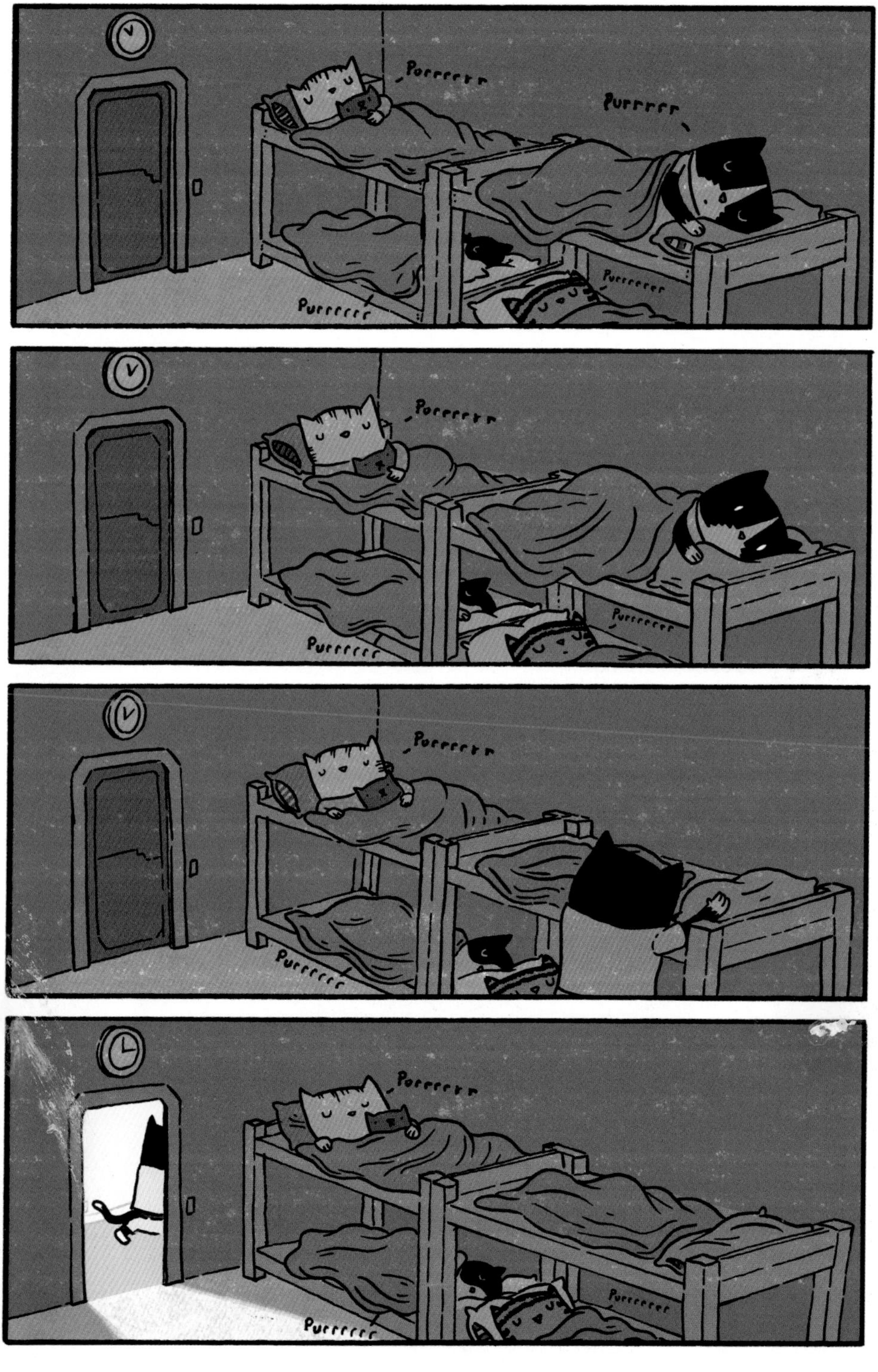
Purrrrrr
Purrrrr
Purrrrrrr
Purrrrrrr
Purrrrrr
Purrrrrrr
Purrrrrrr
Purrrrrr
Purrrrrrr
Purrrrrr
Purrrrrrr
Purrrrrrr

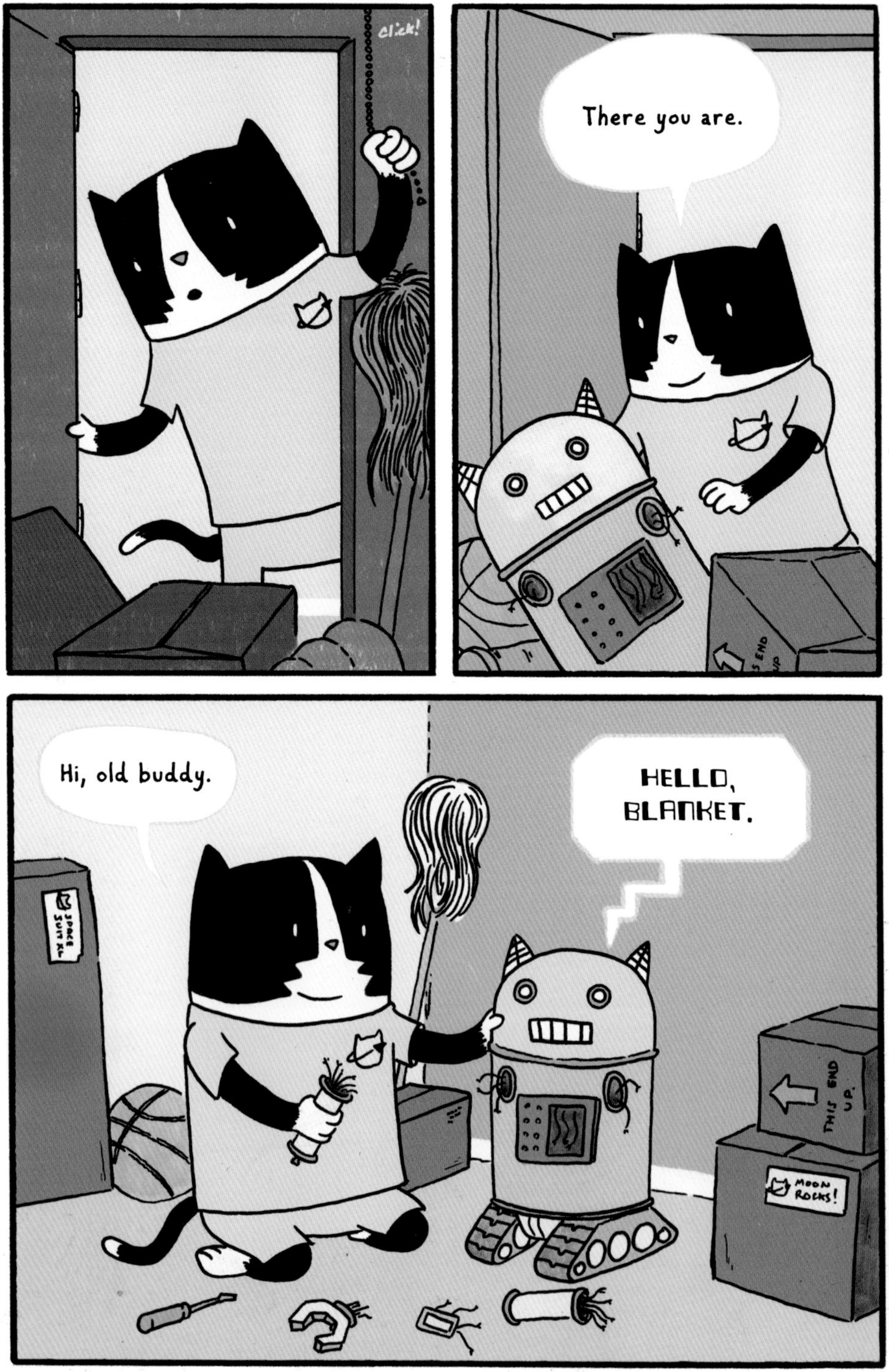
Click!
There you are.
Hi, old buddy.
HELLO, BLANKET.
SPACE SUIT XL
THIS END UP.
MOON ROCKS!

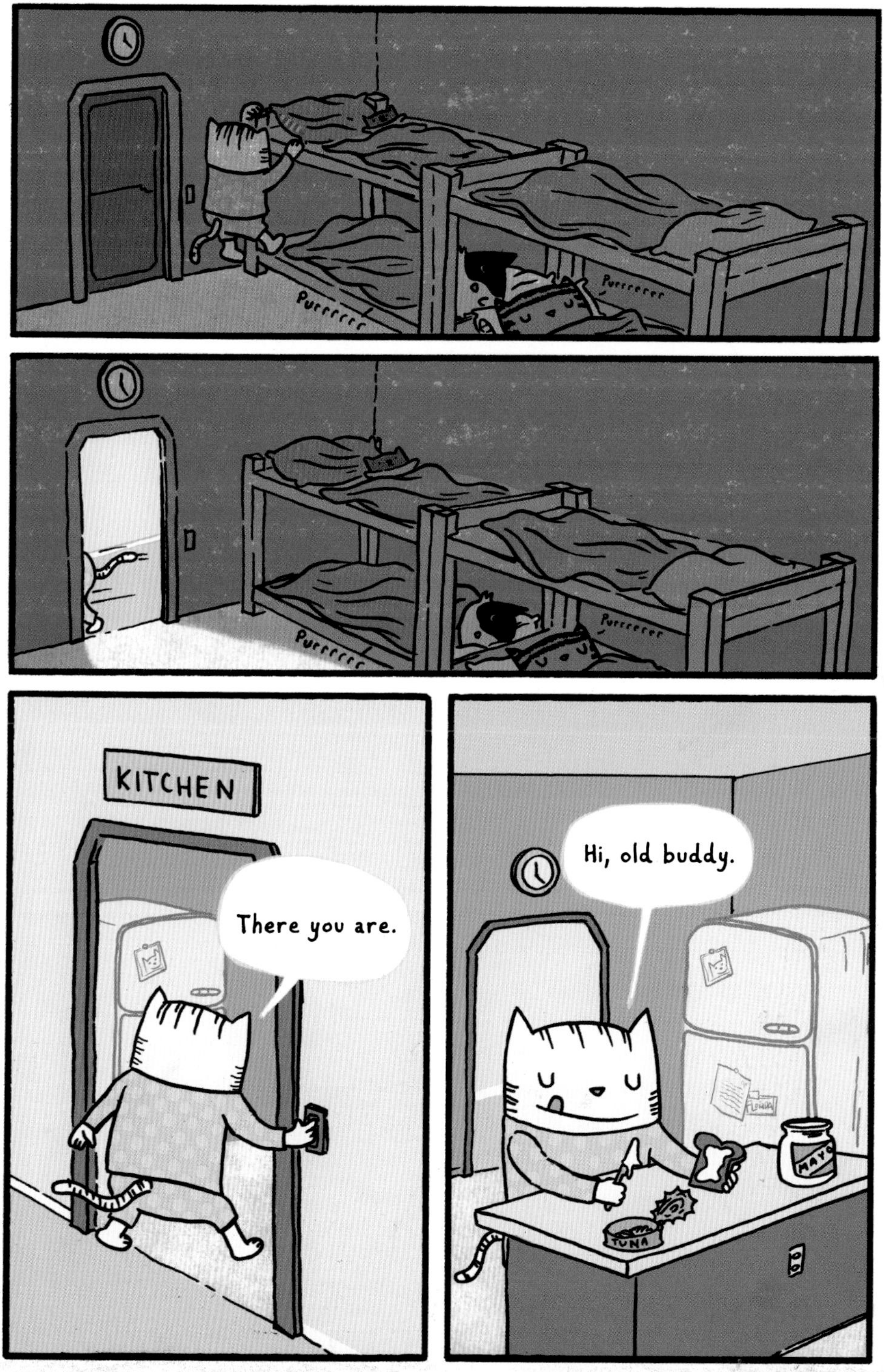

Purrrrrr
Purrrrrr
Purrrrrr
Purrrrrr
KITCHEN
There you are.
Hi, old buddy.
MAYO
TUNA

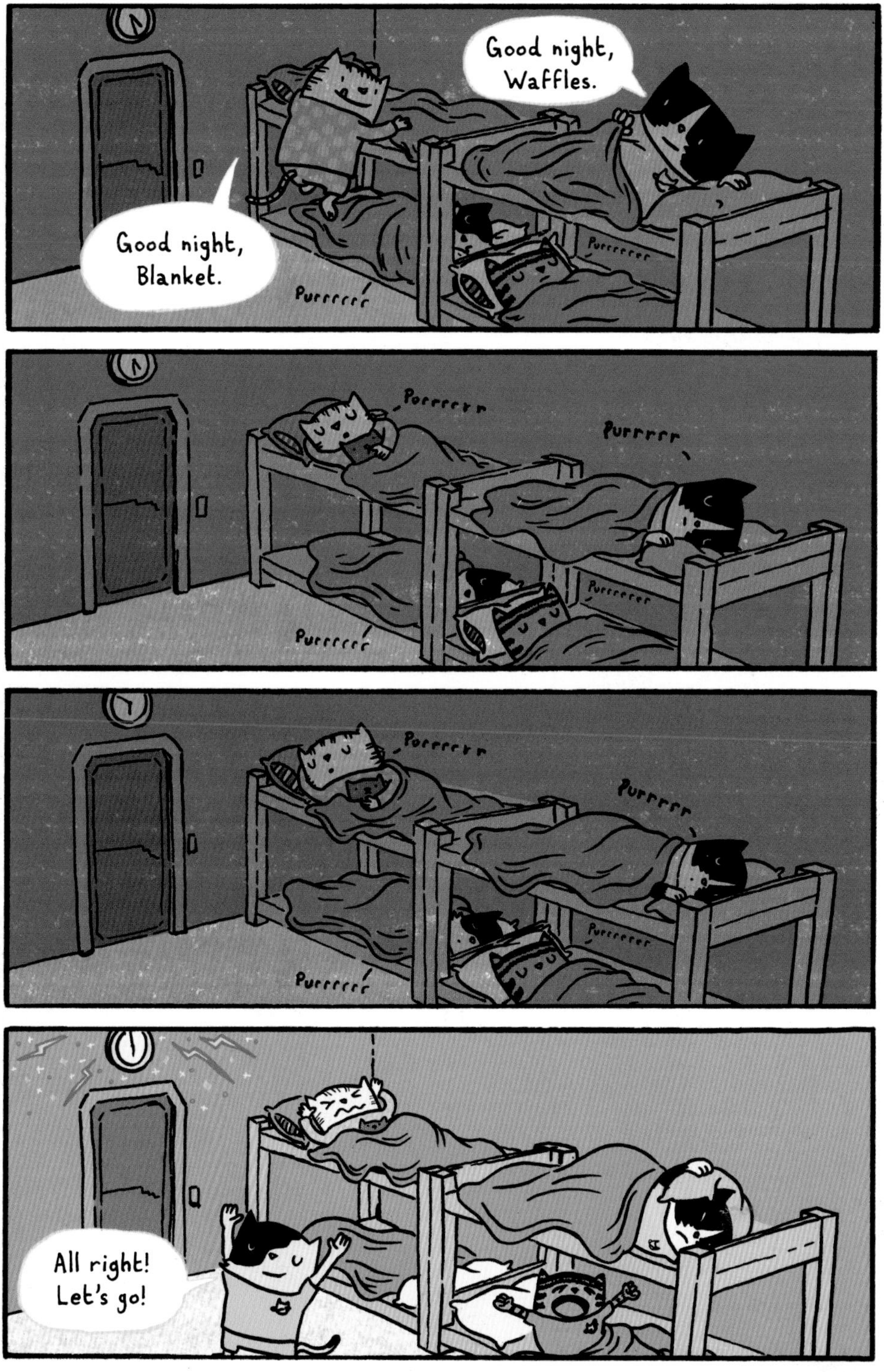
Good night,
Waffles.
Good night,
Blanket.
Purrrrrrr
Purrrrrr
Purrrrrrr
Purrrrr
Purrrrrrr
Purrrrrr
Purrrrr
Purrrrrrr
Purrrrrr
Purrrrrrr
Purrrrrr
All right!
Let's go!

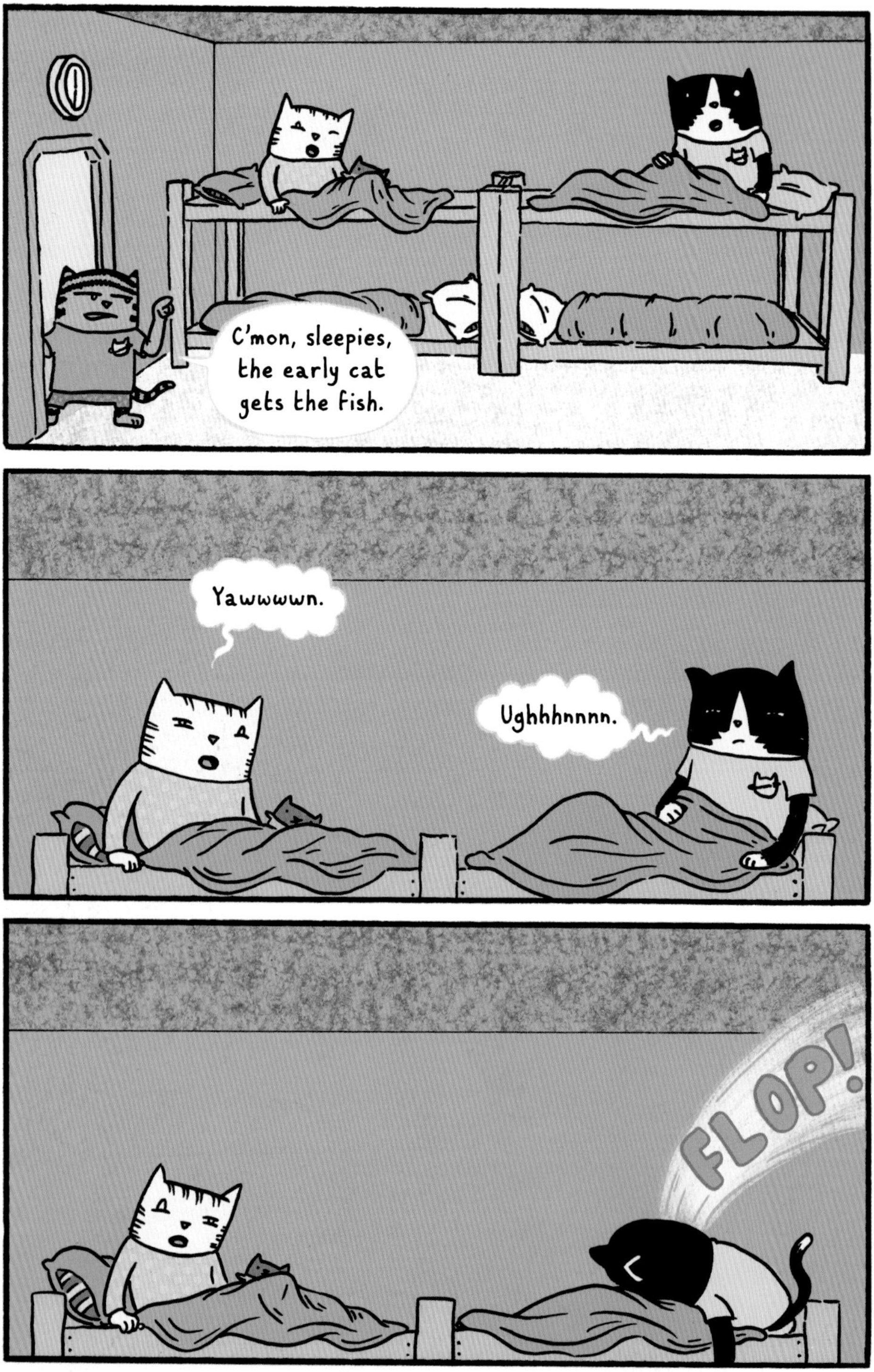
C'mon, sleepies, the early cat gets the fish.
Yawwwwn.
Ughhhnnnn.
FLOP!

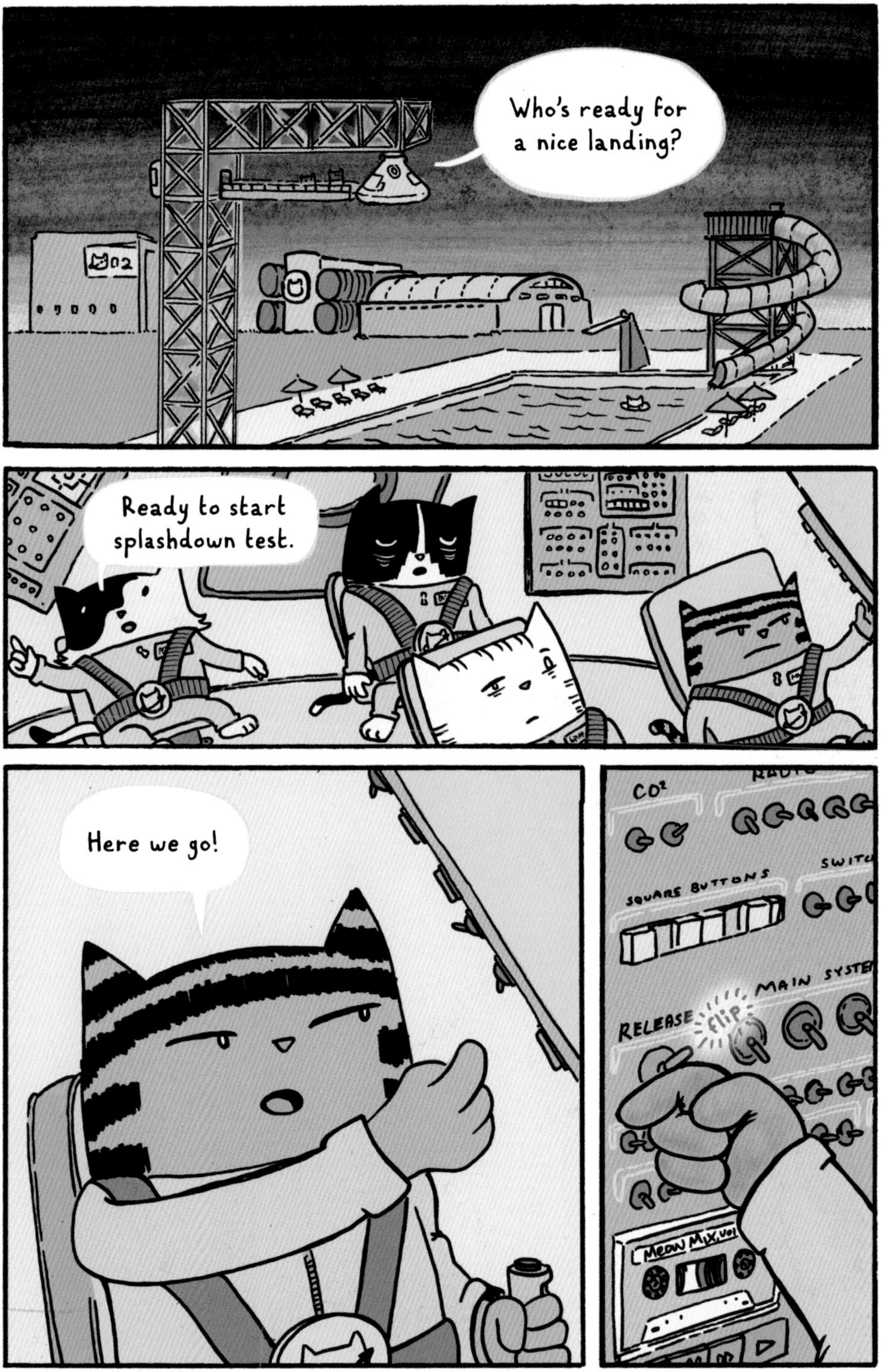
Who's ready for a nice landing?
Ready to start splashdown test.
Here we go!
CO2
SQUARE BUTTONS
RELEASE
flip
MEOW MIX vol

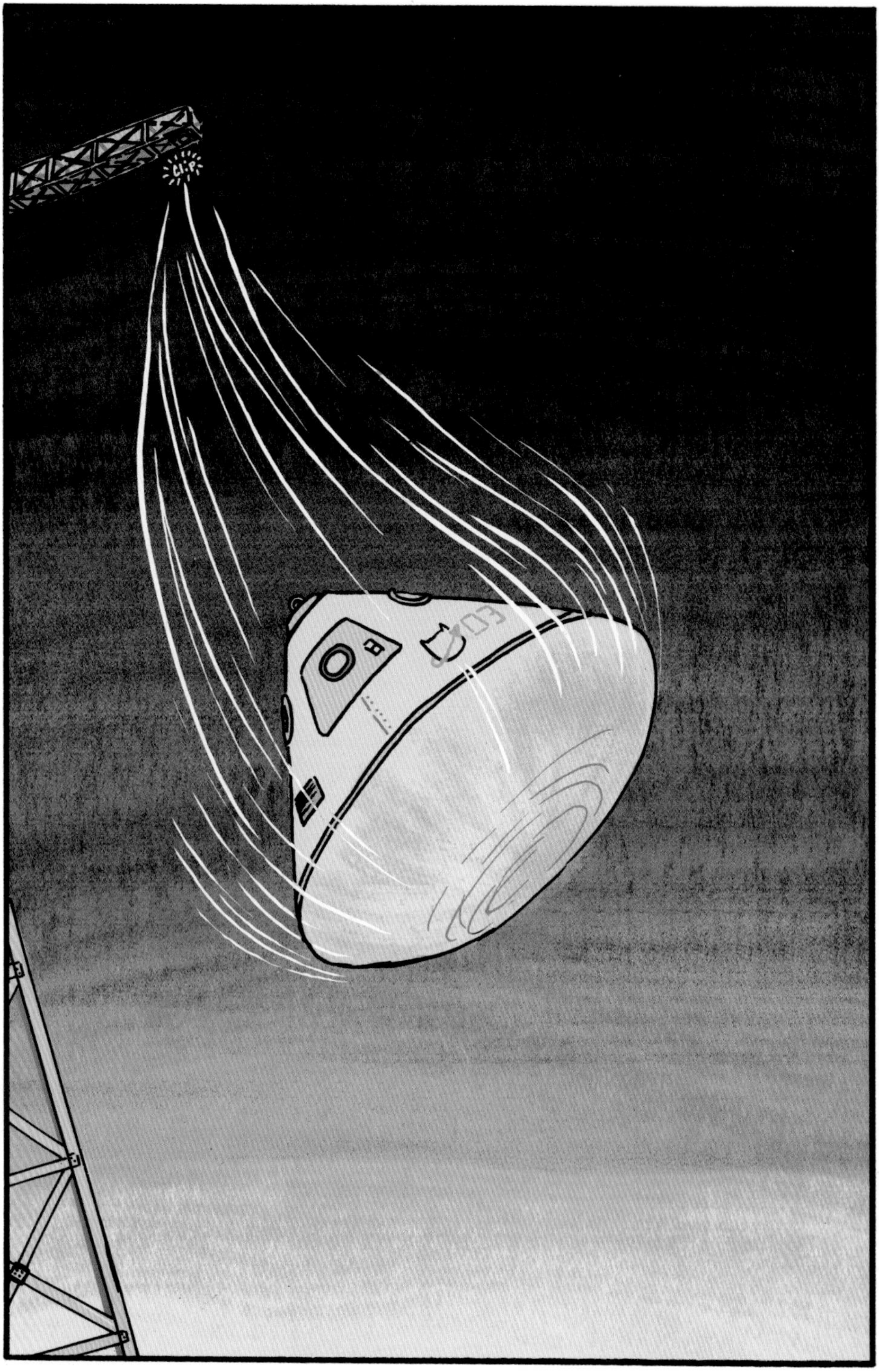
CLIP

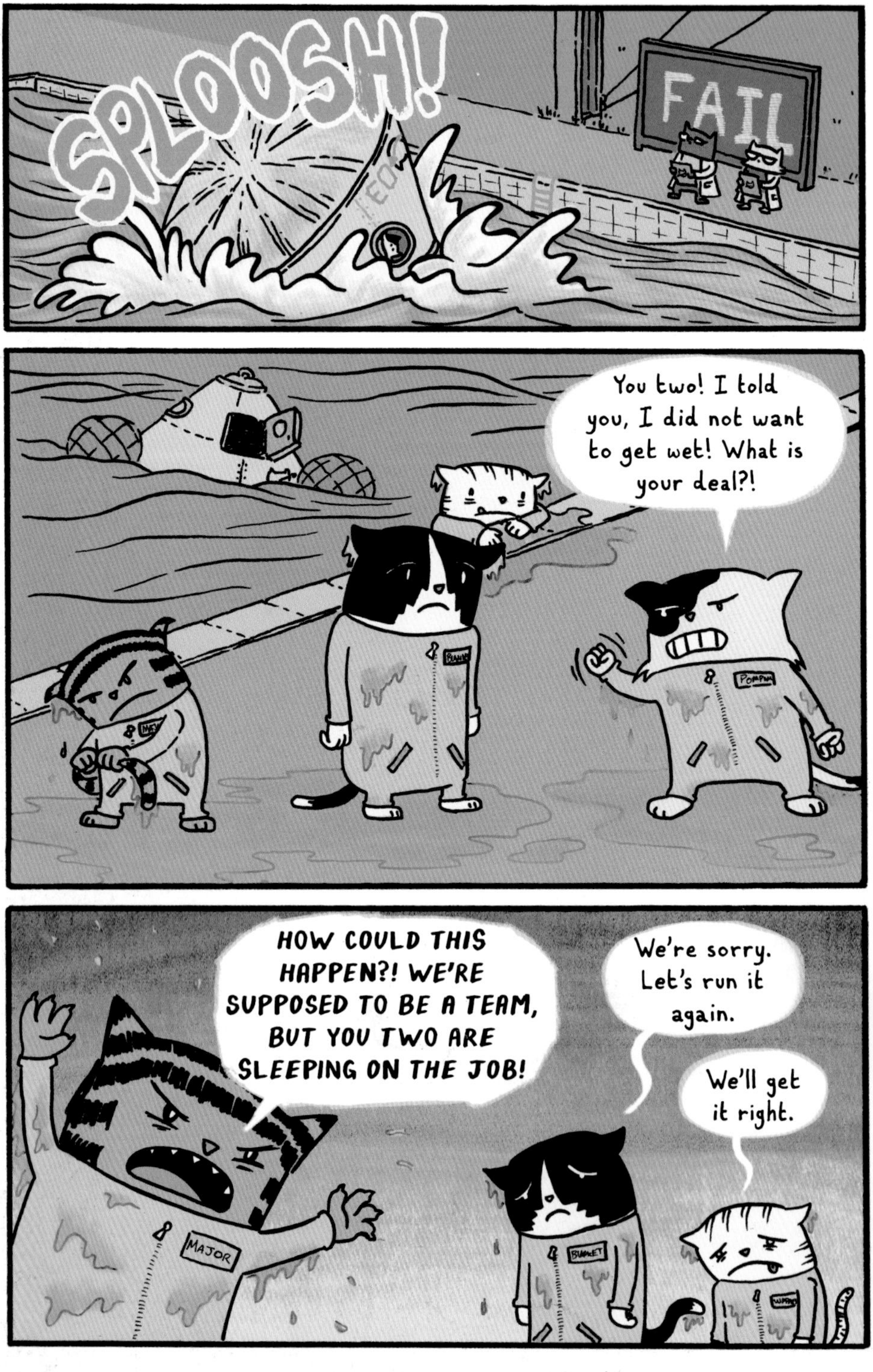
SPLOOSH!
FAIL
You two! I told you, I did not want to get wet! What is your deal?!
HOW COULD THIS HAPPEN?! WE'RE SUPPOSED TO BE A TEAM, BUT YOU TWO ARE SLEEPING ON THE JOB!
We're sorry. Let's run it again.
We'll get it right.
MAJOR

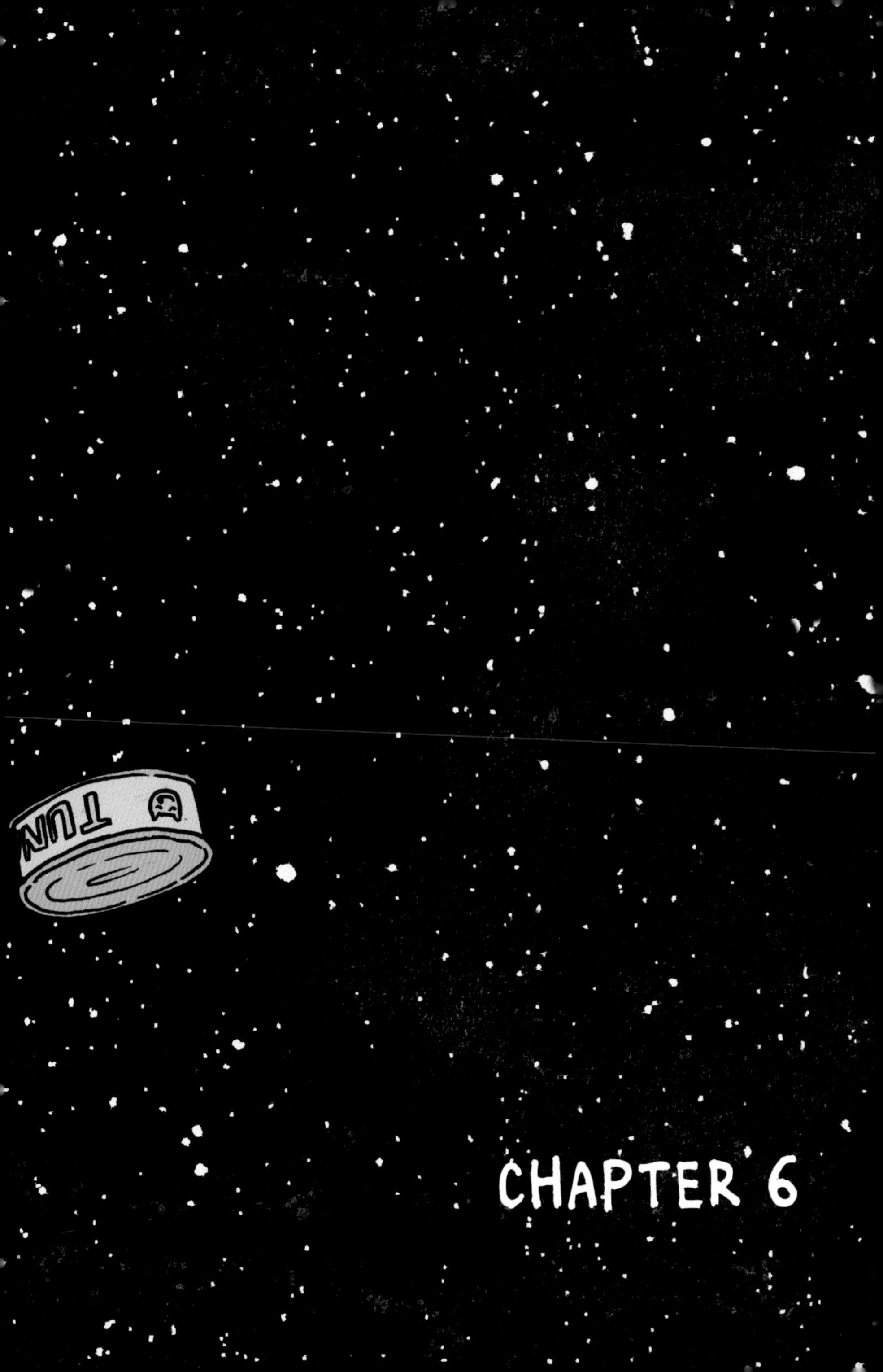
TUN
CHAPTER 6

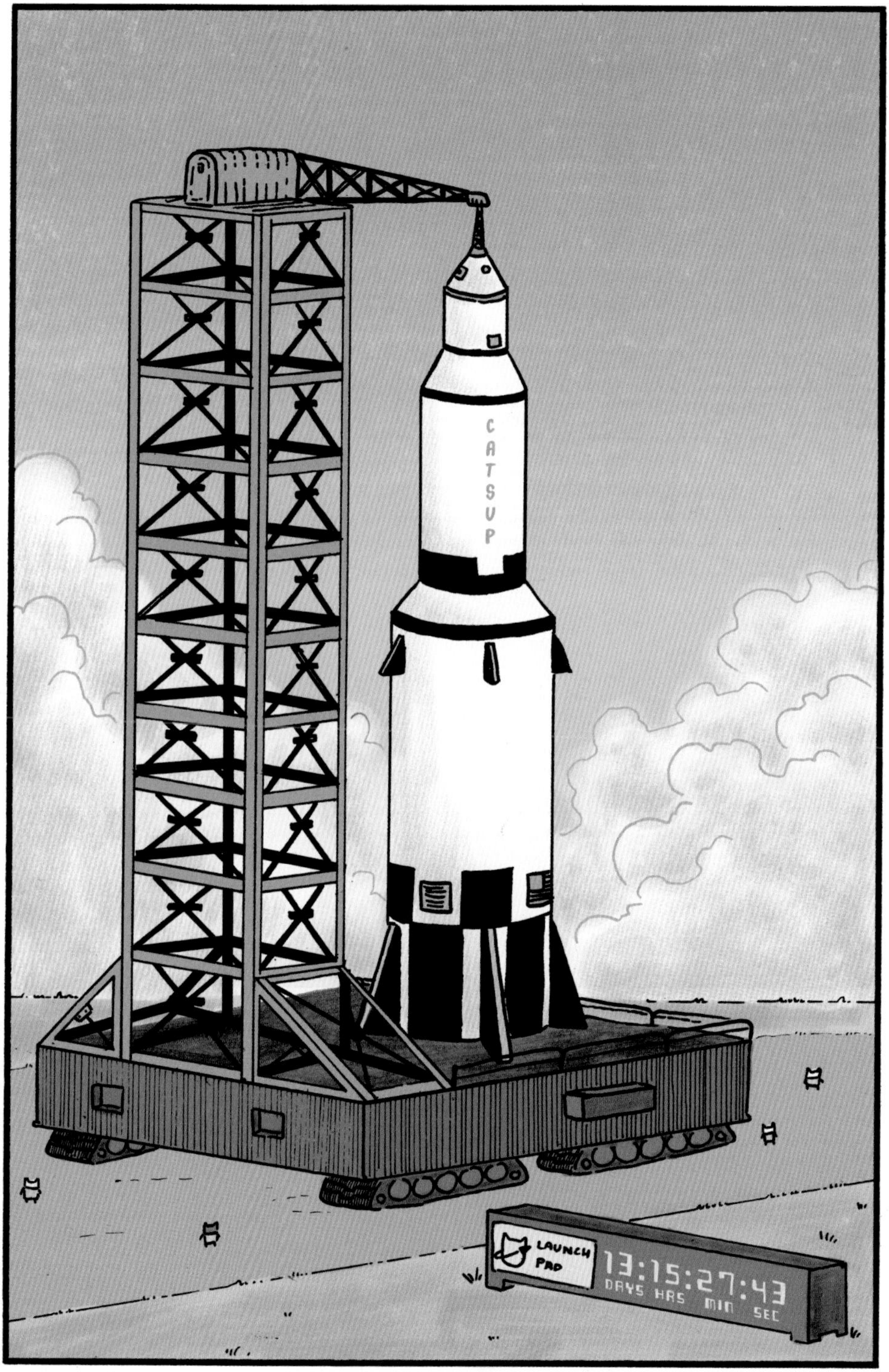
C A T S U P
LAUNCH PAD
13:15:27:43
DAYS HRS MIN SEC

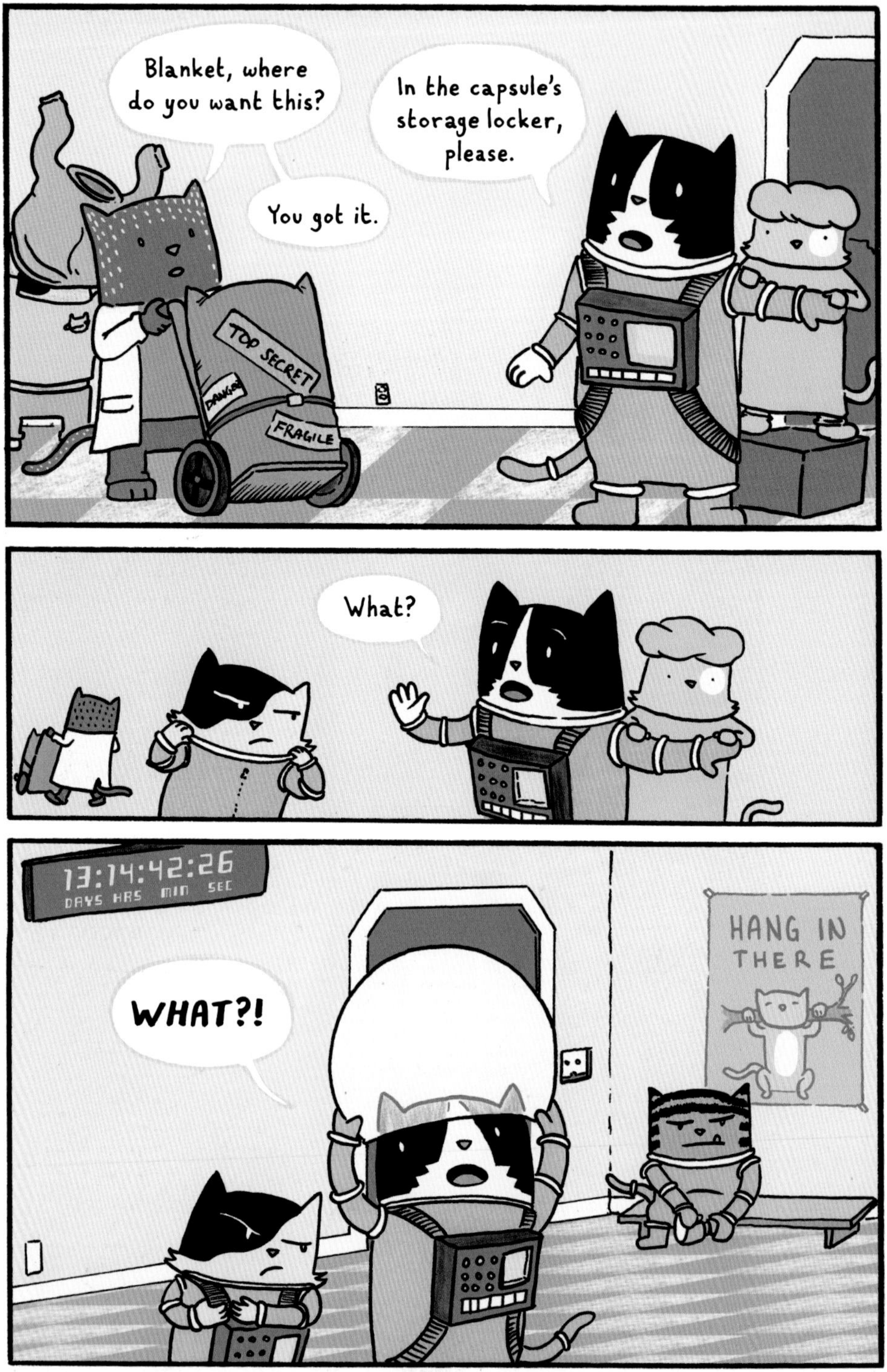
Blanket, where do you want this?
In the capsule's storage locker, please.
You got it.
TOP SECRET
DANGER
FRAGILE
What?
13:14:42:26
DAYS HRS MIN SEC
WHAT?!
HANG IN THERE

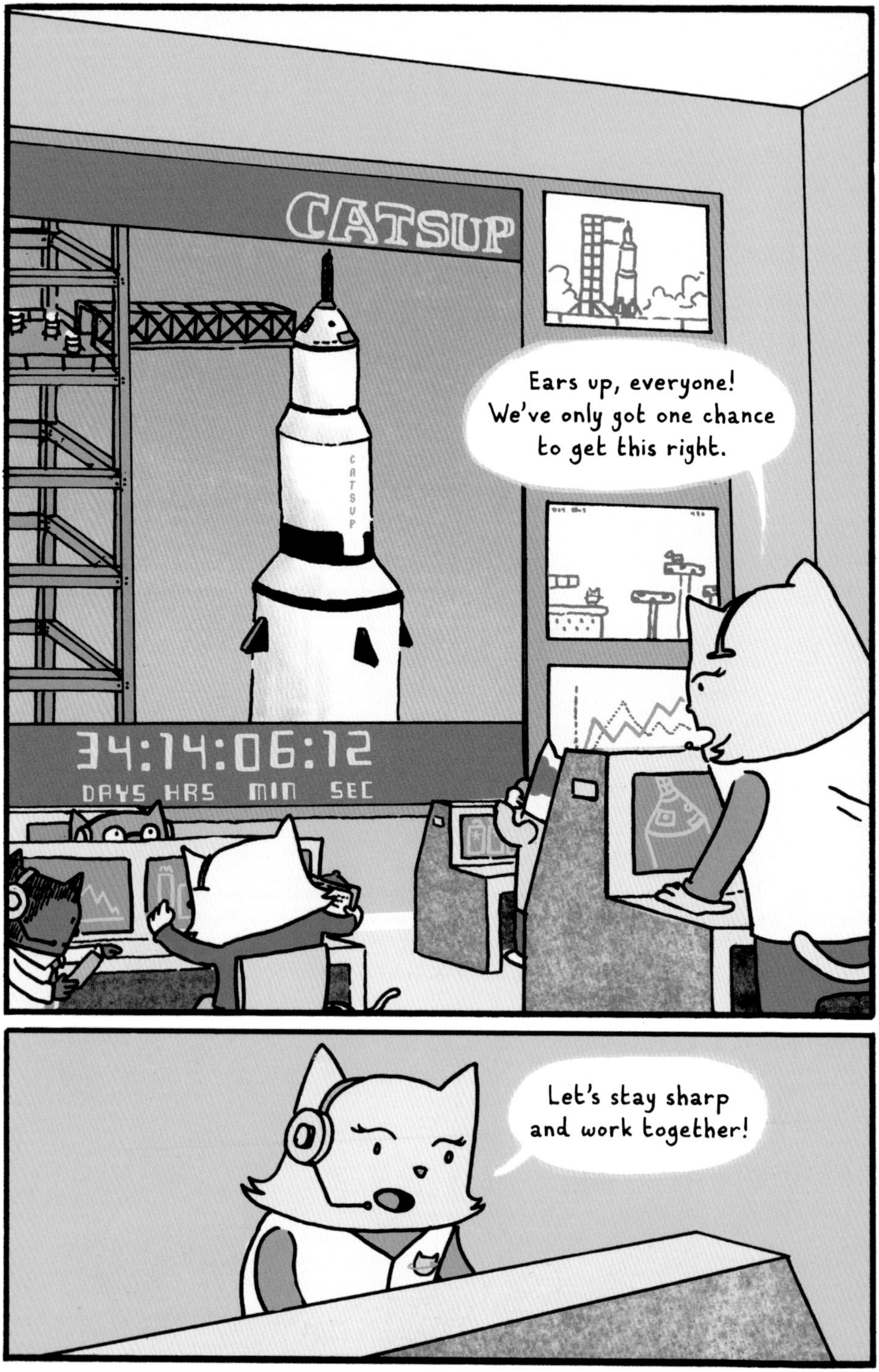
CATSUP
34:14:06:12
DAYS HRS MIN SEC
CATSUP
Ears up, everyone! We've only got one chance to get this right.
Let's stay sharp and work together!

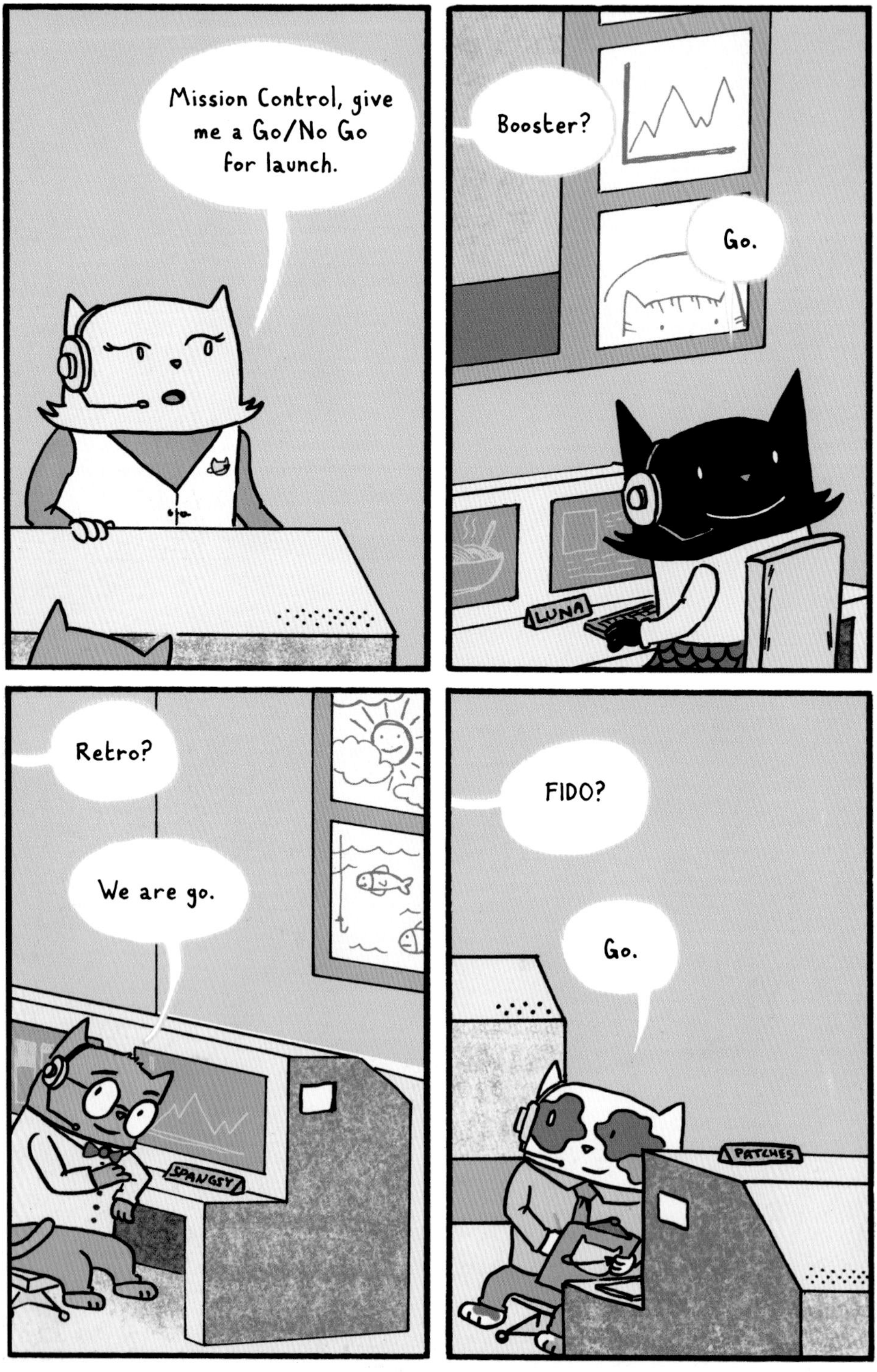
Mission Control, give me a Go/No Go for launch.
Booster?
Go.
LUNA
Retro?
We are go.
SPANGSY
FIDO?
Go.
PATCHES

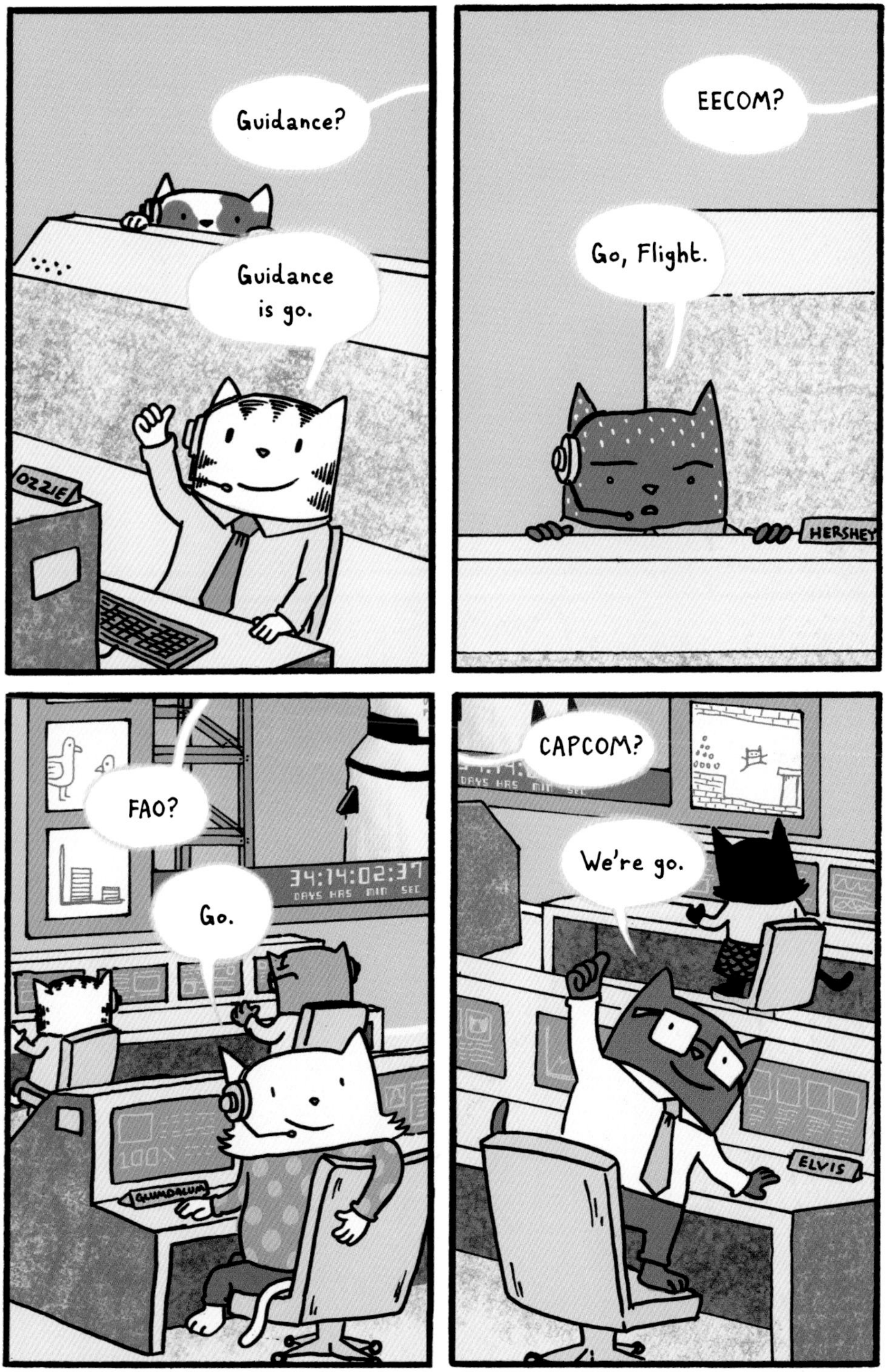
Guidance?
Guidance is go.
OZZIE
EECOM?
Go, Flight.
HERSHEY
FAO?
34:14:02:37
DAYS HRS MIN SEC
Go.
CAPCOM?
We're go.
ELVIS

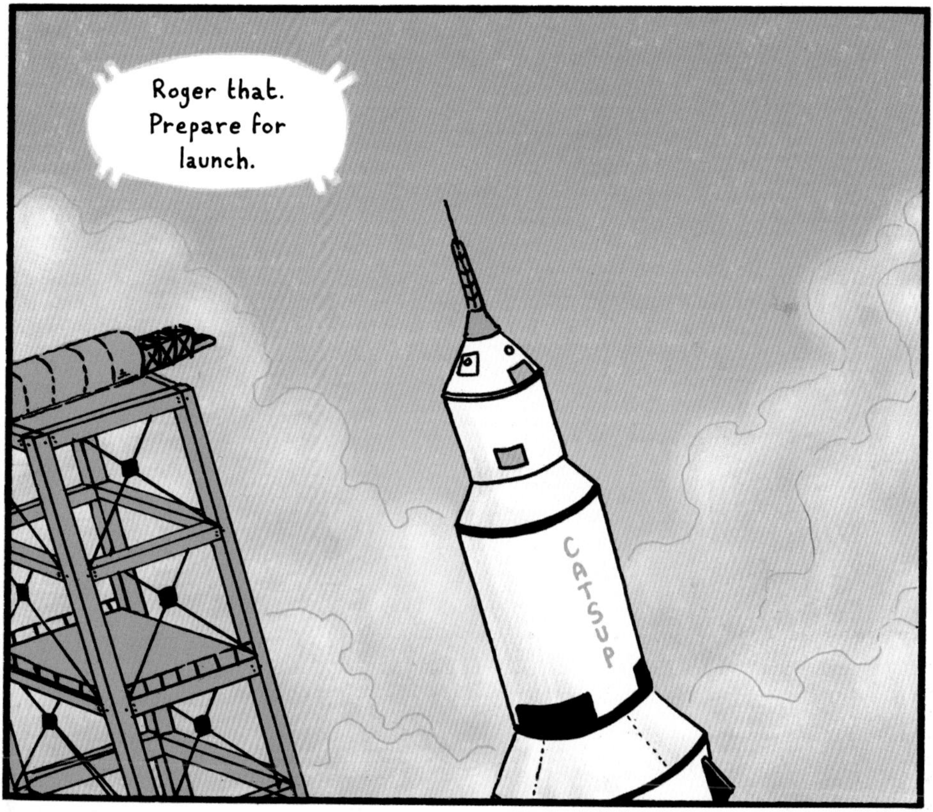
Roger that. Prepare for launch.
CATSUP

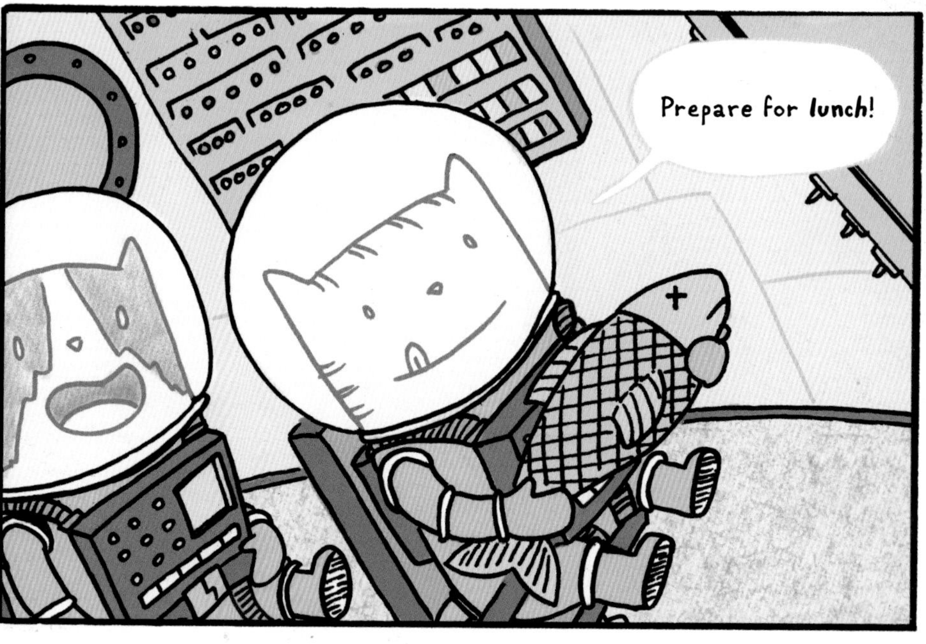
Prepare for **lunch**!

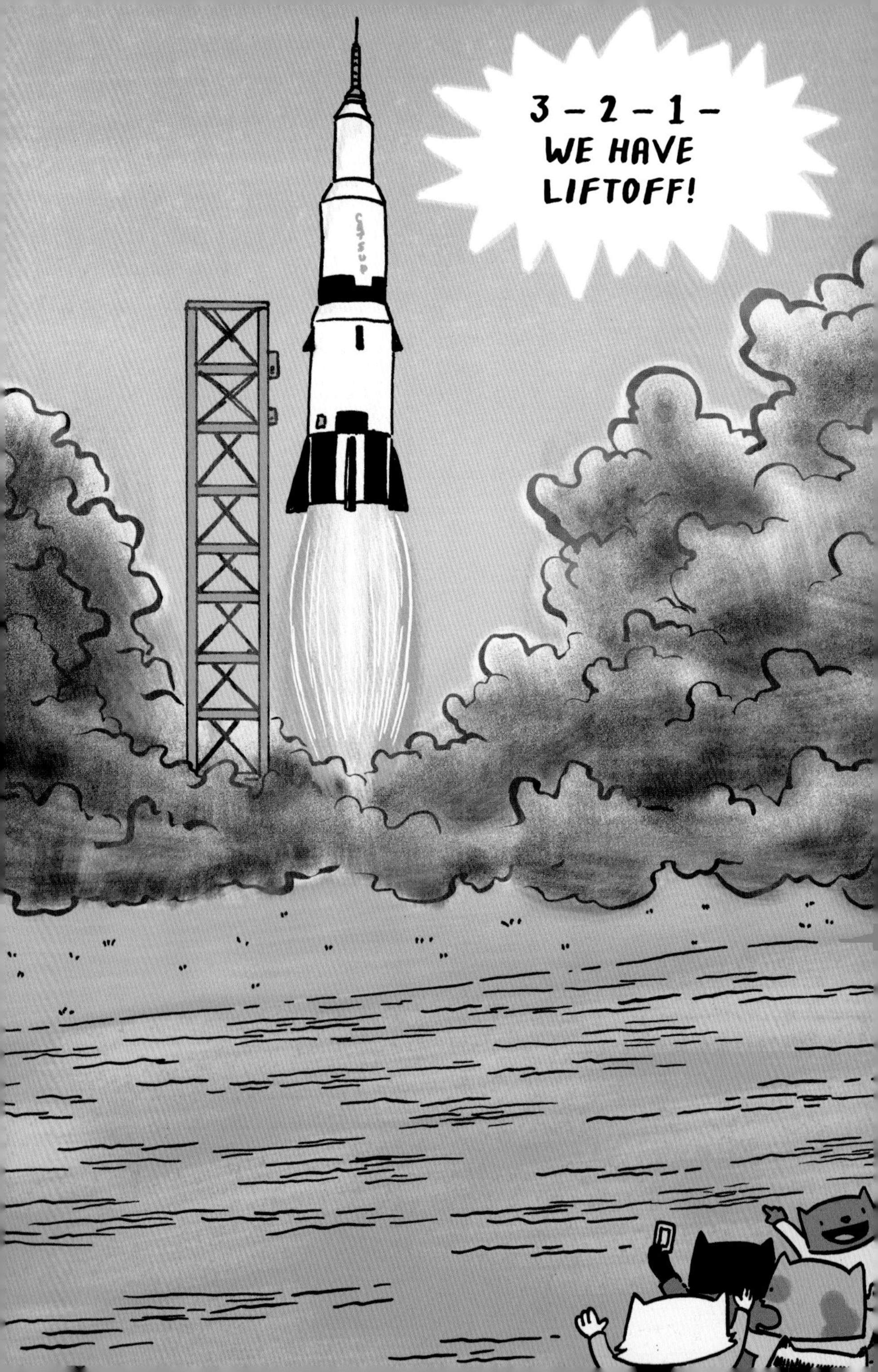
3 – 2 – 1 – WE HAVE LIFTOFF!

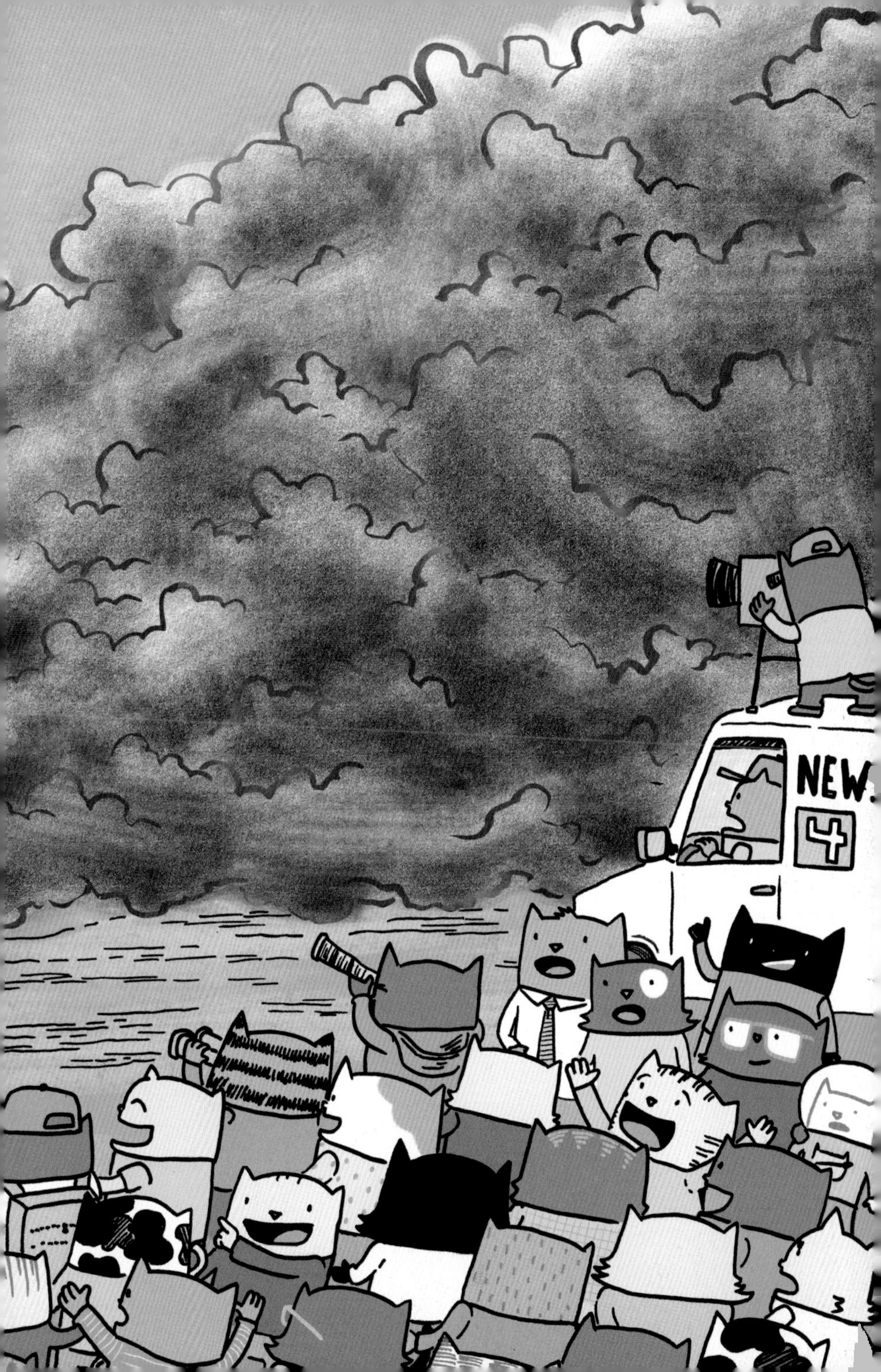
NEW
4

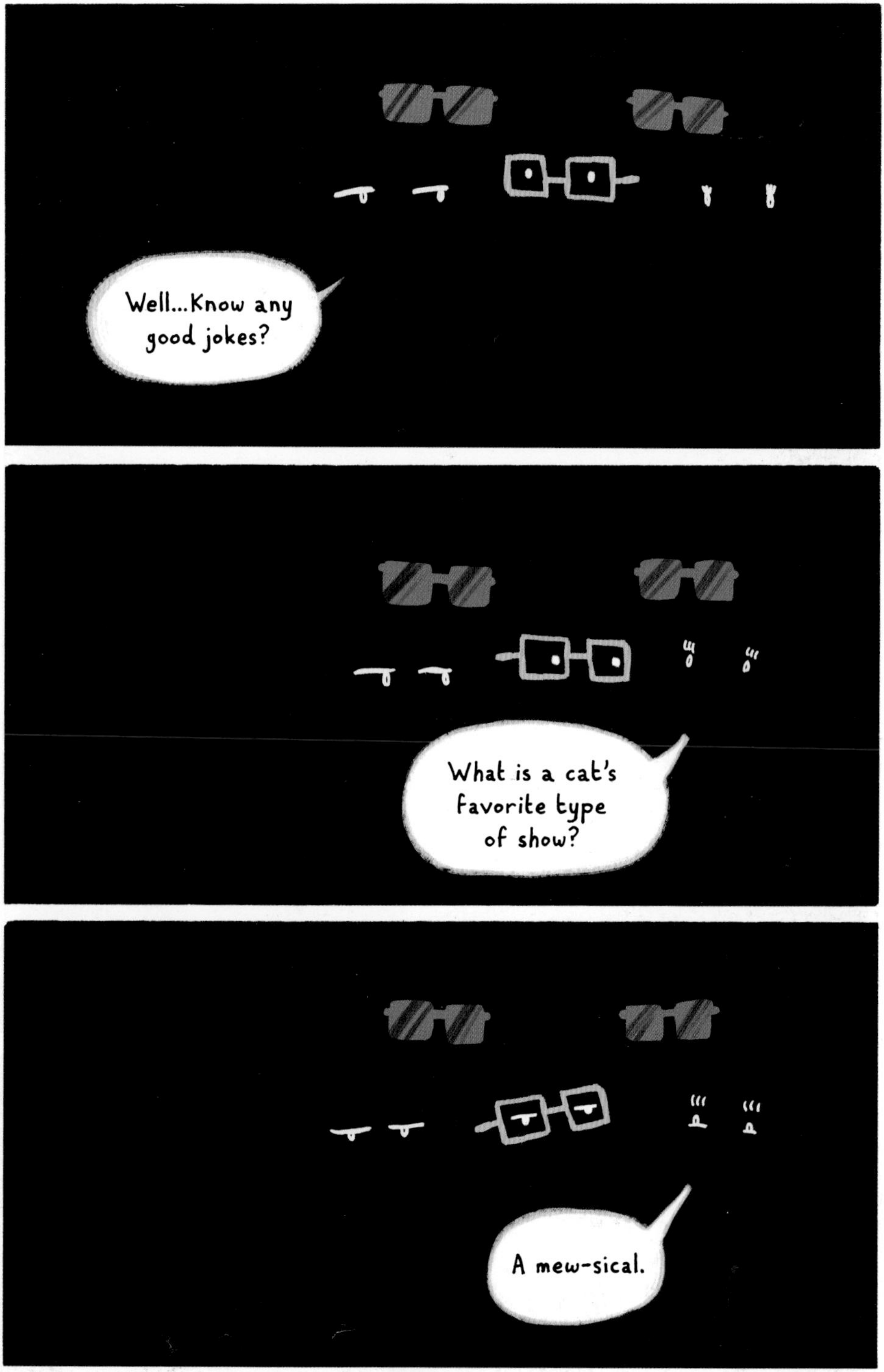
Well...Know any good jokes?
What is a cat's favorite type of show?
A mew-sical.

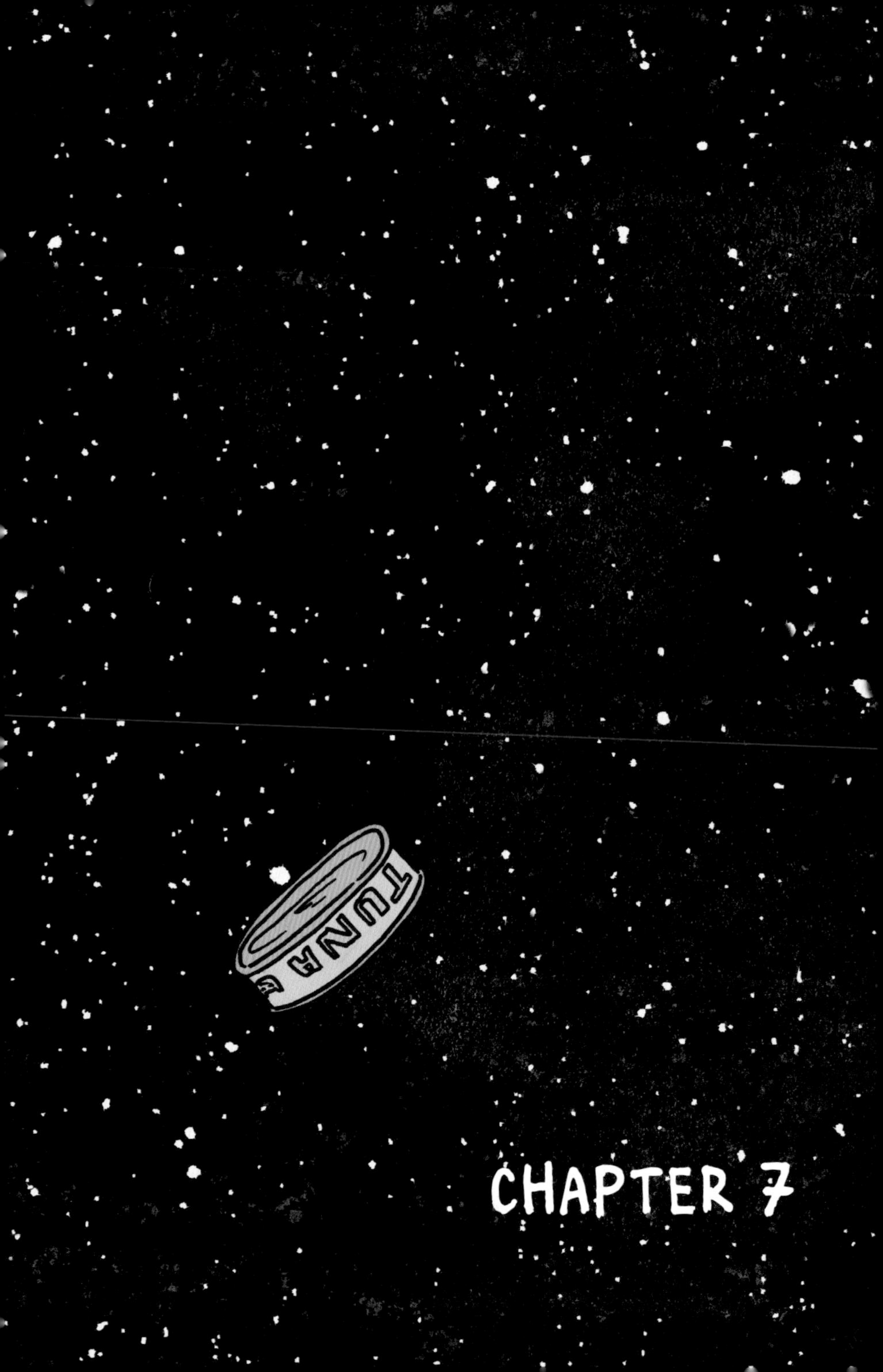
TUNA
CHAPTER 7

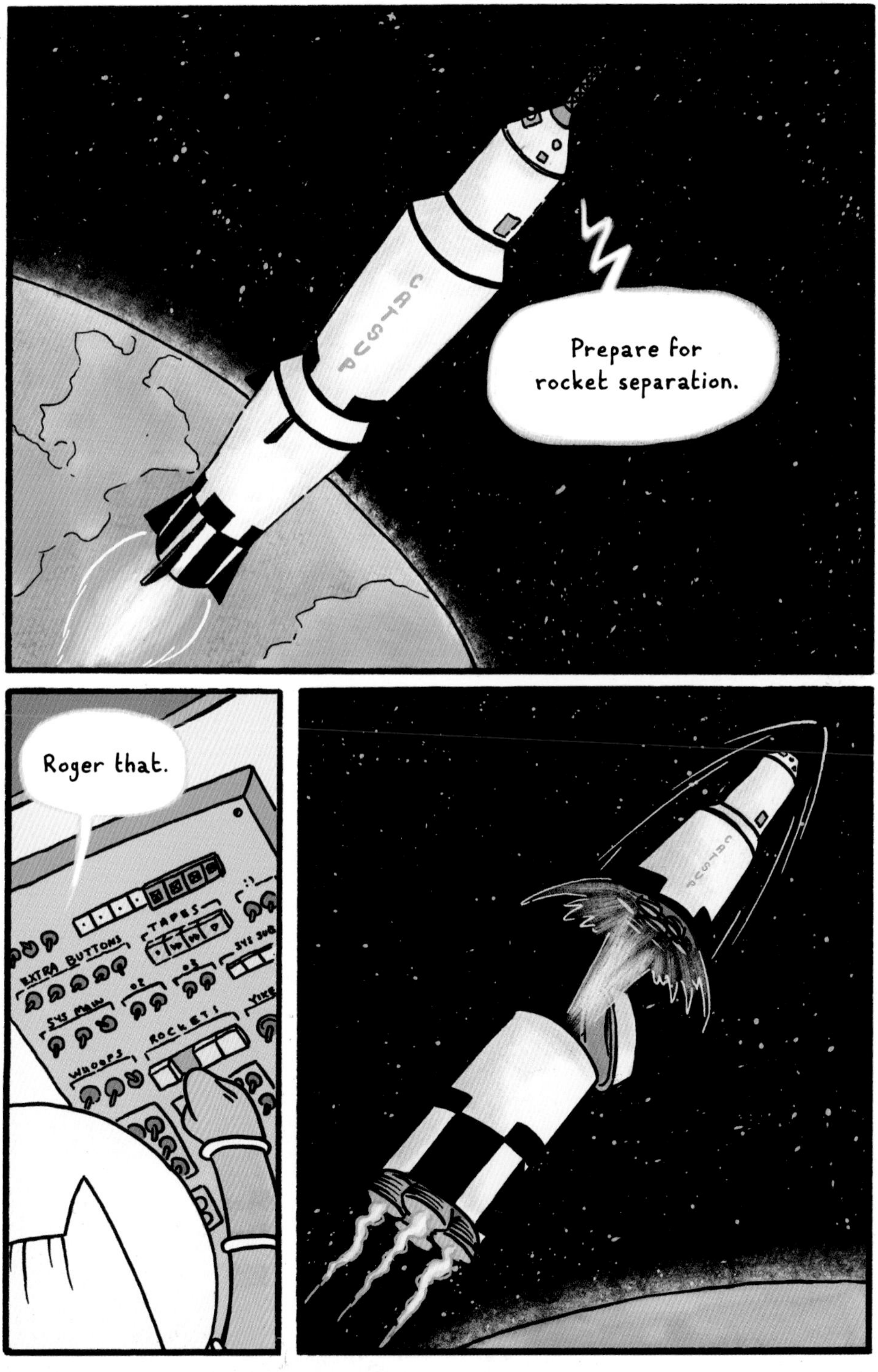
Prepare for rocket separation.
Roger that.
TAPES
EXTRA BUTTONS
SYS MAIN
ROCKETS
WHOOPS

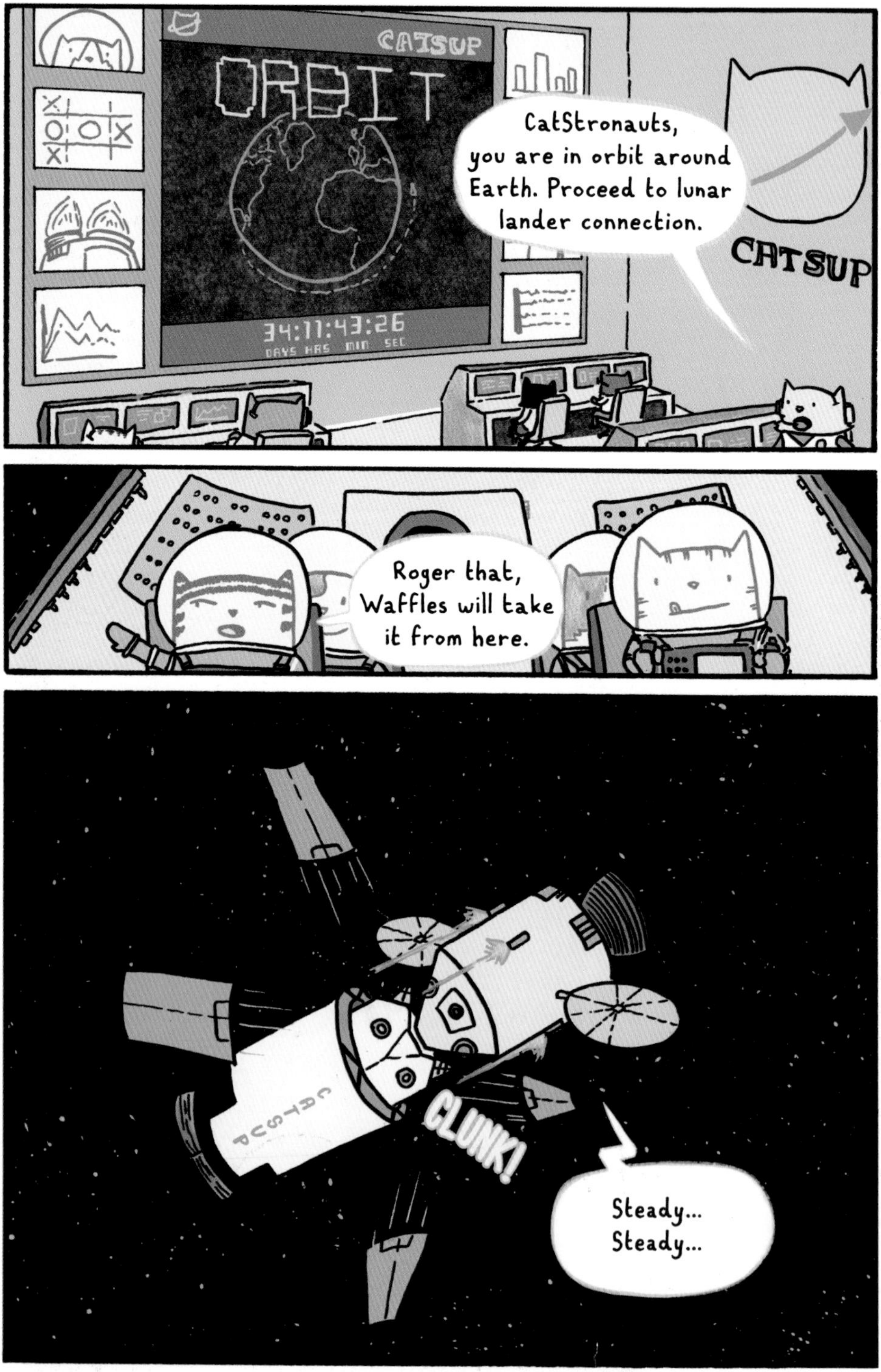
CATSUP
ORBIT
34:11:43:26
DAYS HRS MIN SEC
CatStronauts, you are in orbit around Earth. Proceed to lunar lander connection.
CATSUP
Roger that, Waffles will take it from here.
CATSUP
CLUNK!
Steady... Steady...

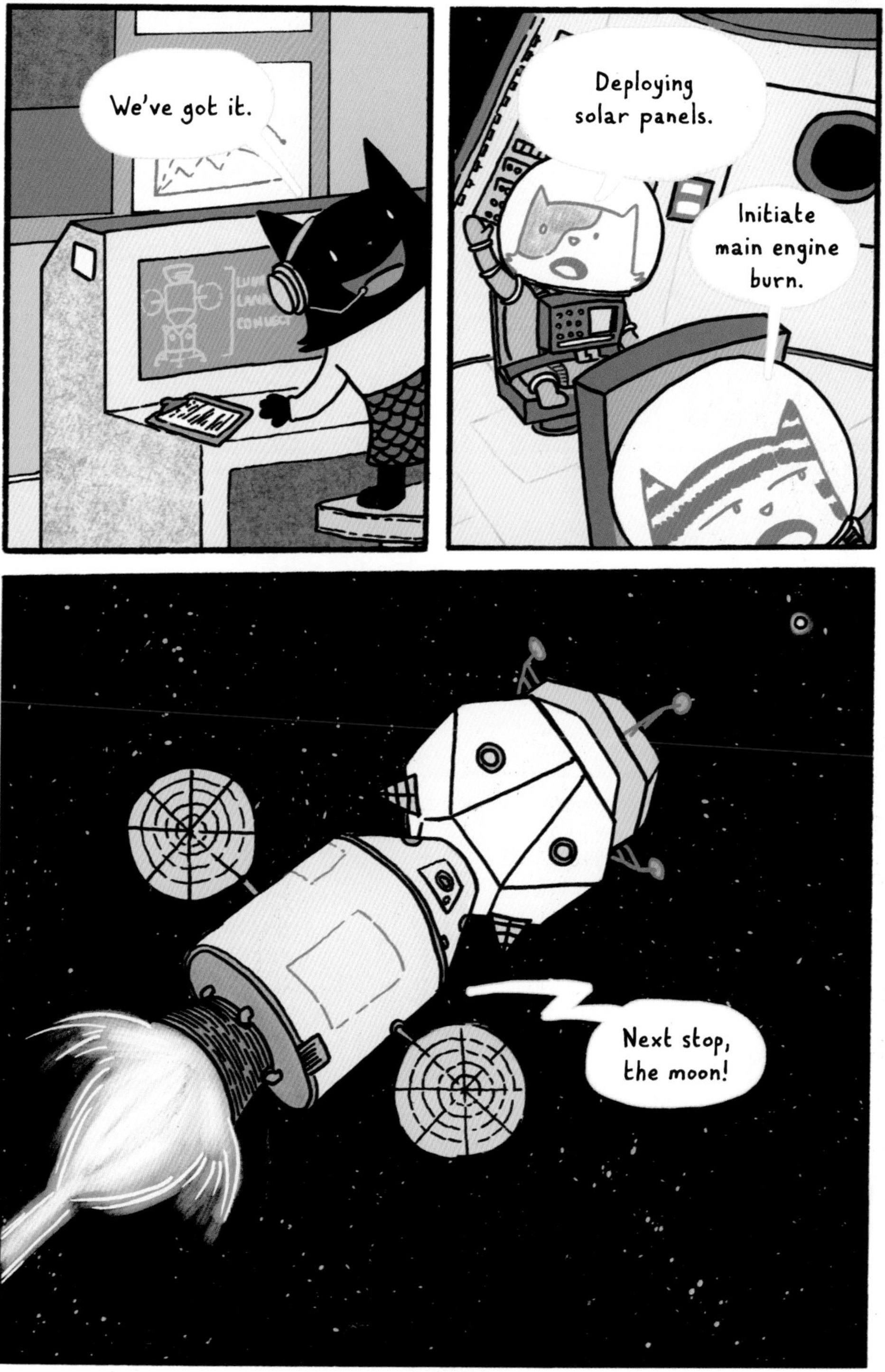
We've got it.
Deploying solar panels.
Initiate main engine burn.
Next stop, the moon!

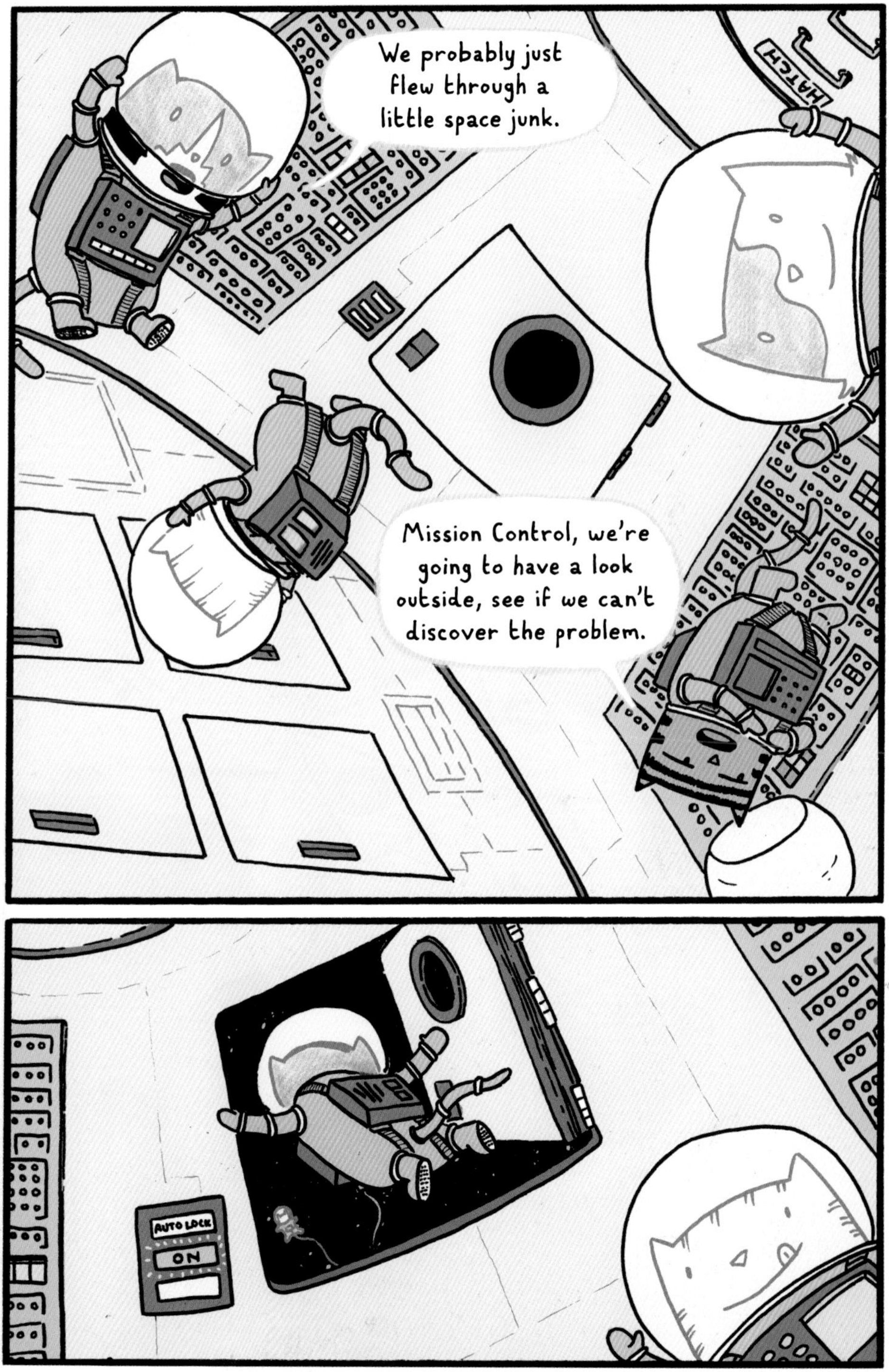
We probably just flew through a little space junk.
HATCH
Mission Control, we're going to have a look outside, see if we can't discover the problem.
AUTO LOCK
ON

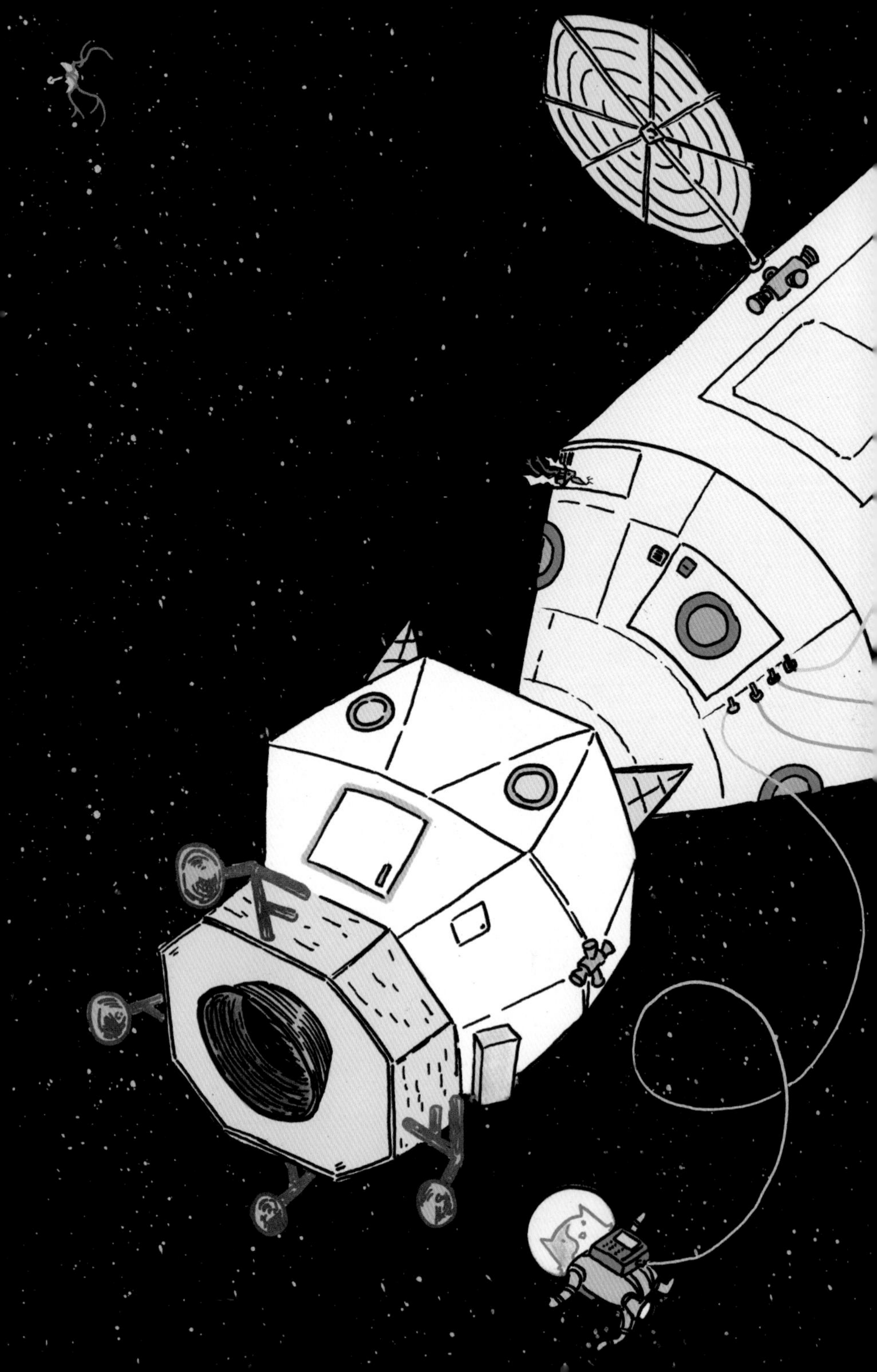

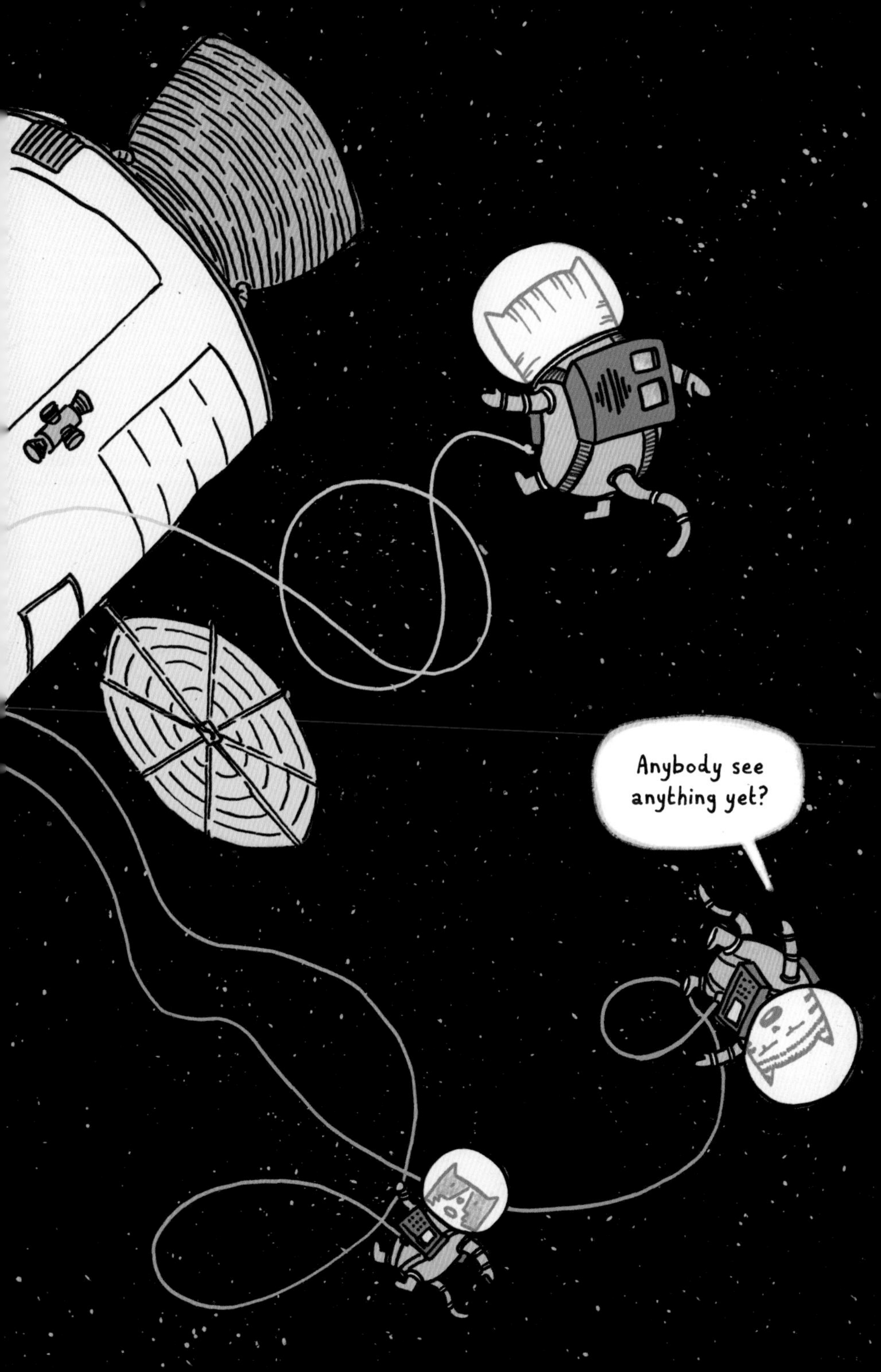
Anybody see anything yet?

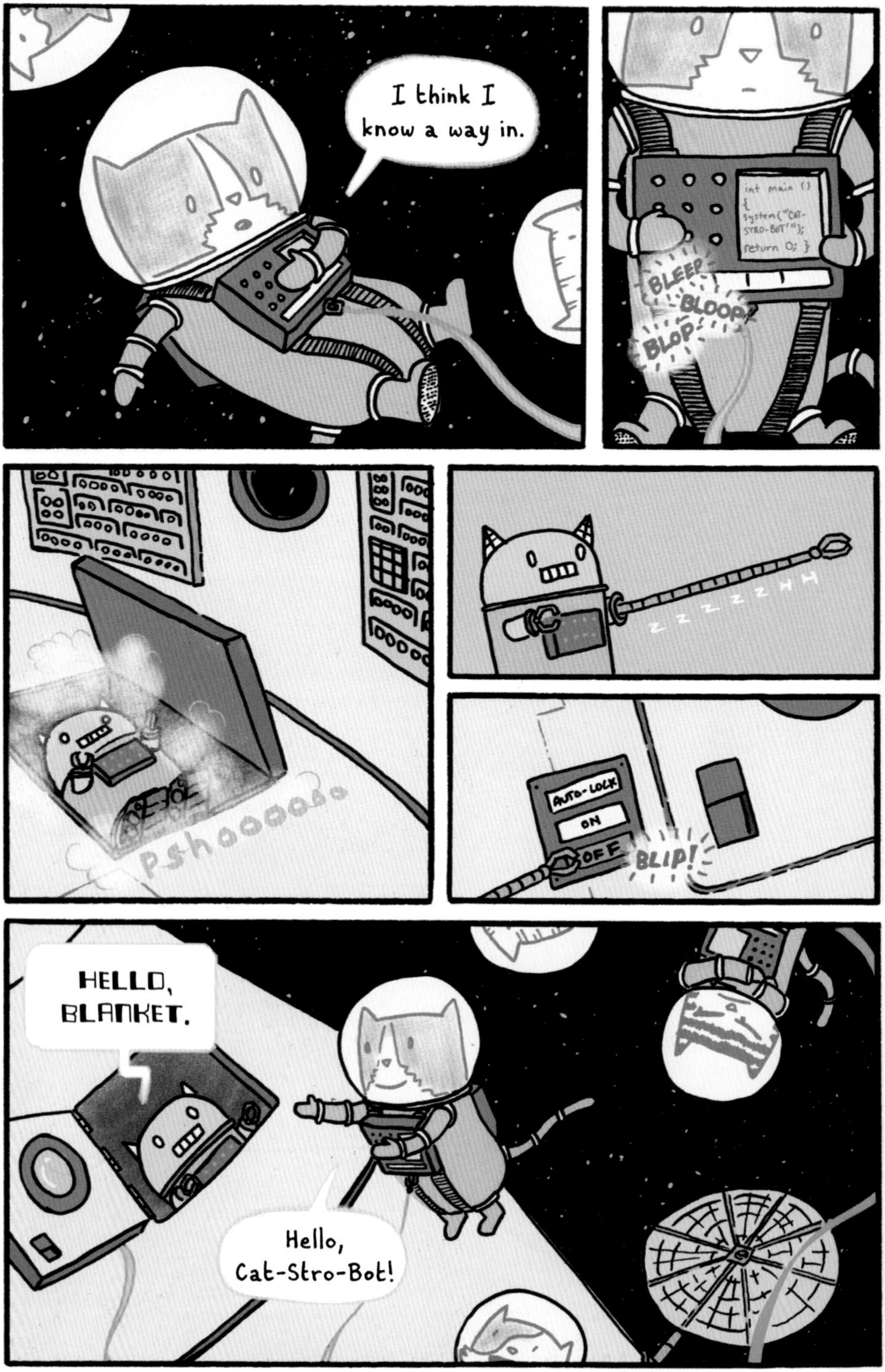
I think I know a way in.
int main ()
{
system("CAT-STRO-BOT");
return 0; }
BLEEP
BLOOP
BLOP!
ZZZZZZHH
Pshoooooo
AUTO-LOCK
ON
OFF
BLIP!
HELLO, BLANKET.
Hello, Cat-Stro-Bot!

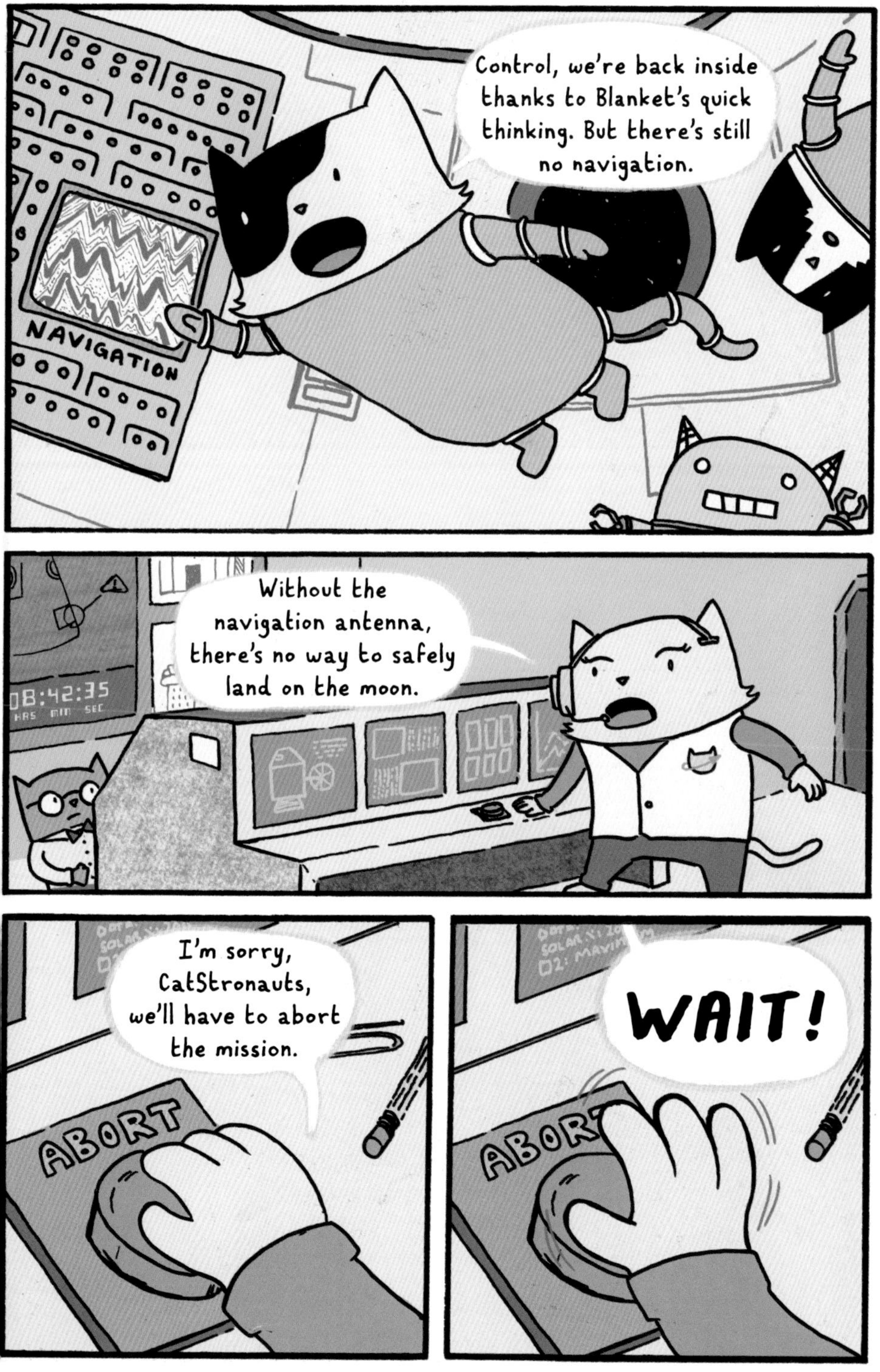
Control, we're back inside thanks to Blanket's quick thinking. But there's still no navigation.
NAVIGATION
Without the navigation antenna, there's no way to safely land on the moon.
08:42:35
HRS MIN SEC
I'm sorry, CatStronauts, we'll have to abort the mission.
ABORT
WAIT!
ABORT

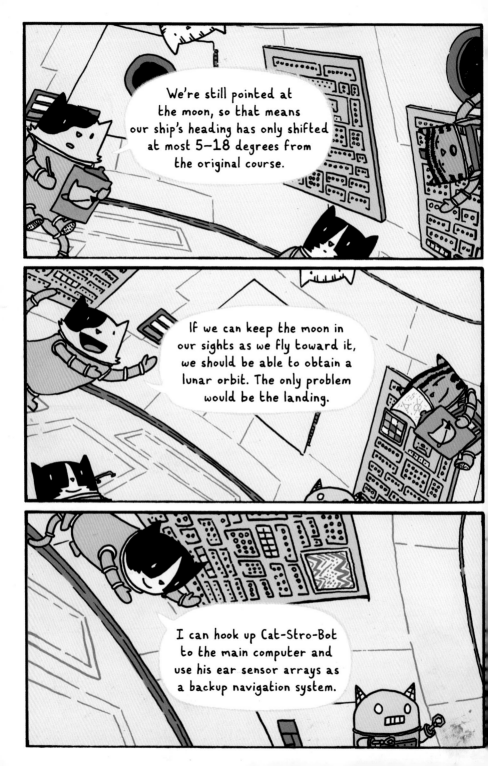

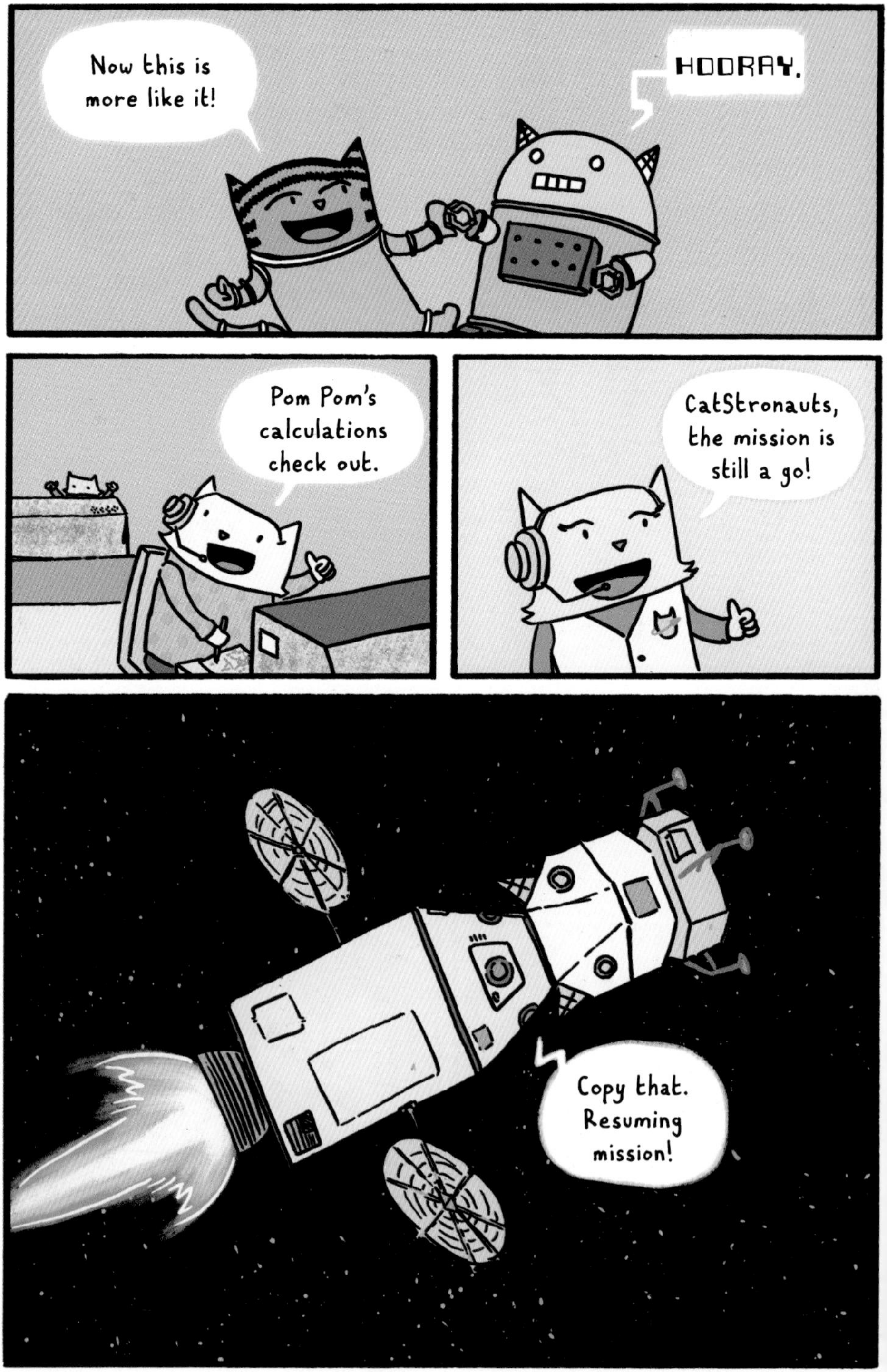
Now this is more like it!
HOORAY.
Pom Pom's calculations check out.
CatStronauts, the mission is still a go!
Copy that. Resuming mission!

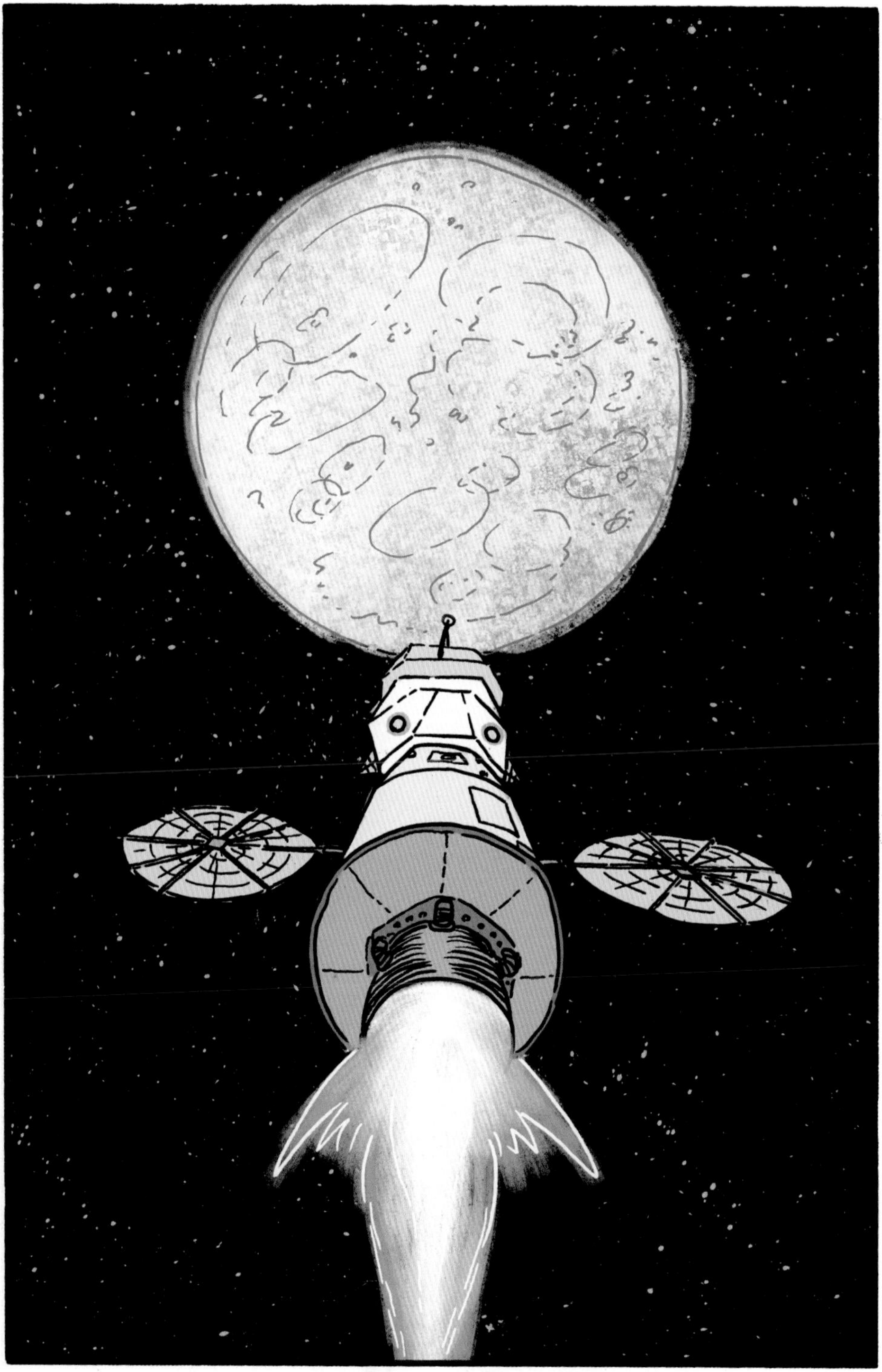

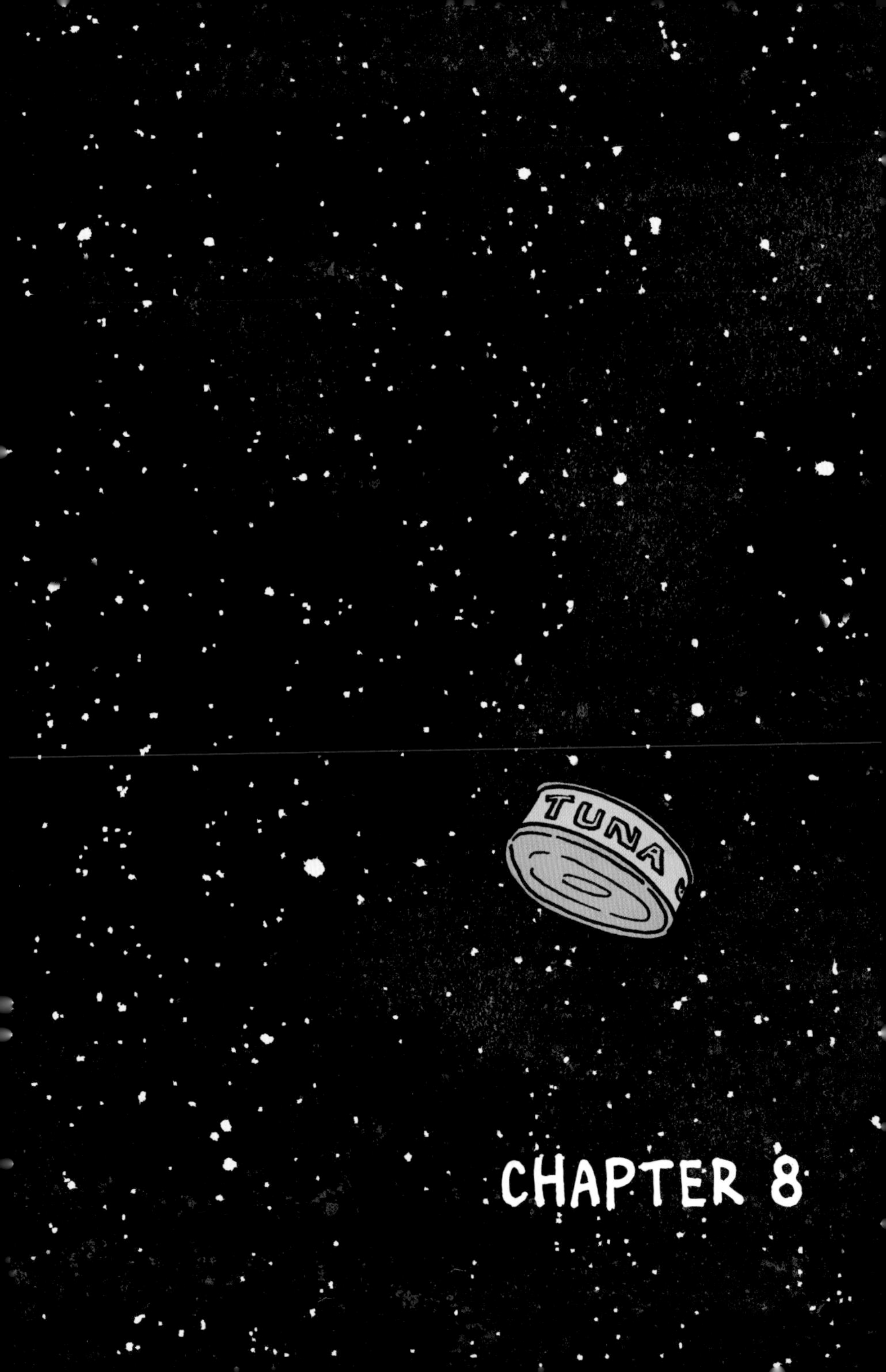
TUNA
CHAPTER 8

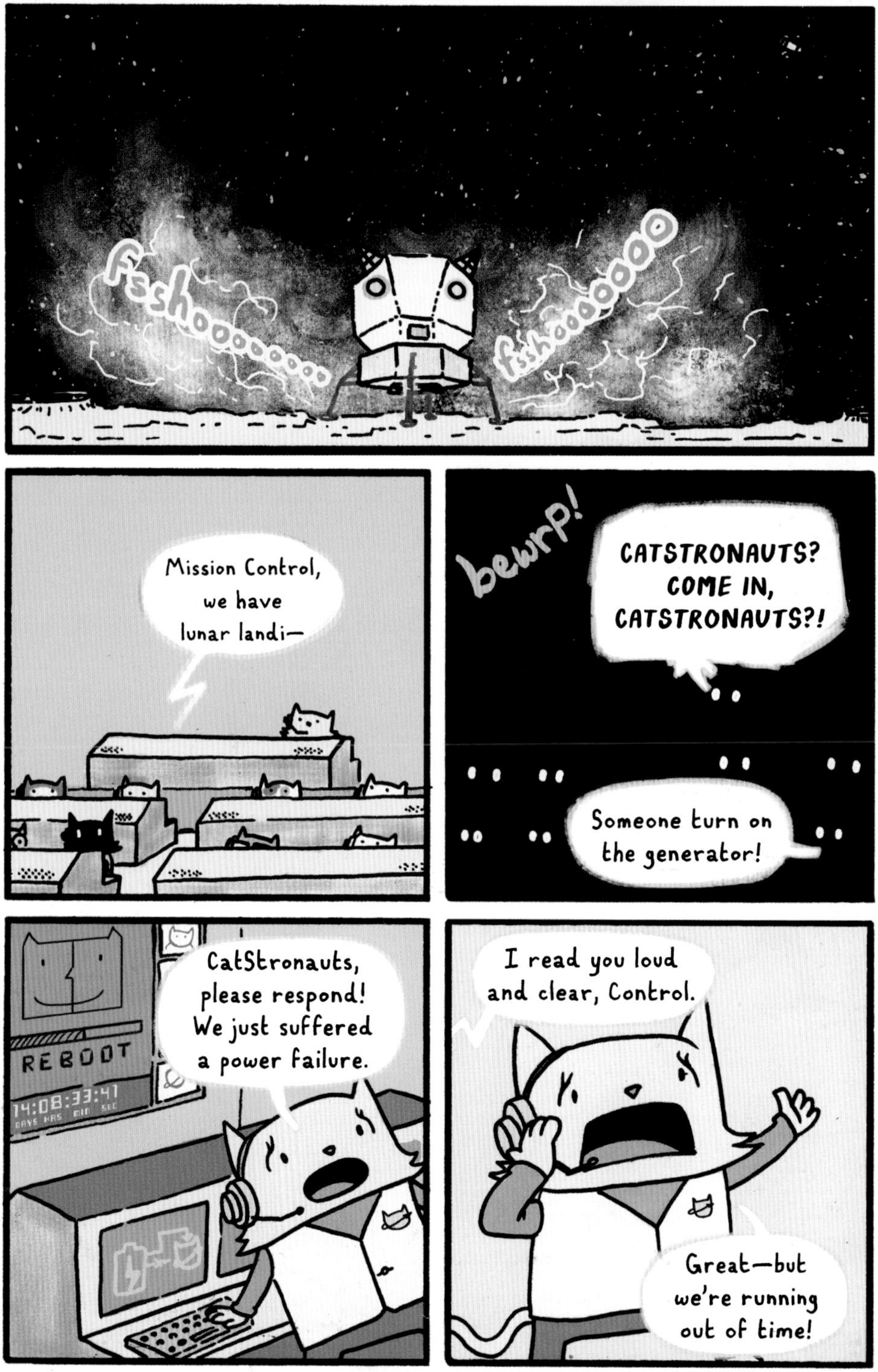
fsshoooooooooo
fsshoooooooo
Mission Control, we have lunar landi—
bewrp!
CATSTRONAUTS? COME IN, CATSTRONAUTS?!
Someone turn on the generator!
REBOOT
14:08:33:41
DAYS HRS MIN SEC
CatStronauts, please respond! We just suffered a power failure.
I read you loud and clear, Control.
Great—but we're running out of time!

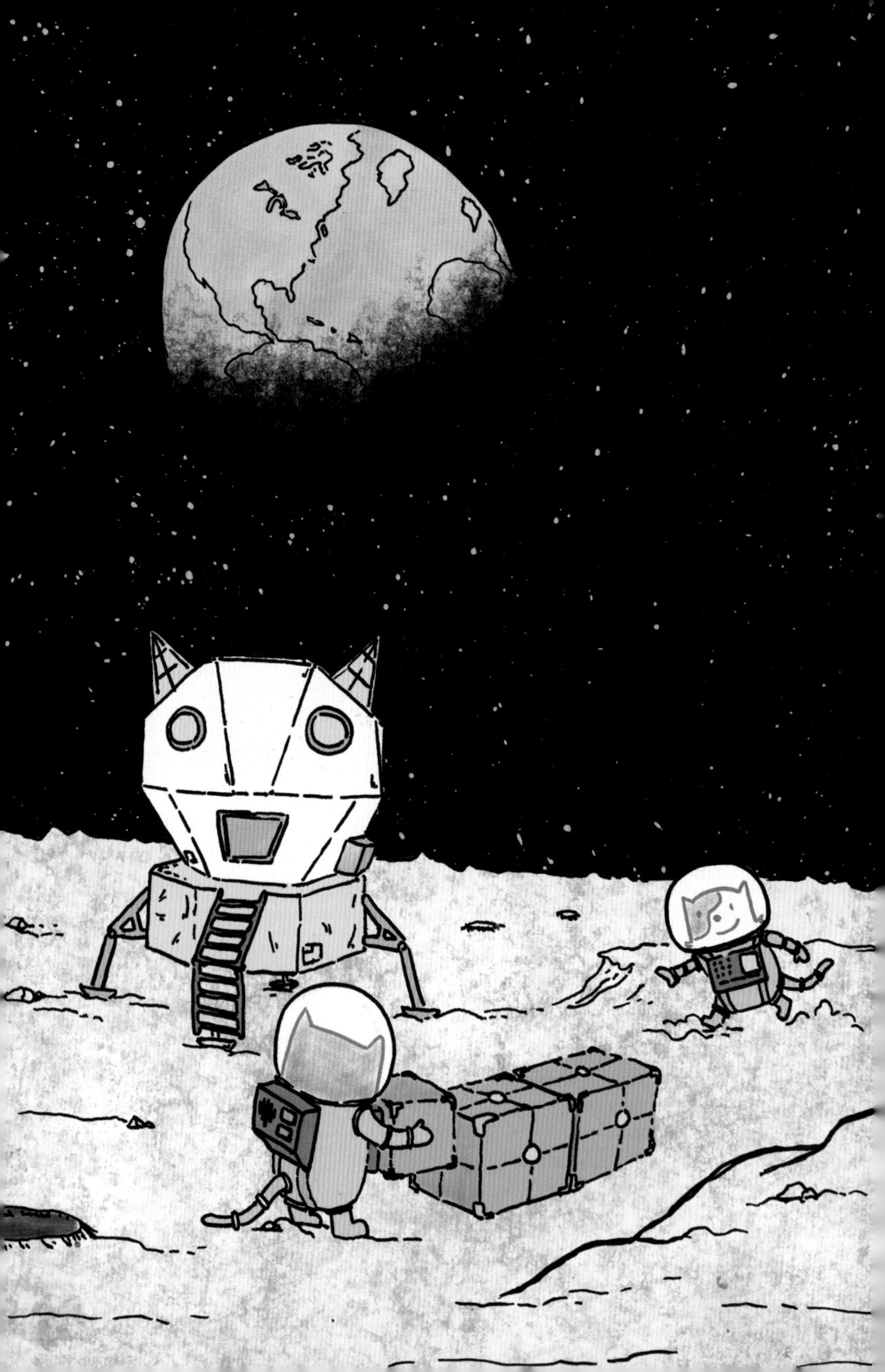

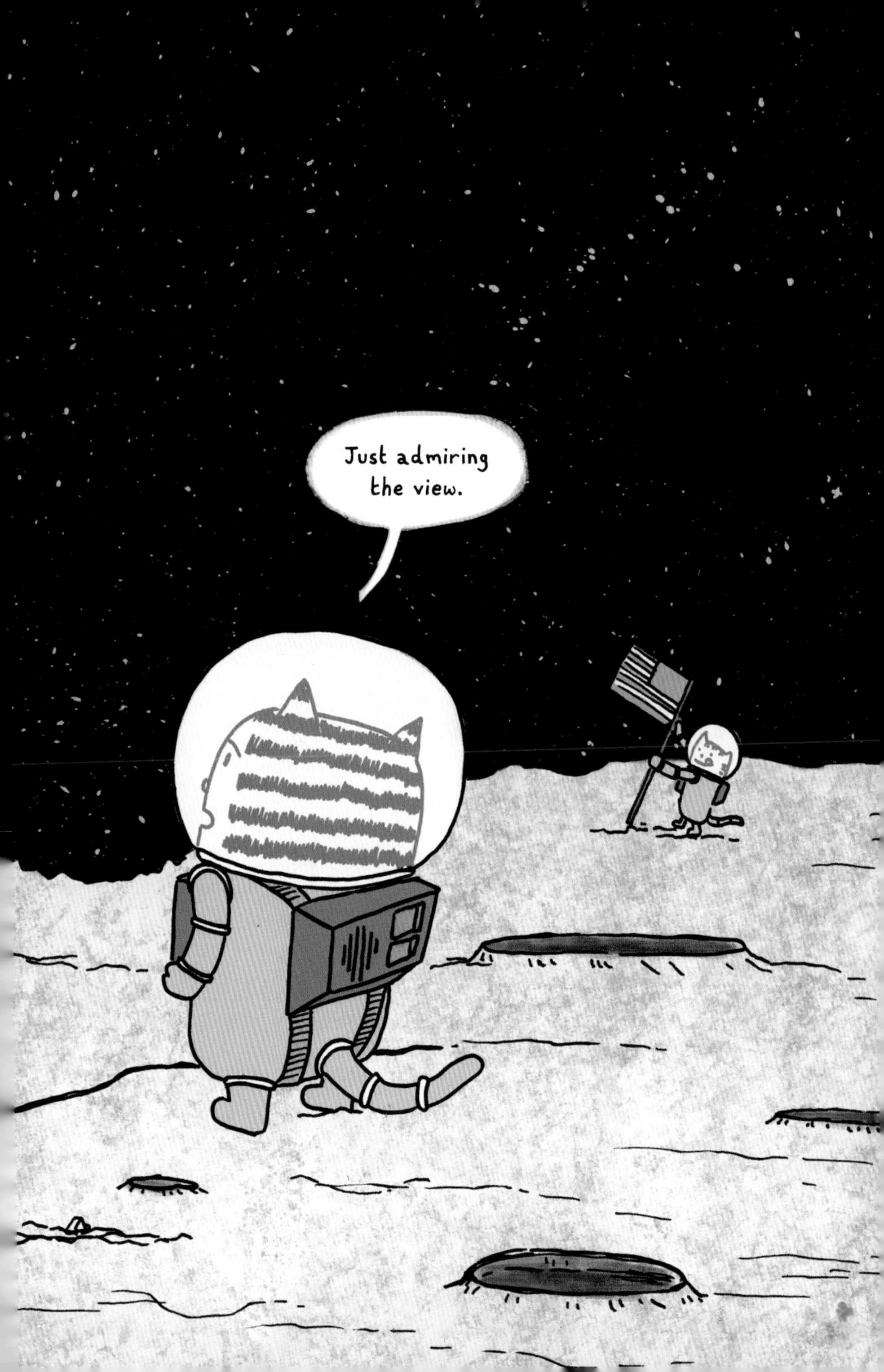
Just admiring the view.

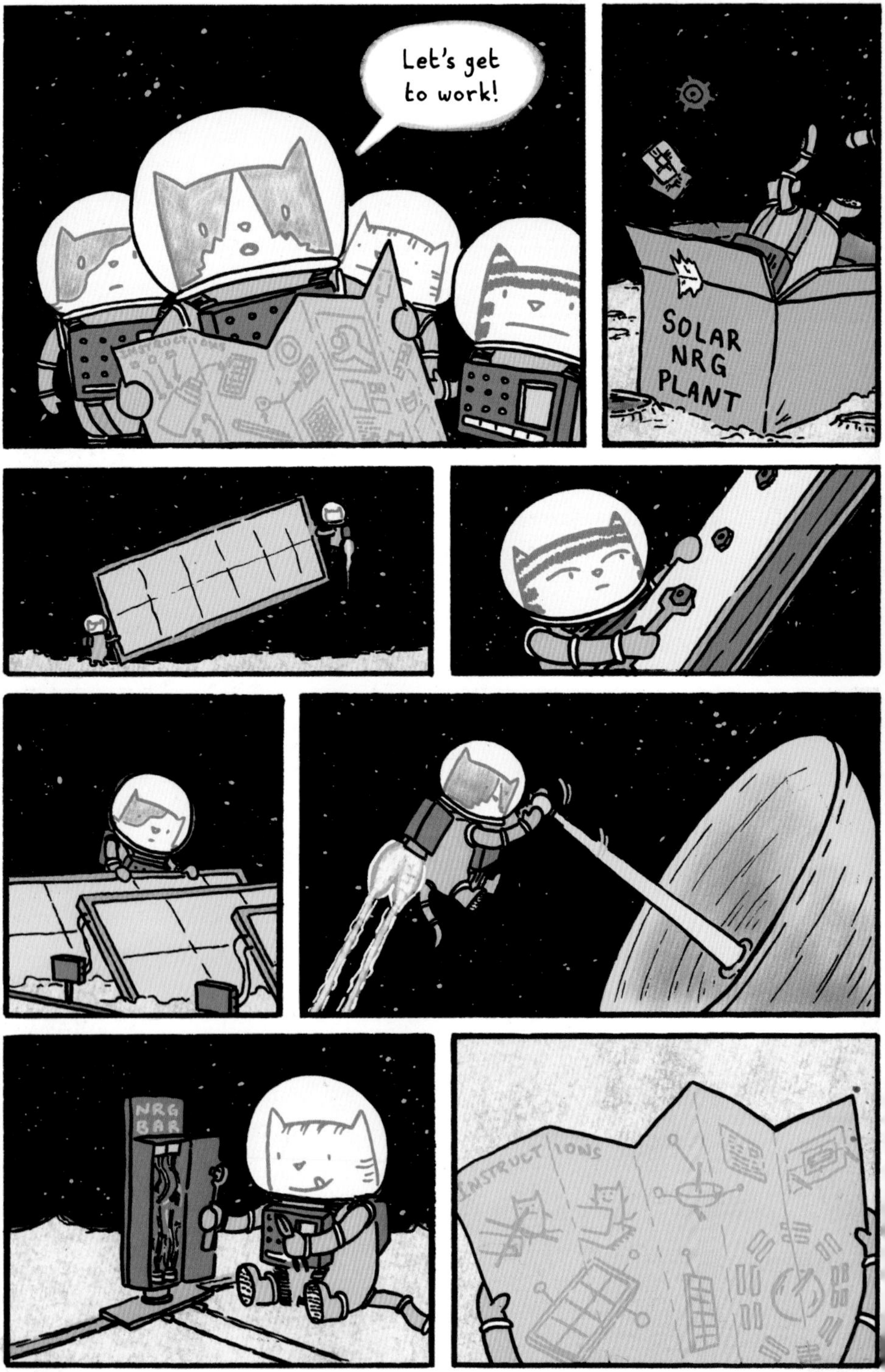
Let's get to work!
INSTRUCTIONS
SOLAR NRG PLANT
NRG BAR
INSTRUCT IONS

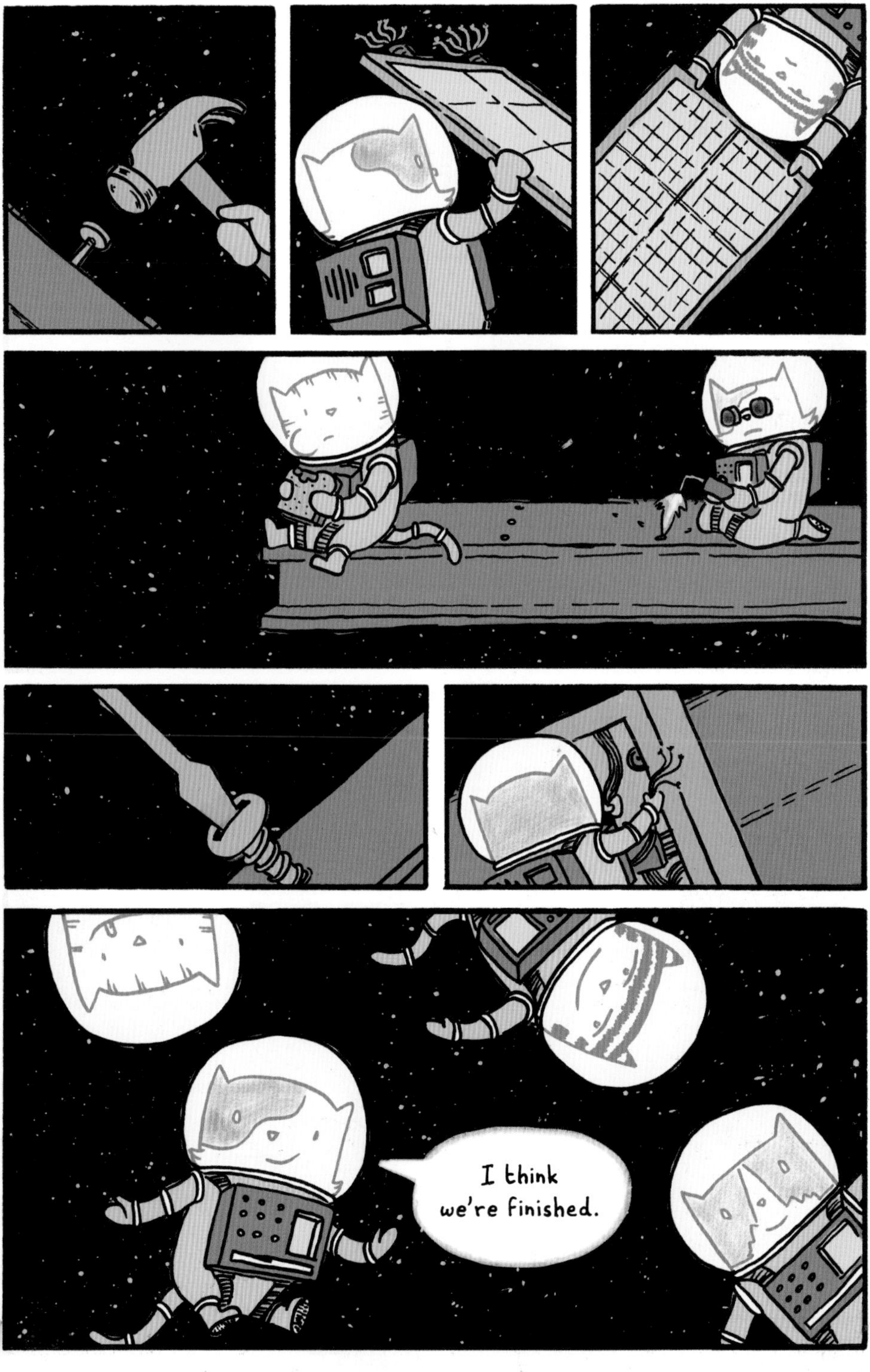
I think we're finished.

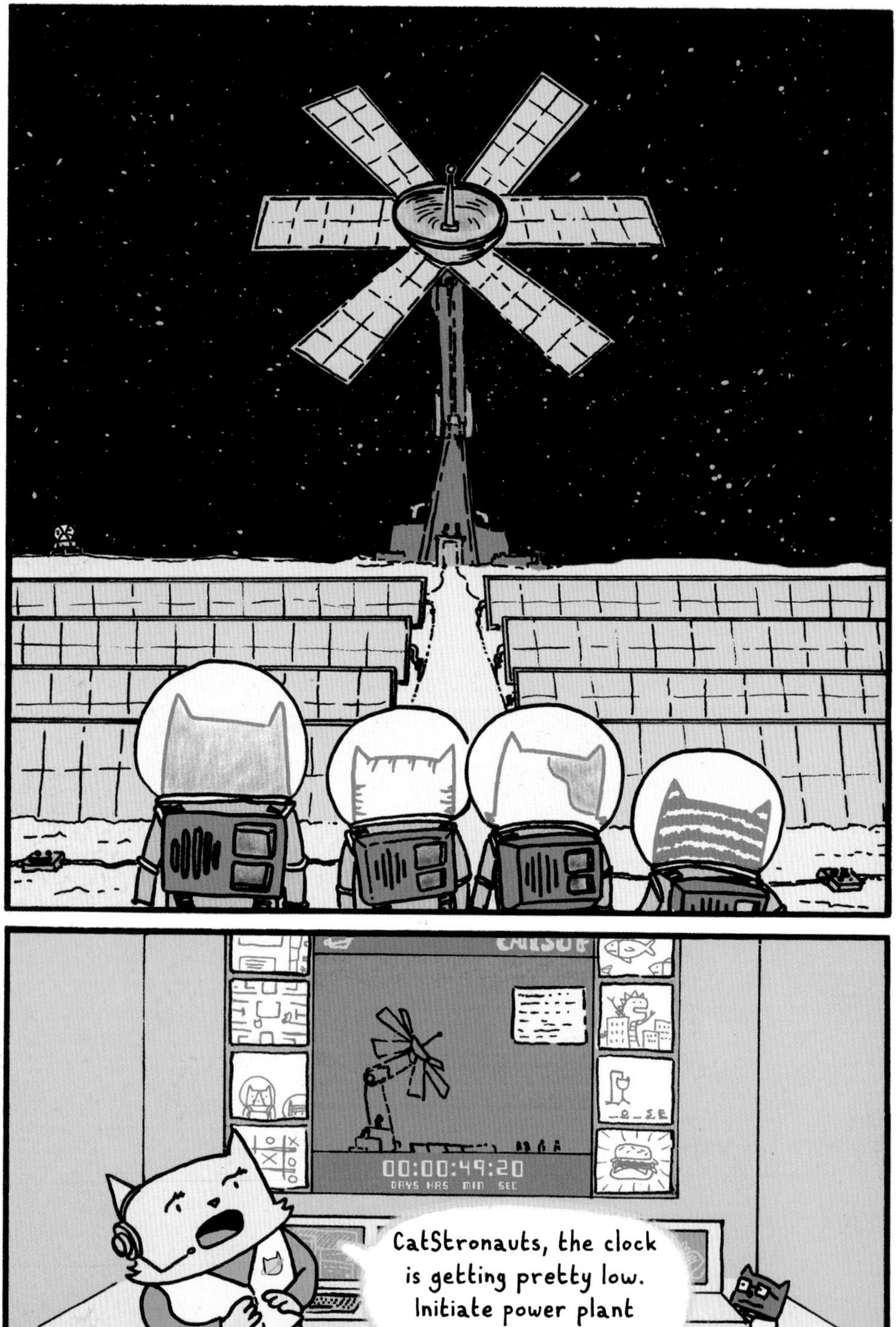
00:00:49:20
DAYS HRS MIN SEC
CatStronauts, the clock is getting pretty low. Initiate power plant power-up sequence.

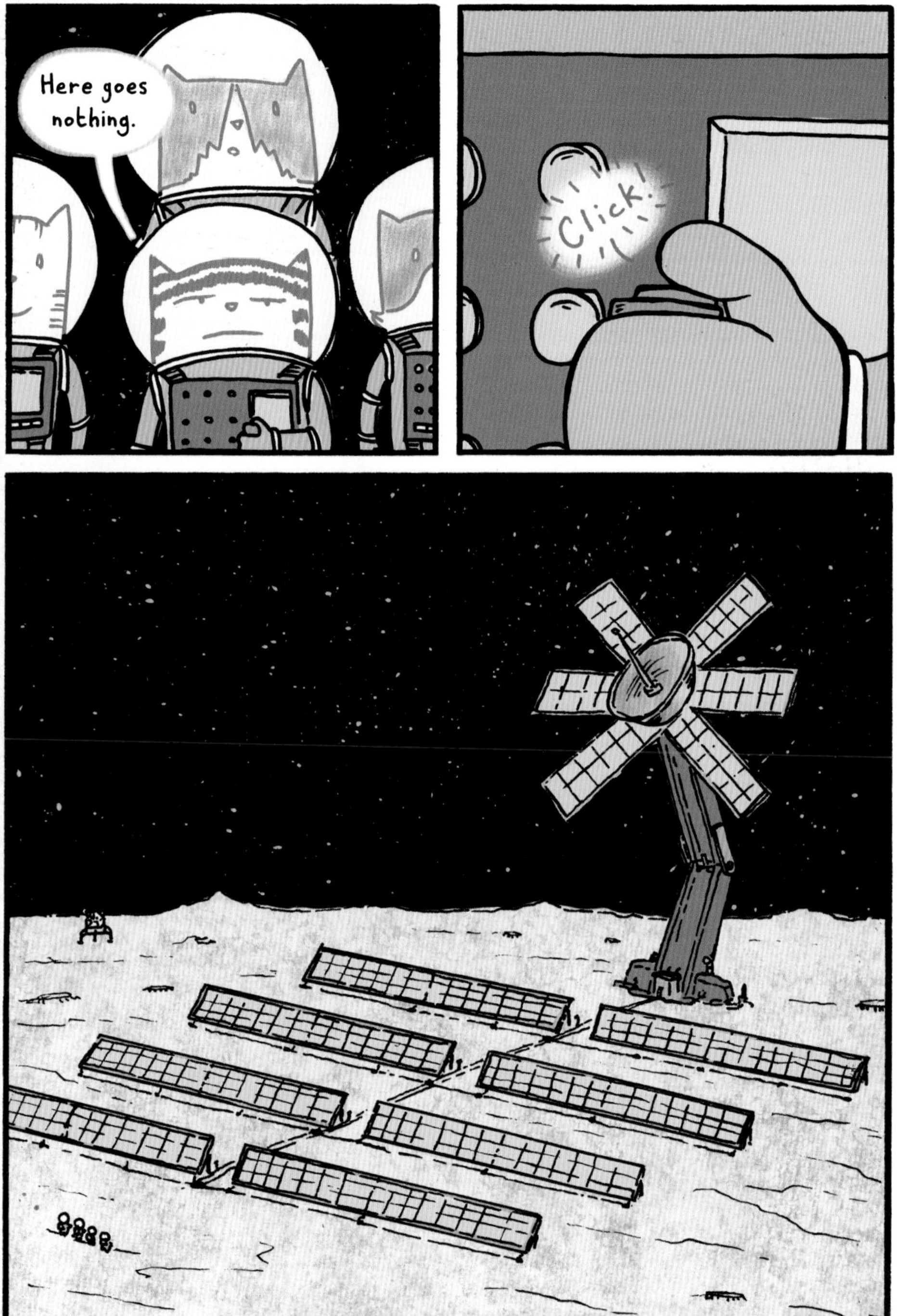
Here goes nothing.
Click!

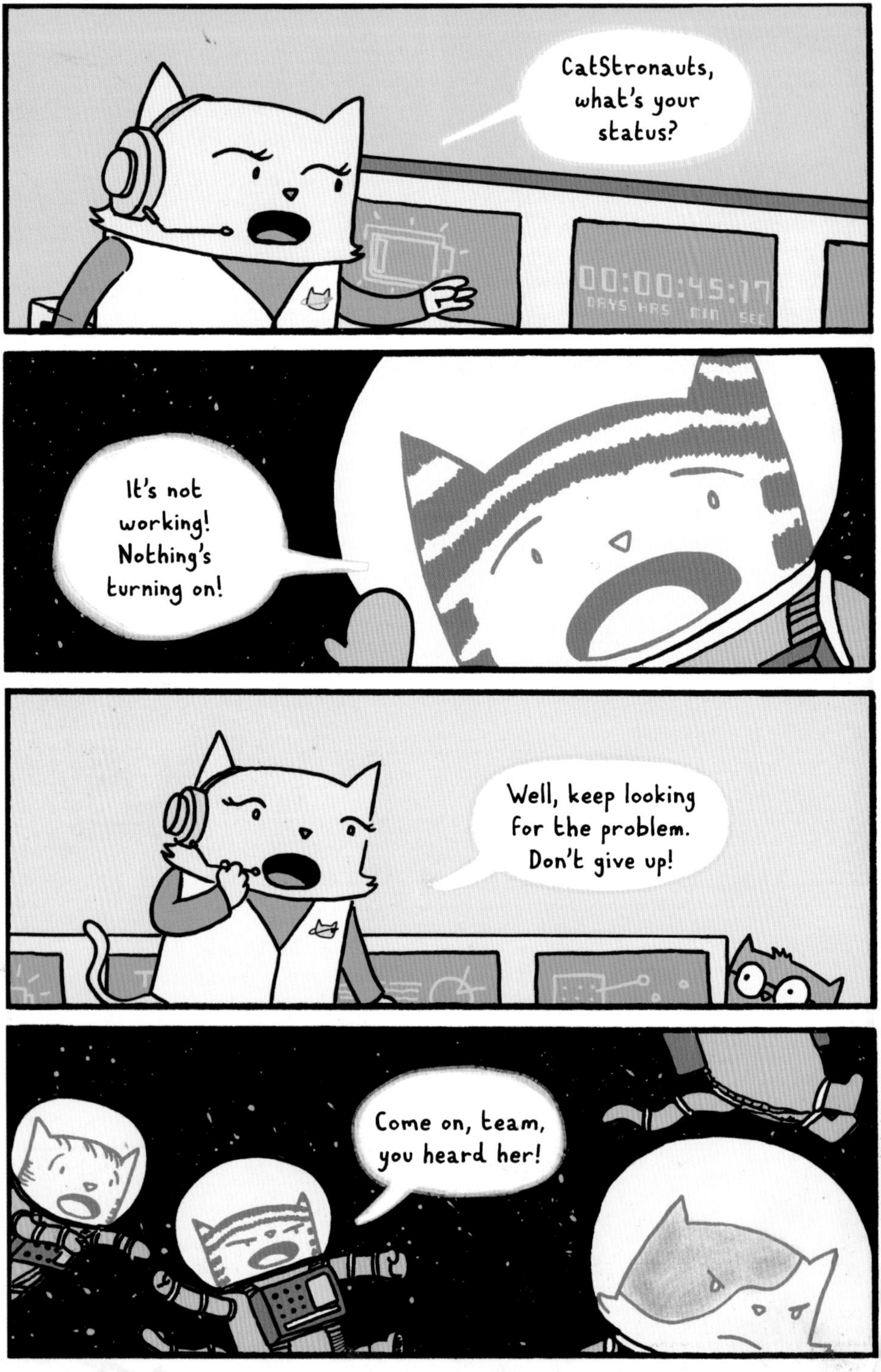
CatStronauts, what's your status?
00:00:45:17
DAYS HRS MIN SEC
It's not working! Nothing's turning on!
Well, keep looking for the problem. Don't give up!
Come on, team, you heard her!

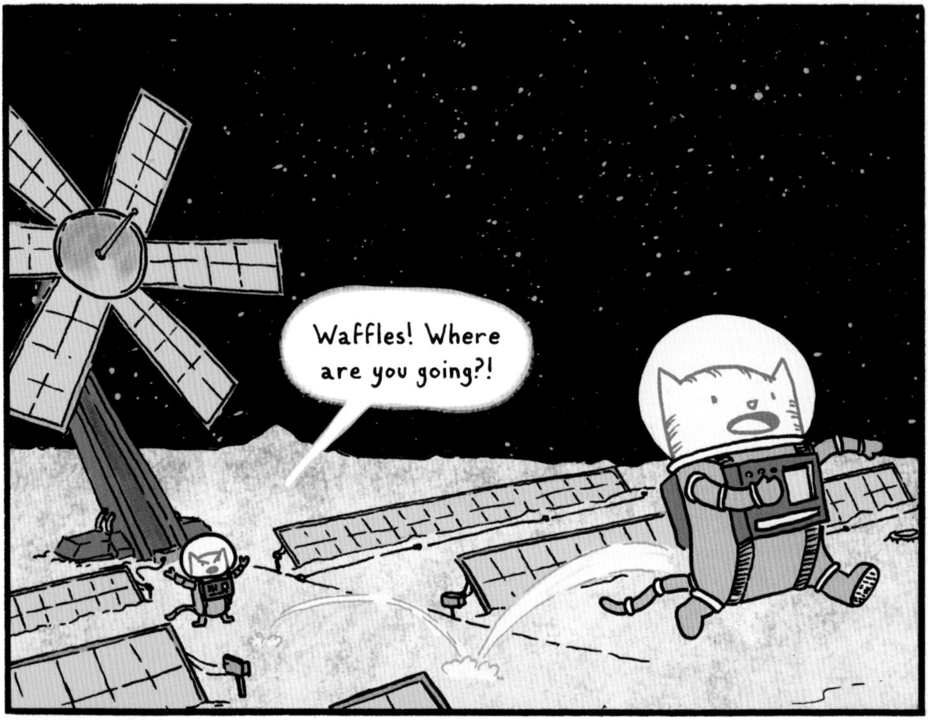
Waffles! Where are you going?!

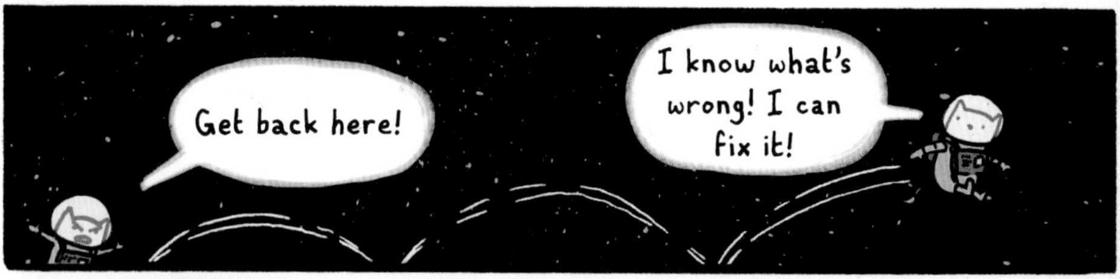
Get back here!
I know what's wrong! I can fix it!

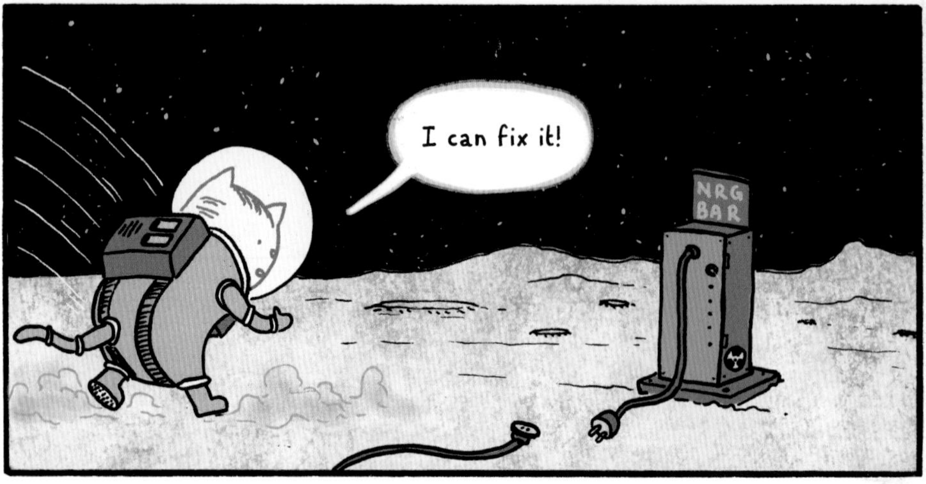
I can fix it!
NRG BAR

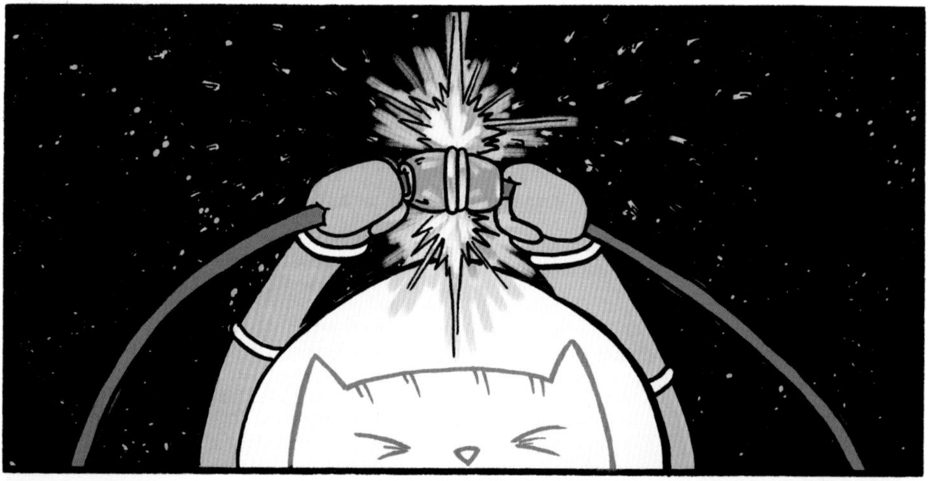

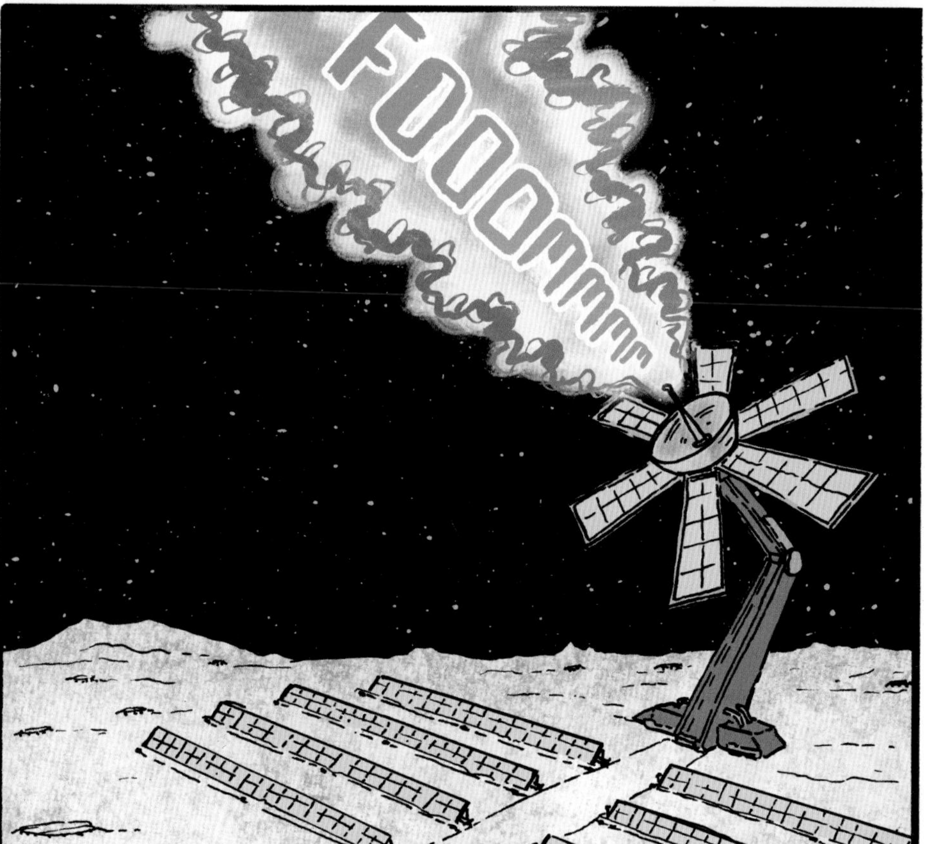
FOOOMMMMM

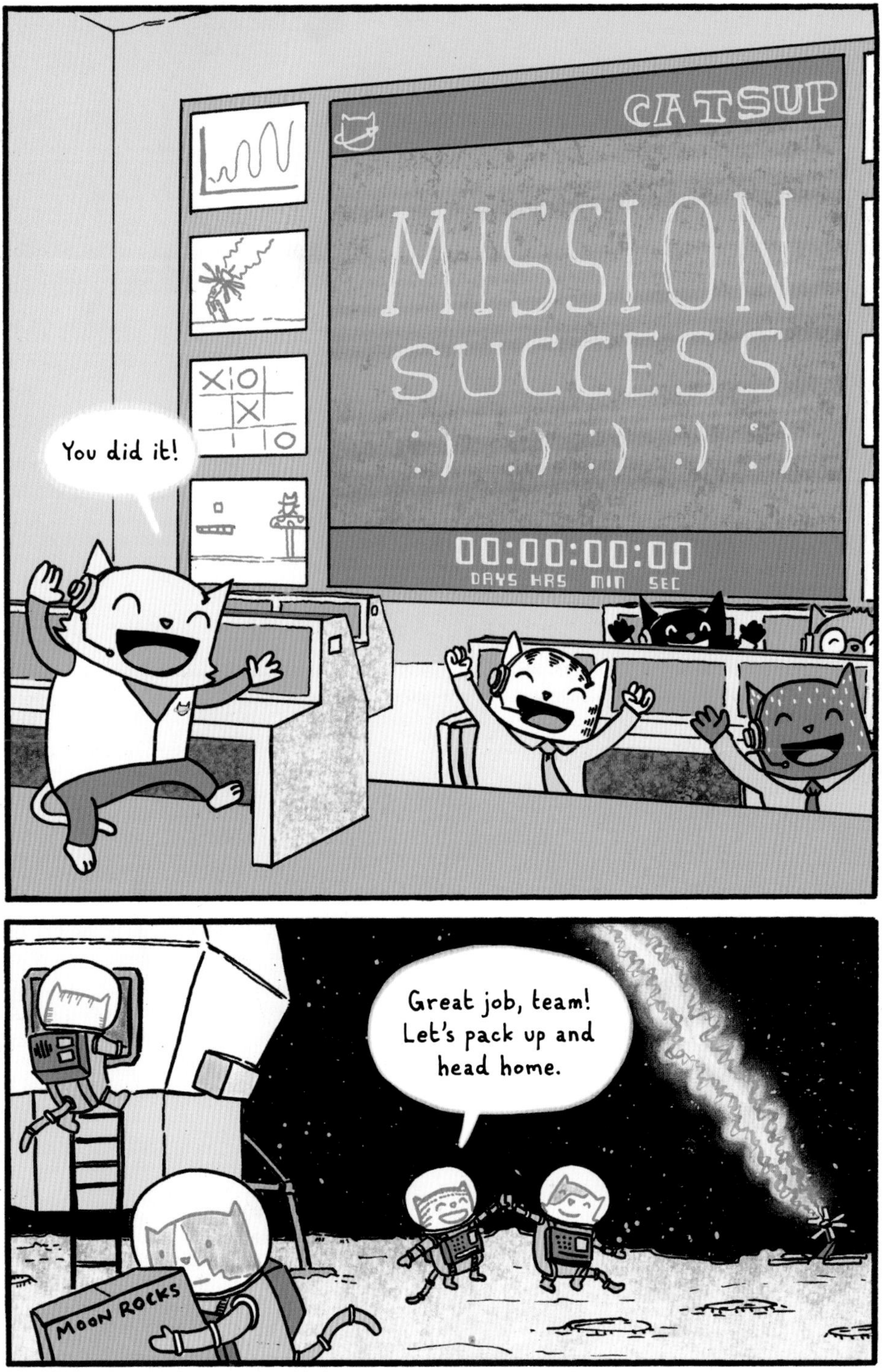
CATSUP
MISSION SUCCESS
:) :) :) :) :)
00:00:00:00
DAYS HRS MIN SEC
You did it!
Great job, team! Let's pack up and head home.
MOON ROCKS

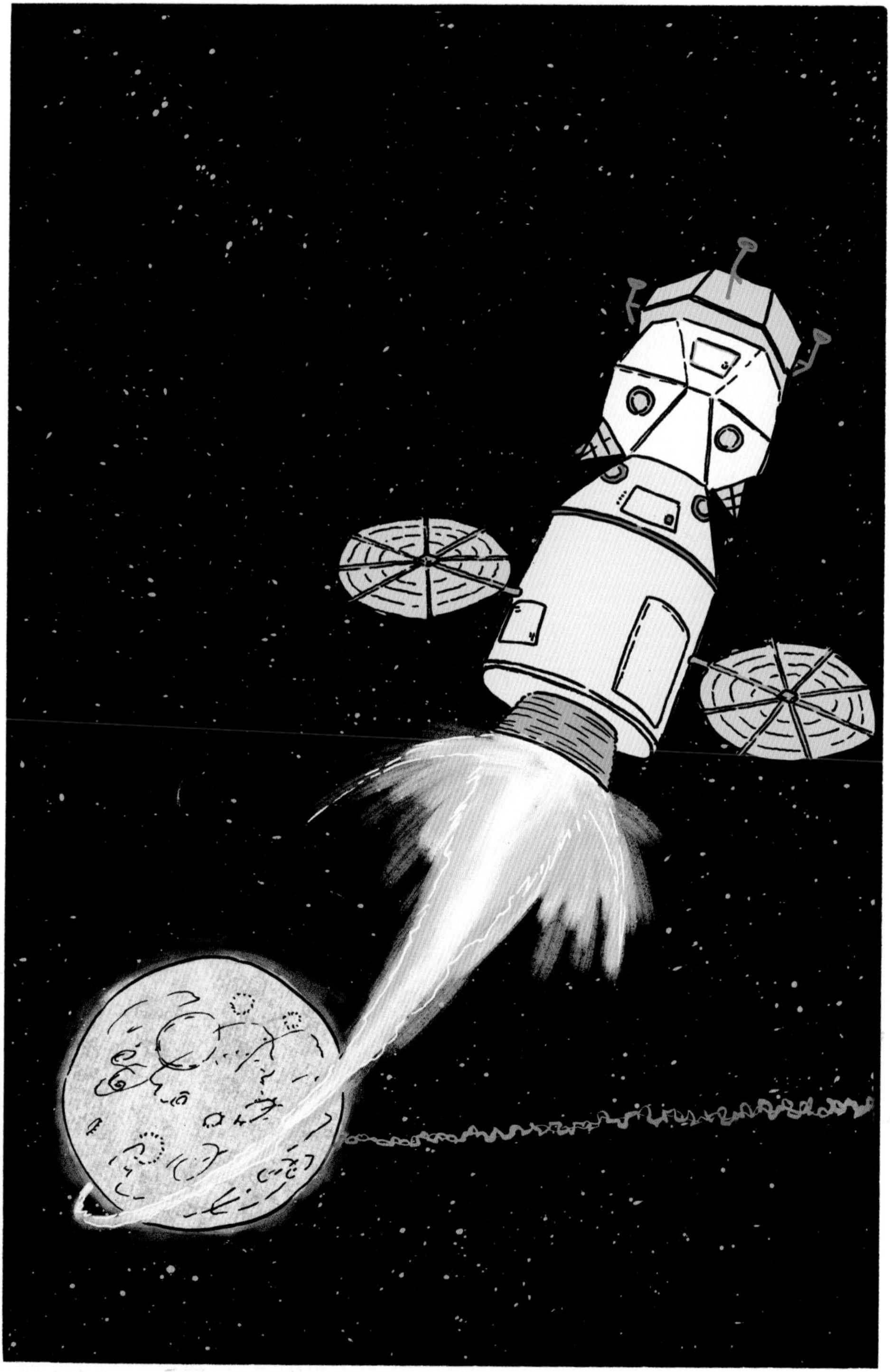

CHAPTER 9

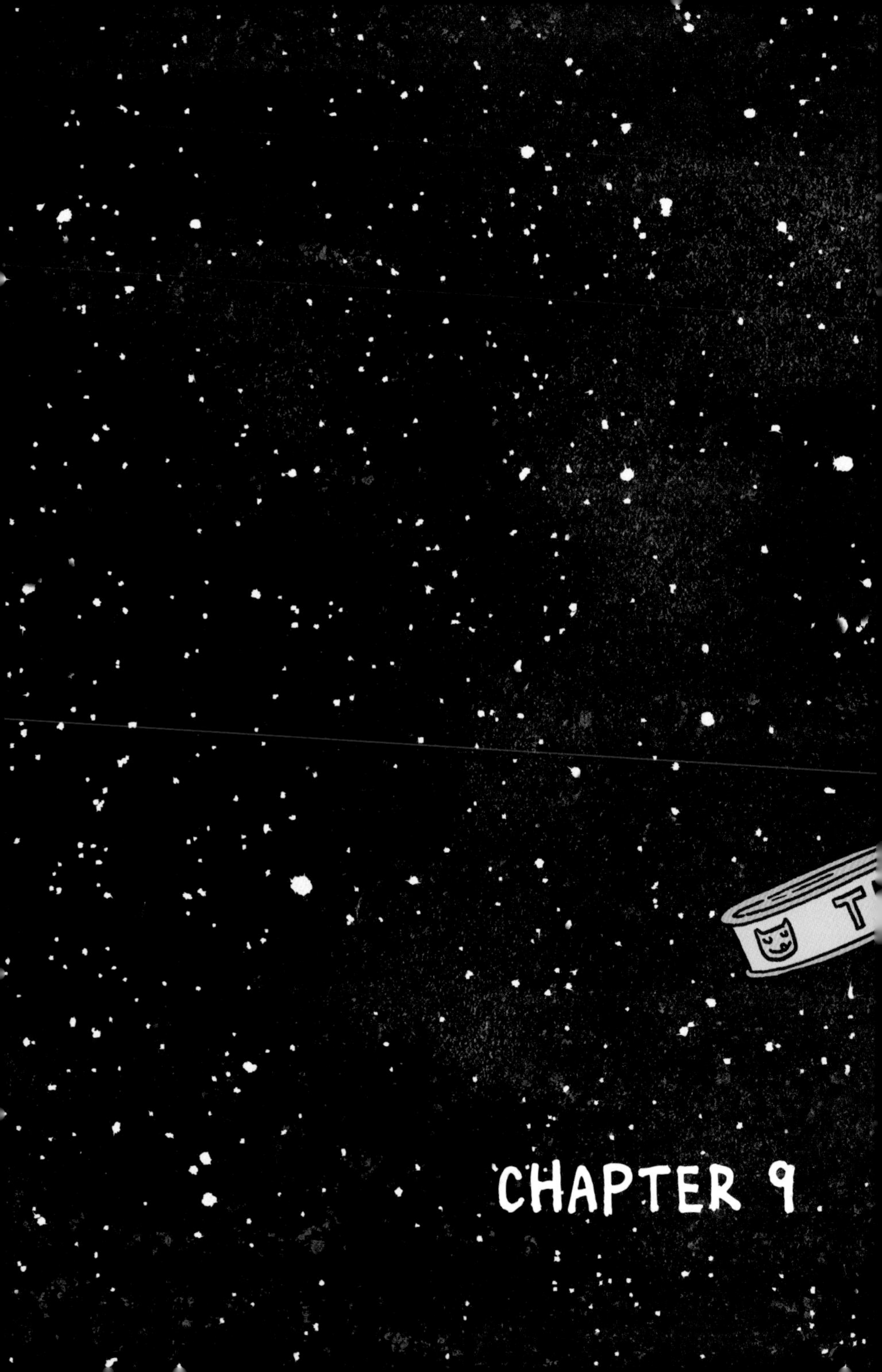

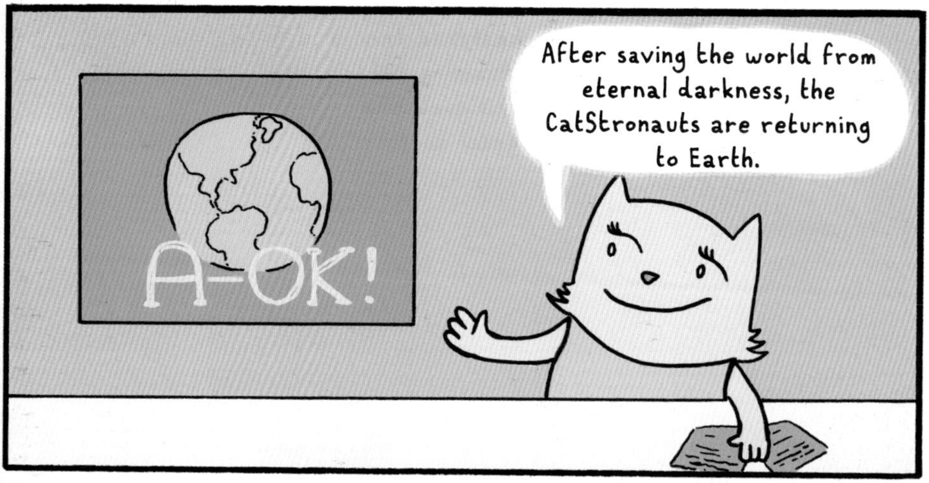
A-OK!
After saving the world from eternal darkness, the CatStronauts are returning to Earth.

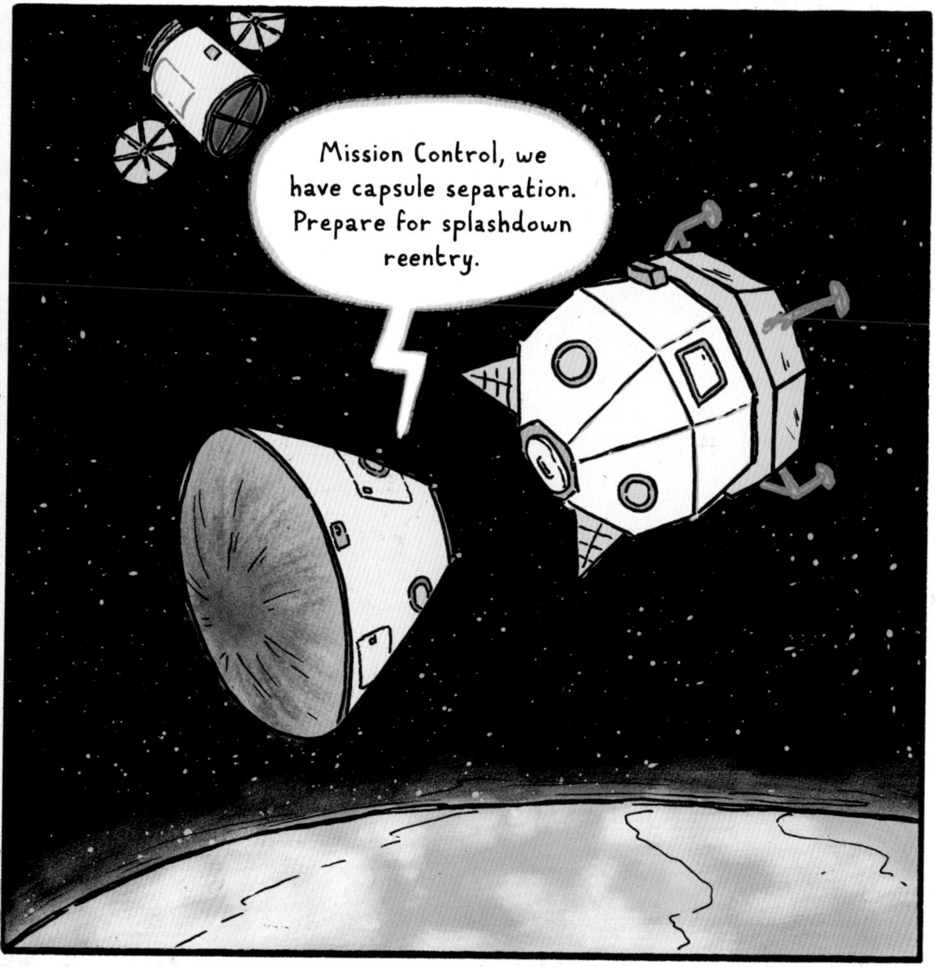
Mission Control, we have capsule separation. Prepare for splashdown reentry.

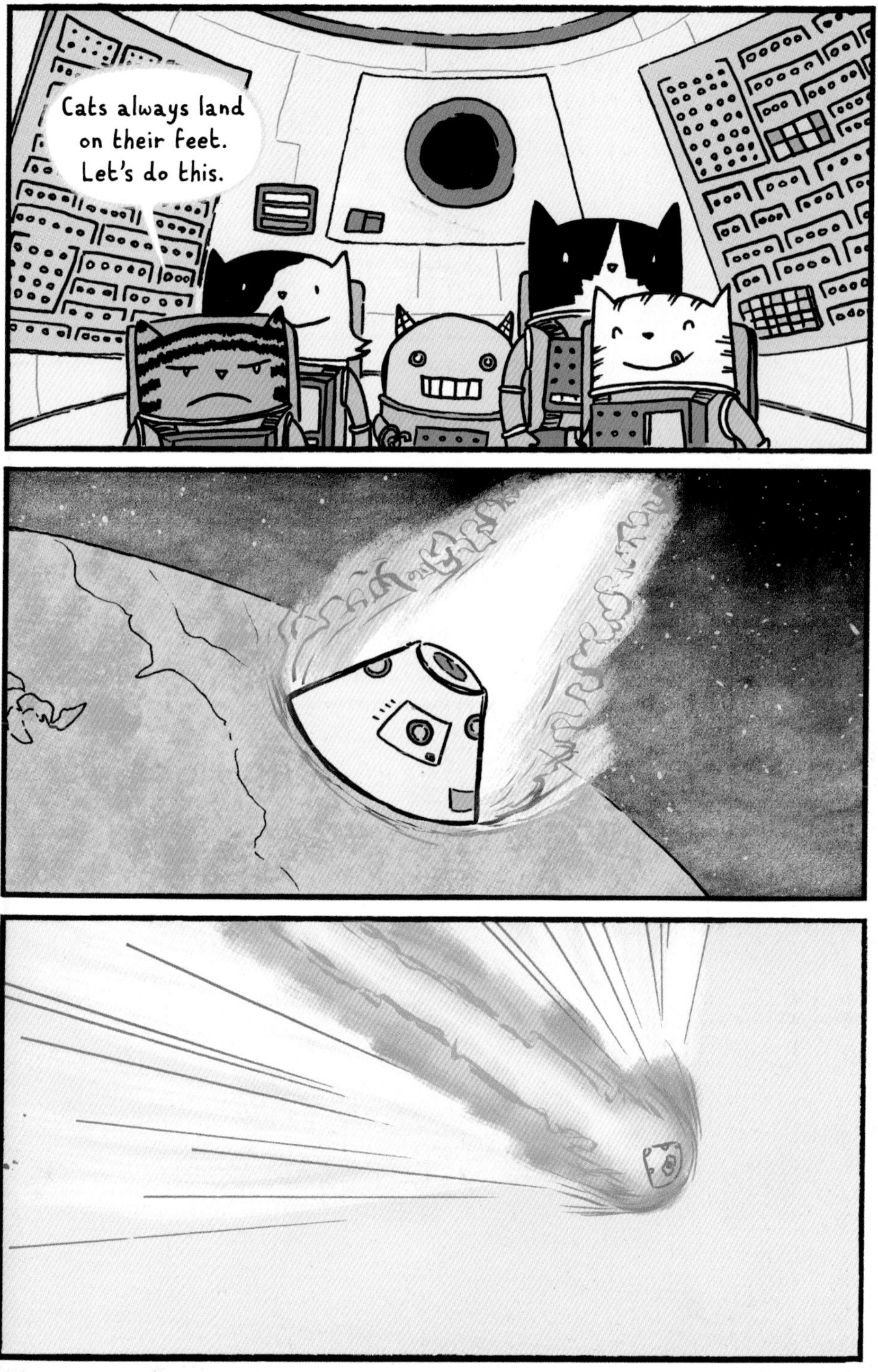
Cats always land on their feet. Let's do this.

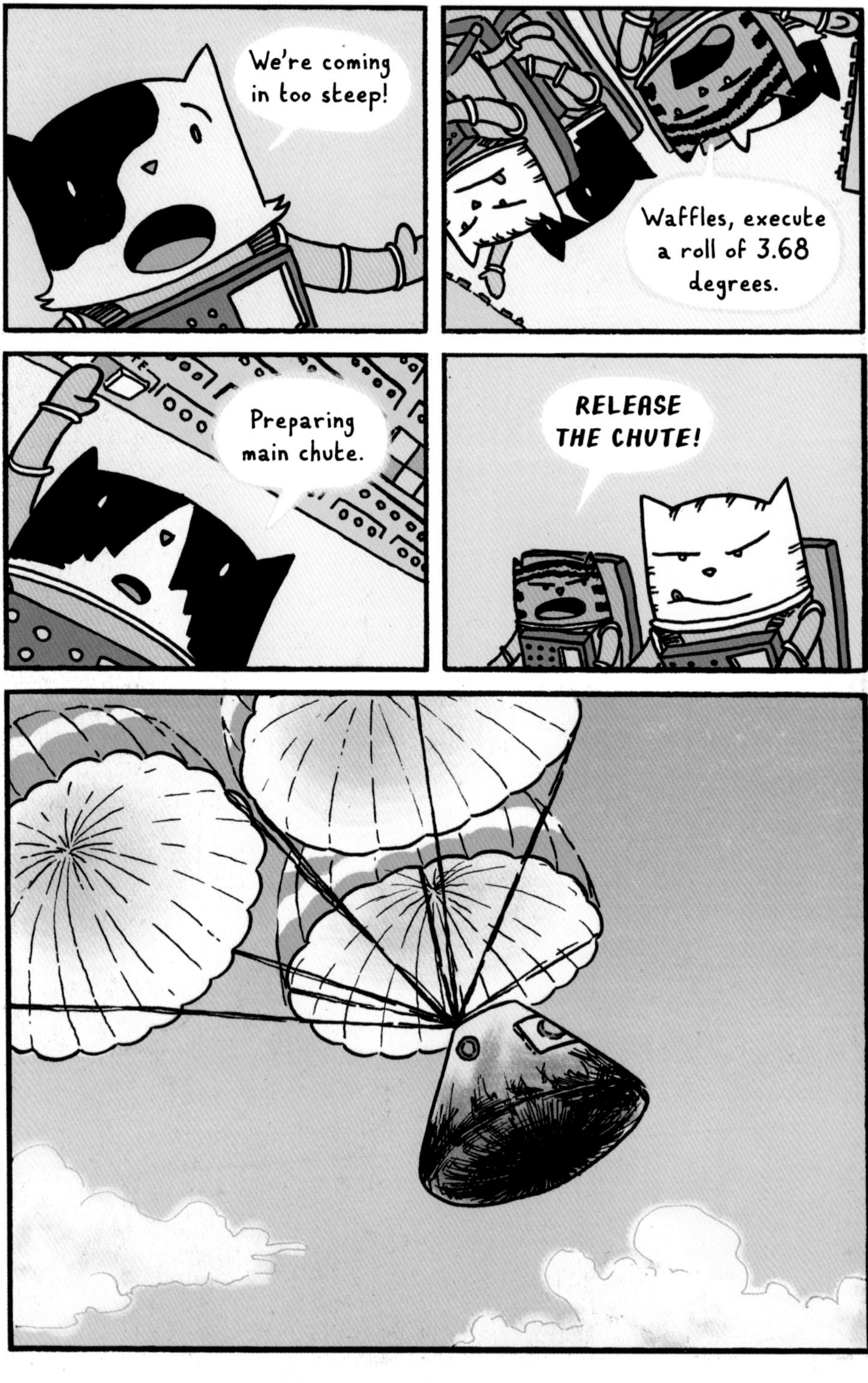
We're coming in too steep!
Waffles, execute a roll of 3.68 degrees.
Preparing main chute.
RELEASE THE CHUTE!

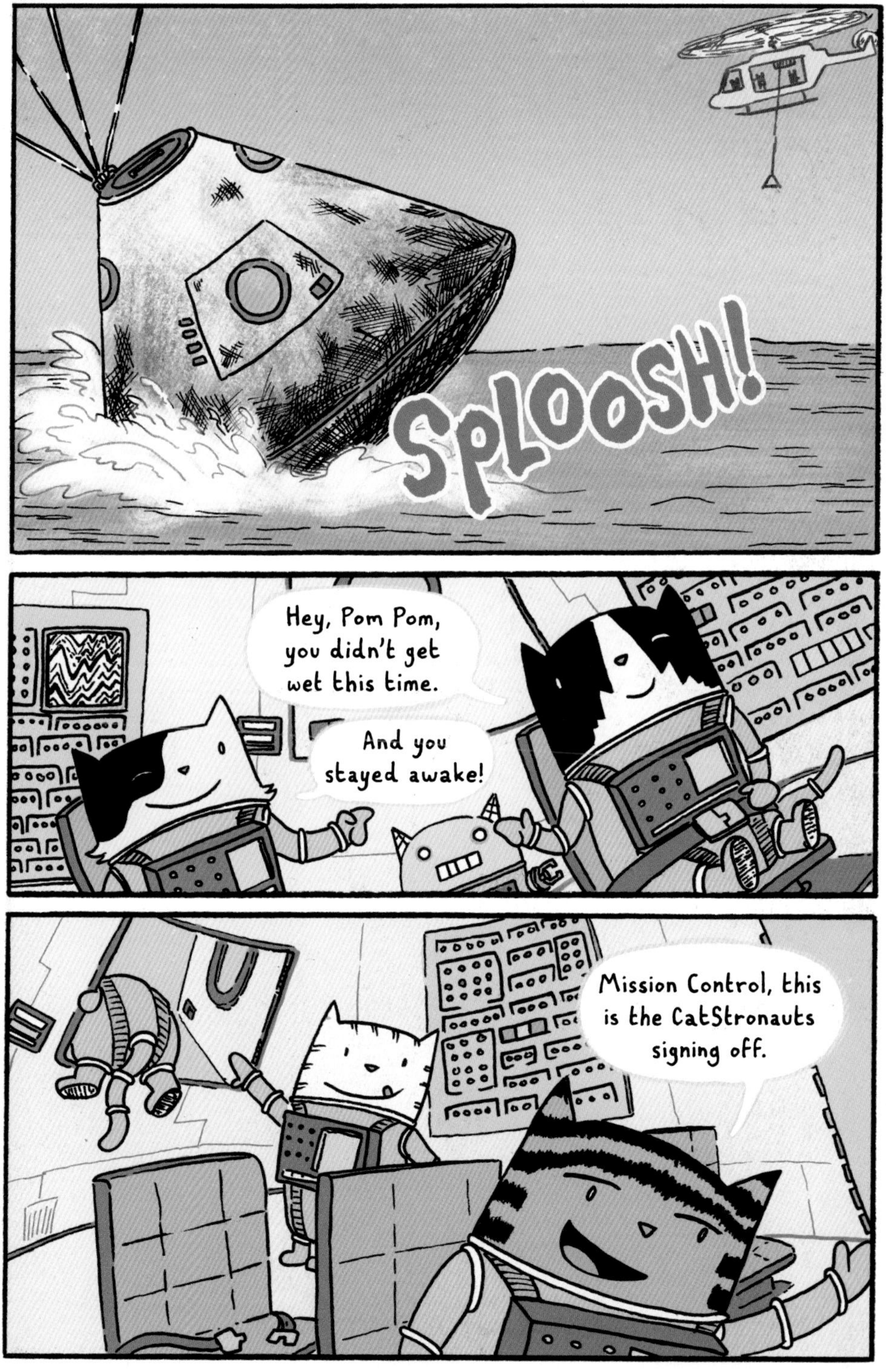
SPLOOSH!
Hey, Pom Pom, you didn't get wet this time.
And you stayed awake!
Mission Control, this is the CatStronauts signing off.

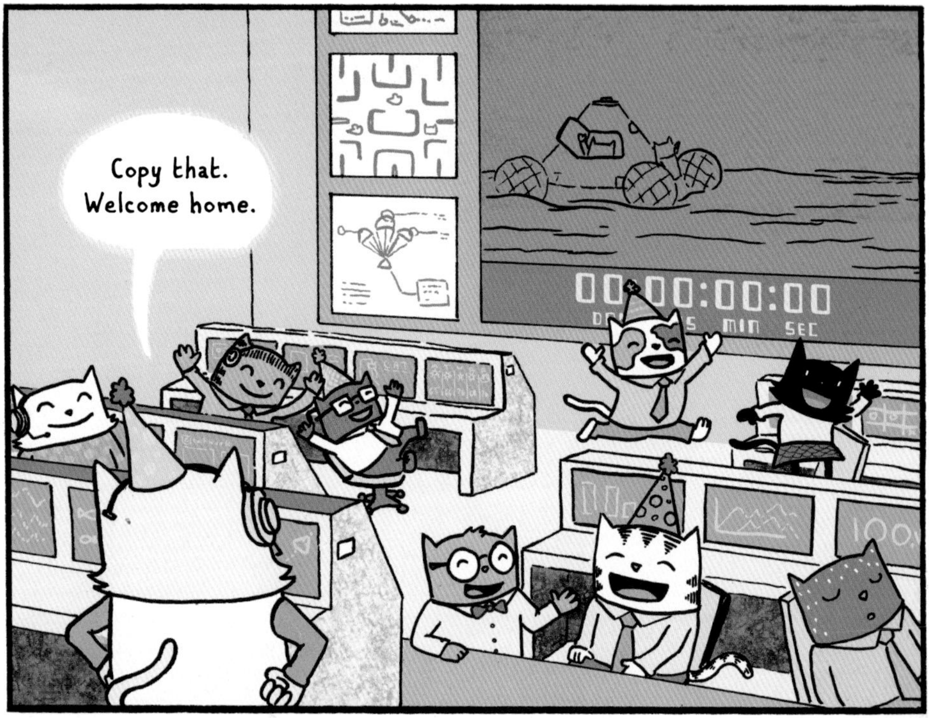
Copy that. Welcome home.
00:00:00:00
MIN SEC

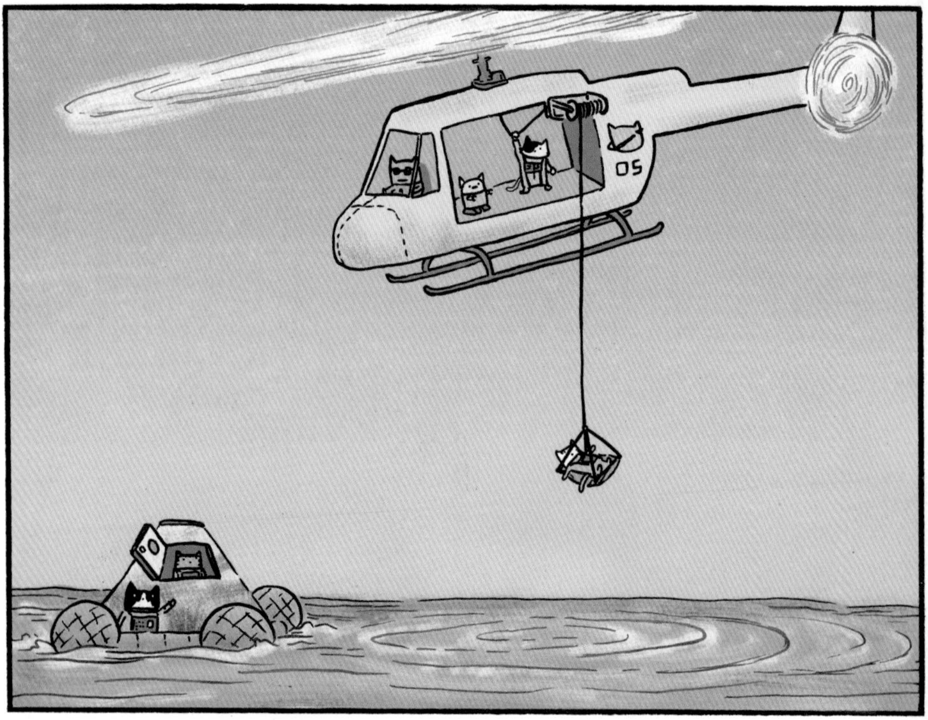
05

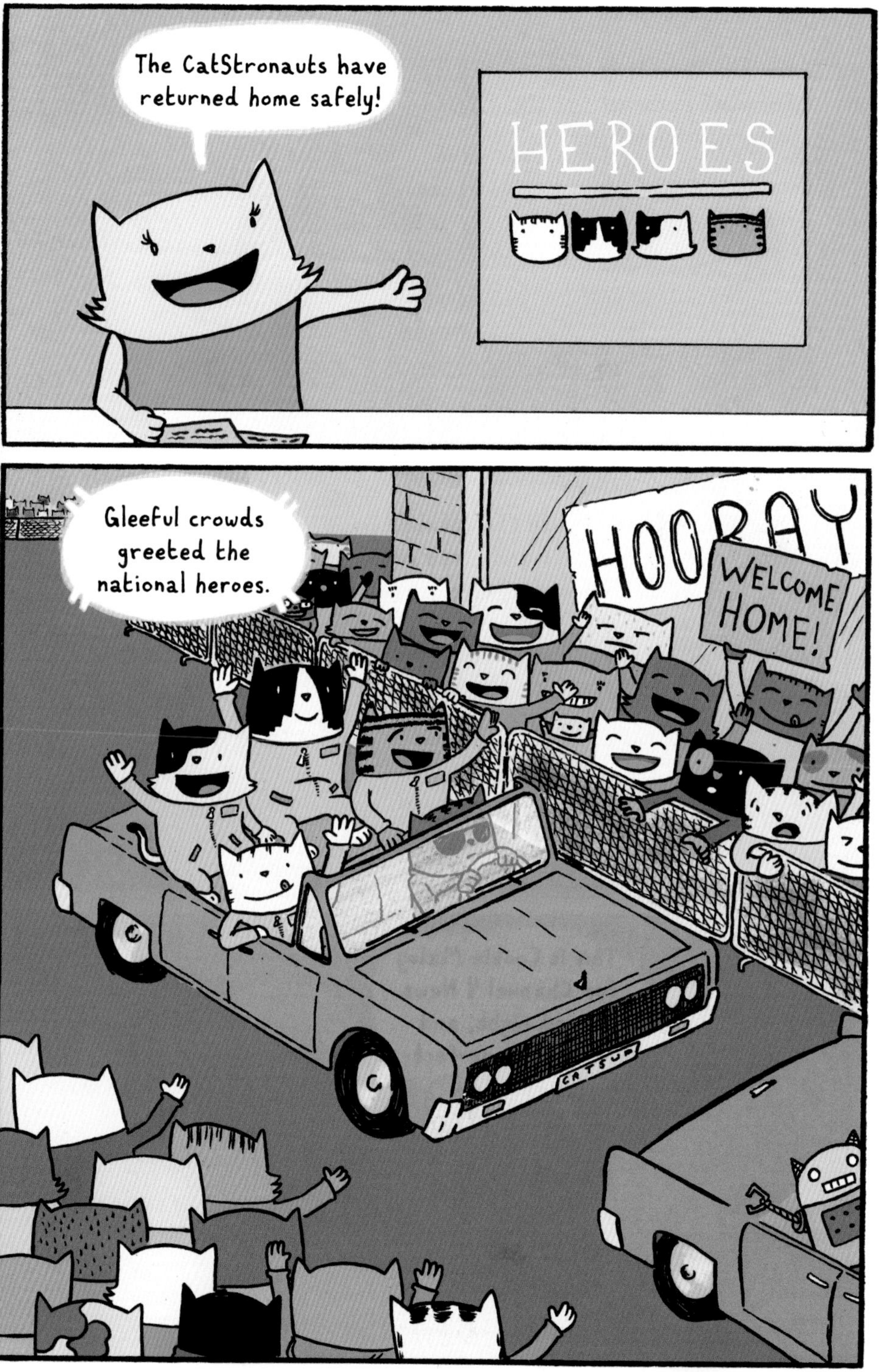

The CatStronauts have returned home safely!
HEROES
Gleeful crowds greeted the national heroes.
HOORAY
WELCOME HOME!
CATSUP

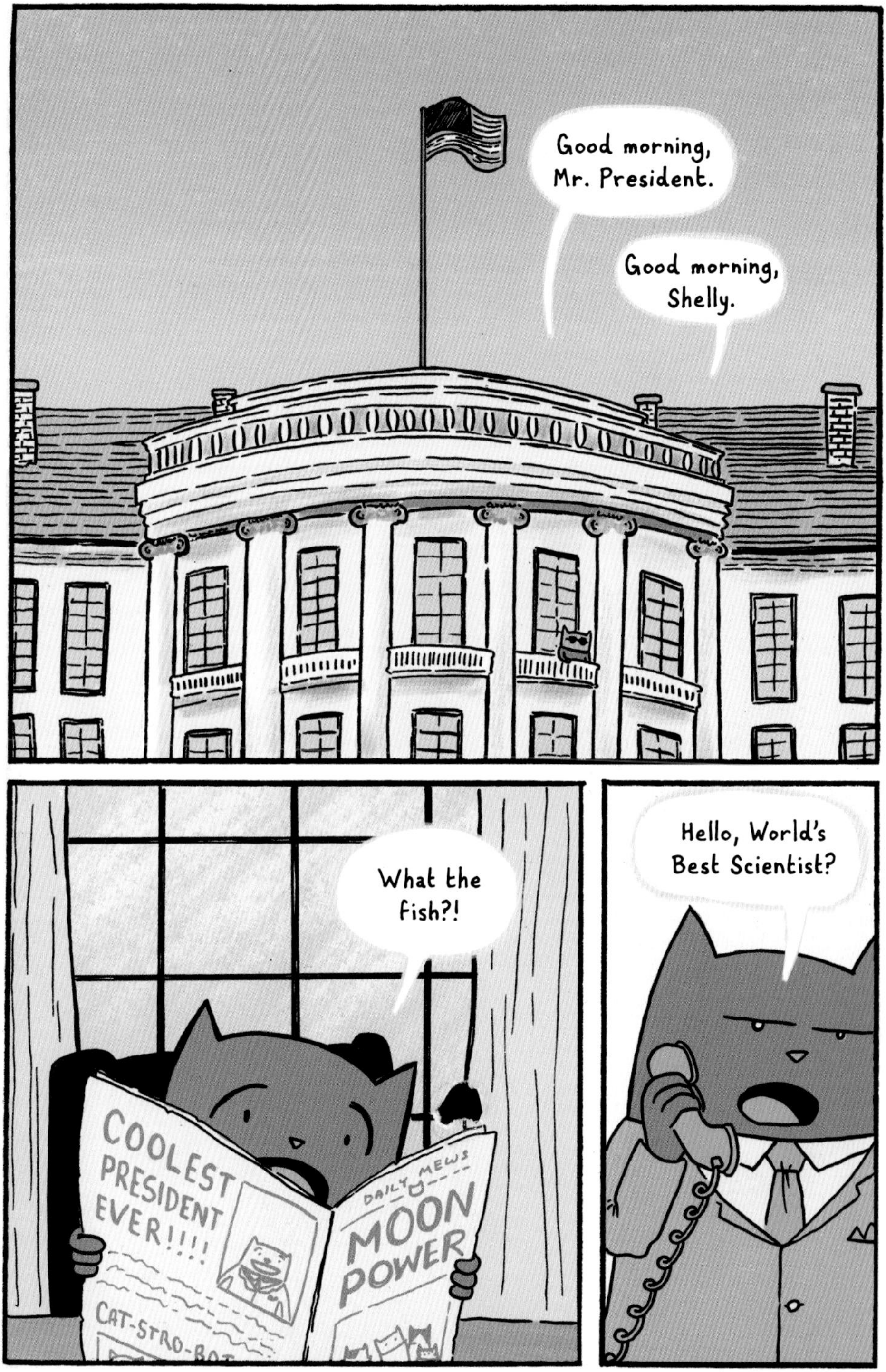
Good morning, Mr. President.
Good morning, Shelly.
What the fish?!
COOLEST PRESIDENT EVER!!!!
DAILY MEWS
MOON POWER
Hello, World's Best Scientist?

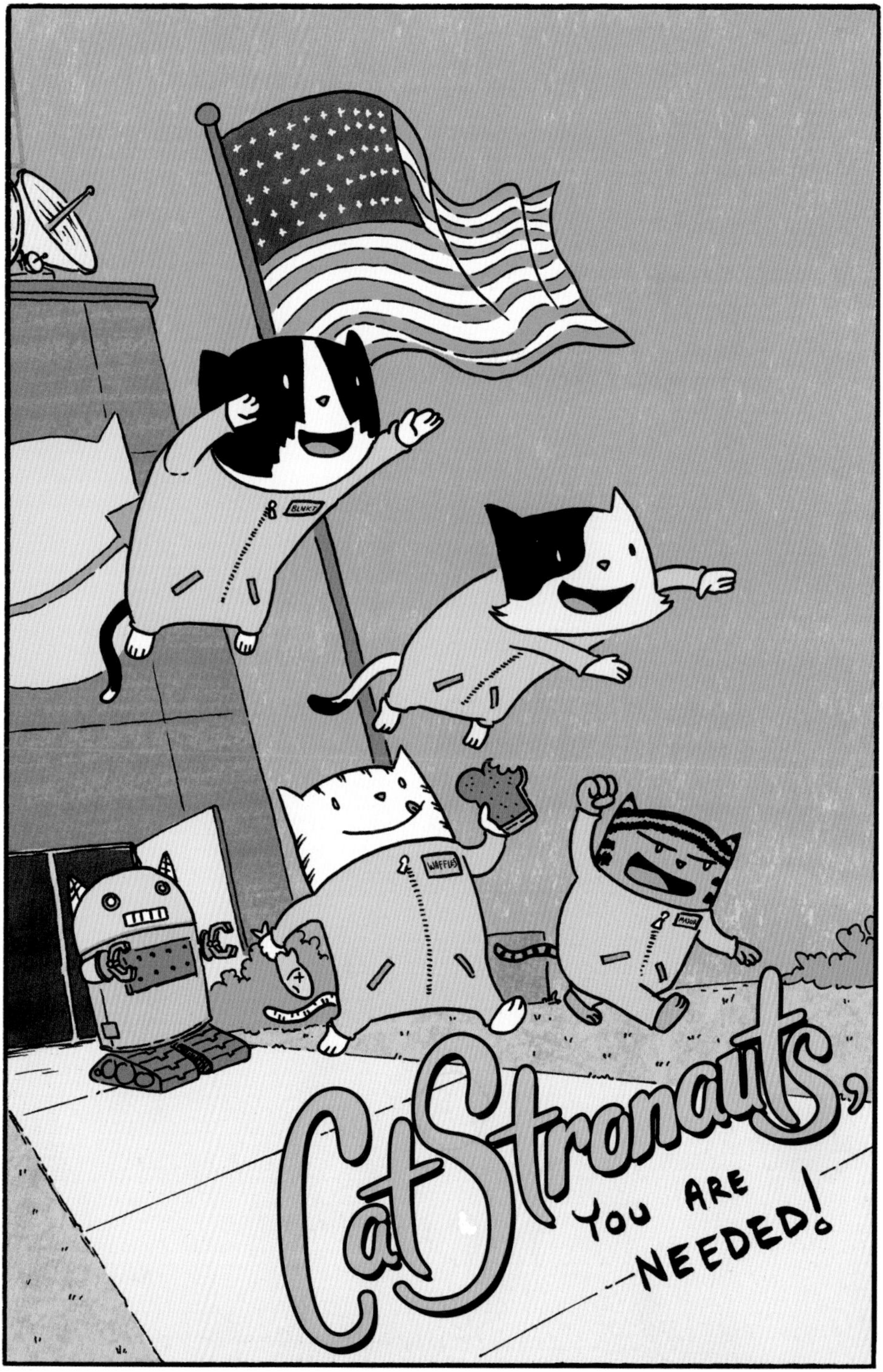
CatStronauts,
YOU ARE NEEDED!

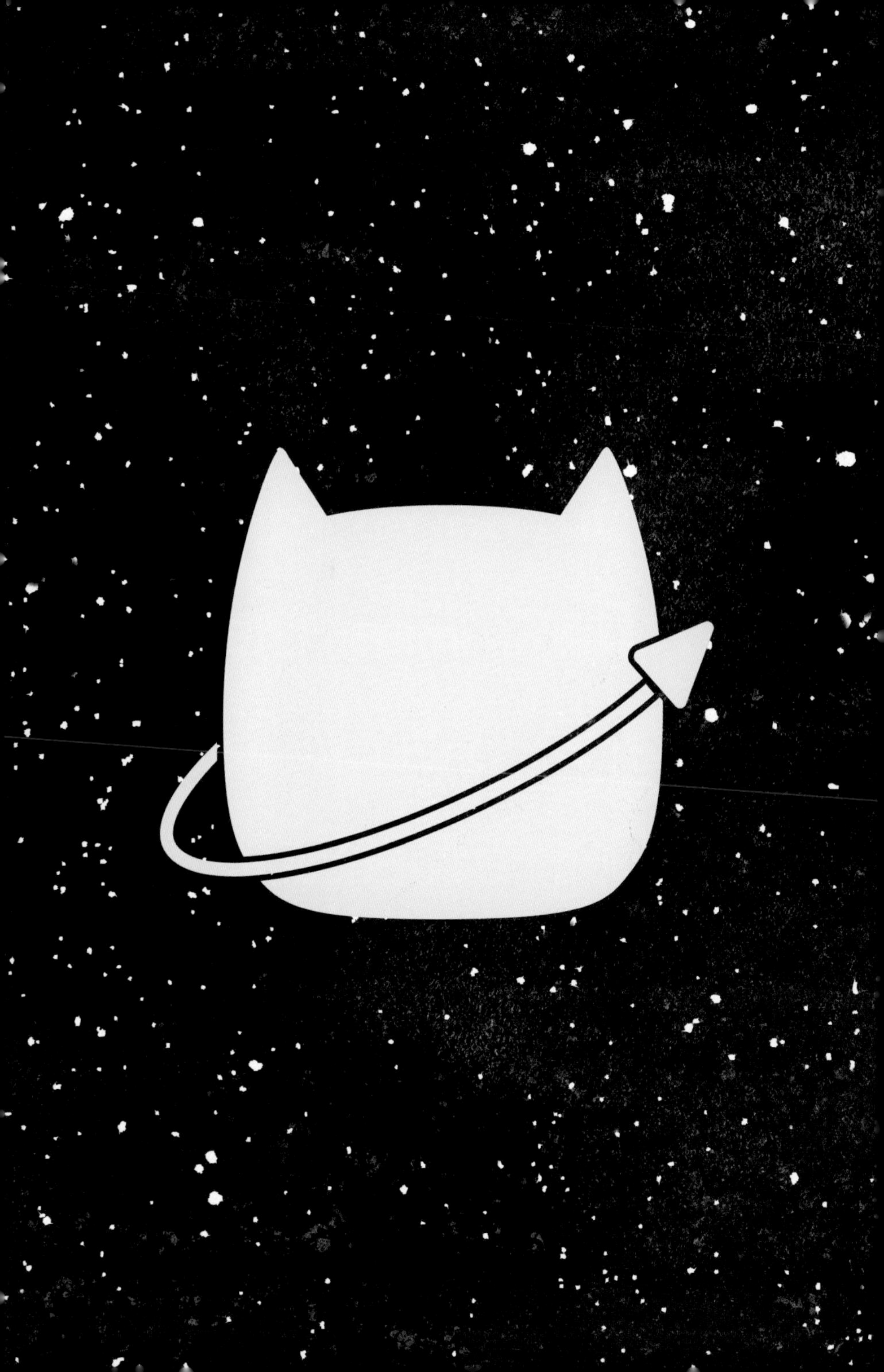

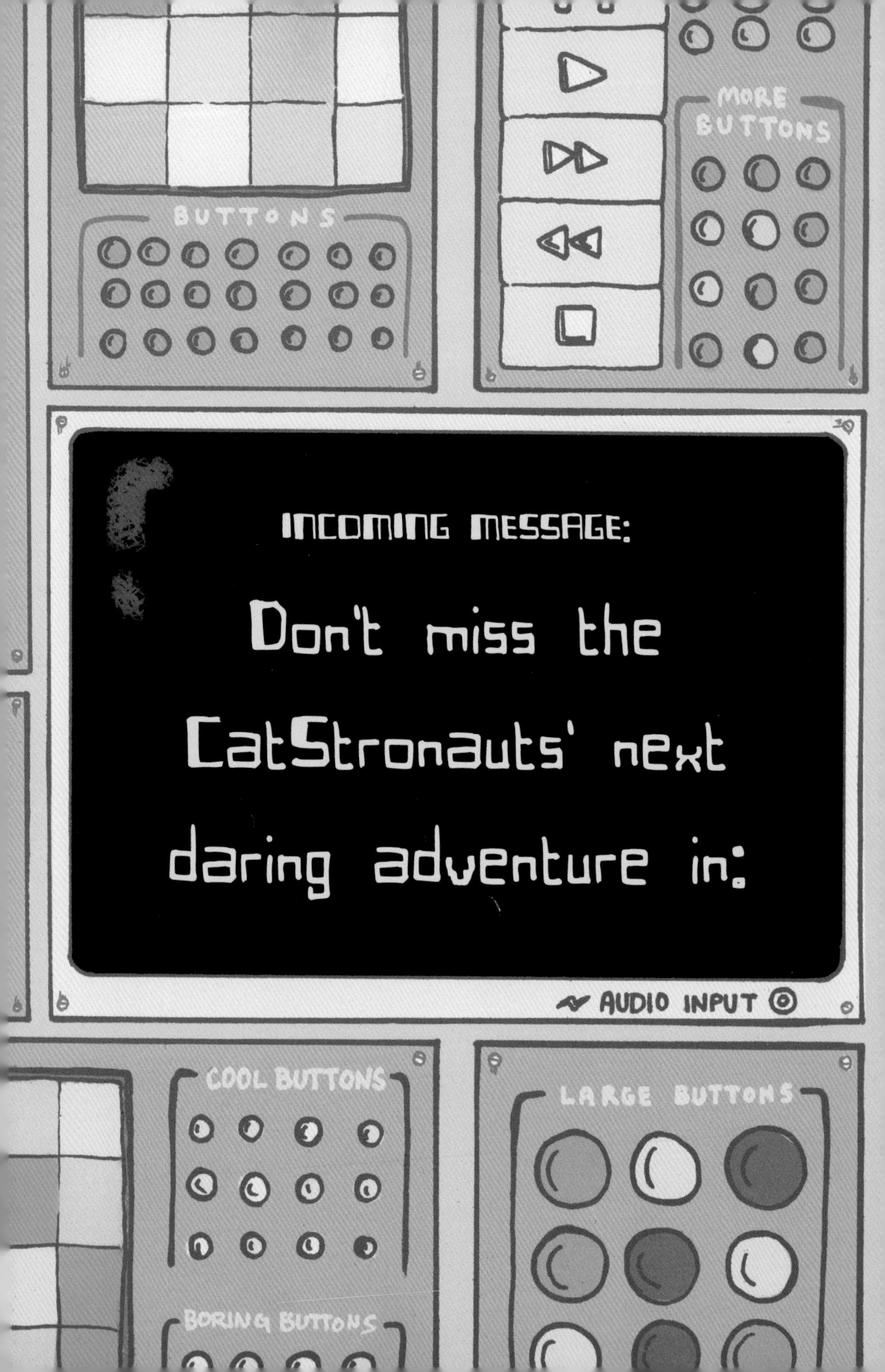
BUTTONS
MORE BUTTONS
INCOMING MESSAGE:
Don't miss the CatStronauts' next daring adventure in:
AUDIO INPUT
COOL BUTTONS
LARGE BUTTONS
BORING BUTTONS

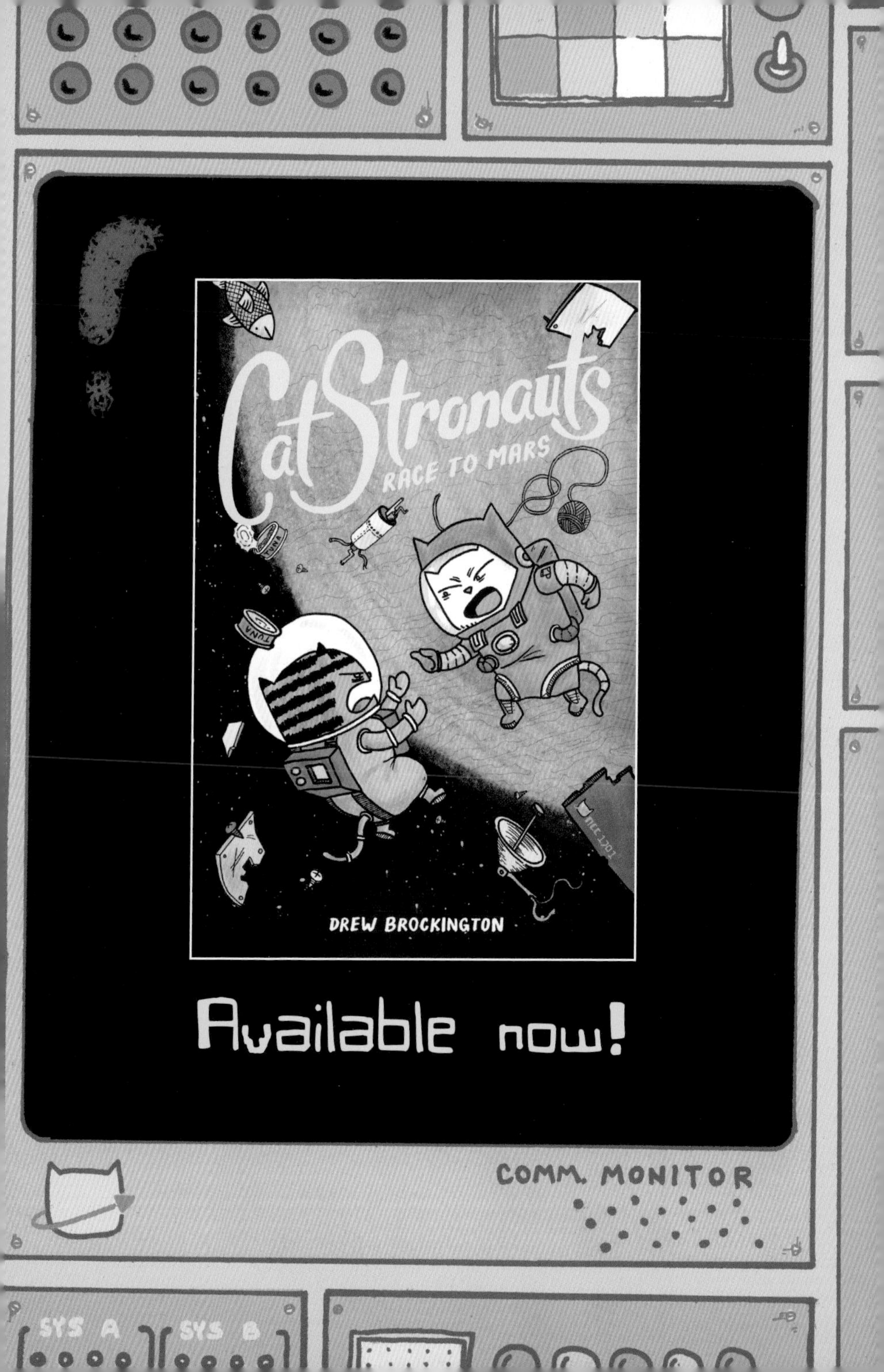
CatStronauts
RACE TO MARS
DREW BROCKINGTON
Available now!
COMM. MONITOR
SYS A
SYS B

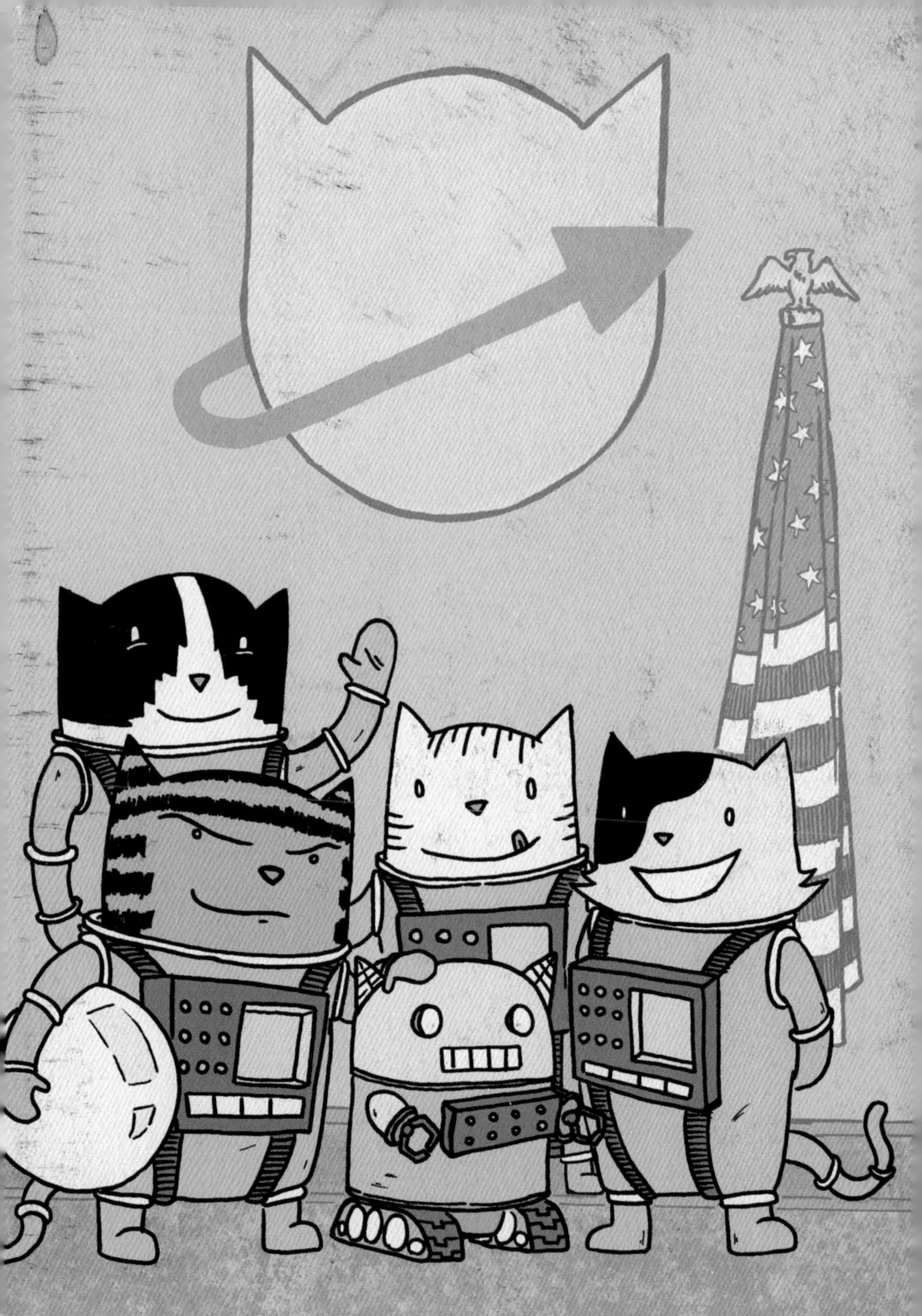

CatStronauts, Mission Moon

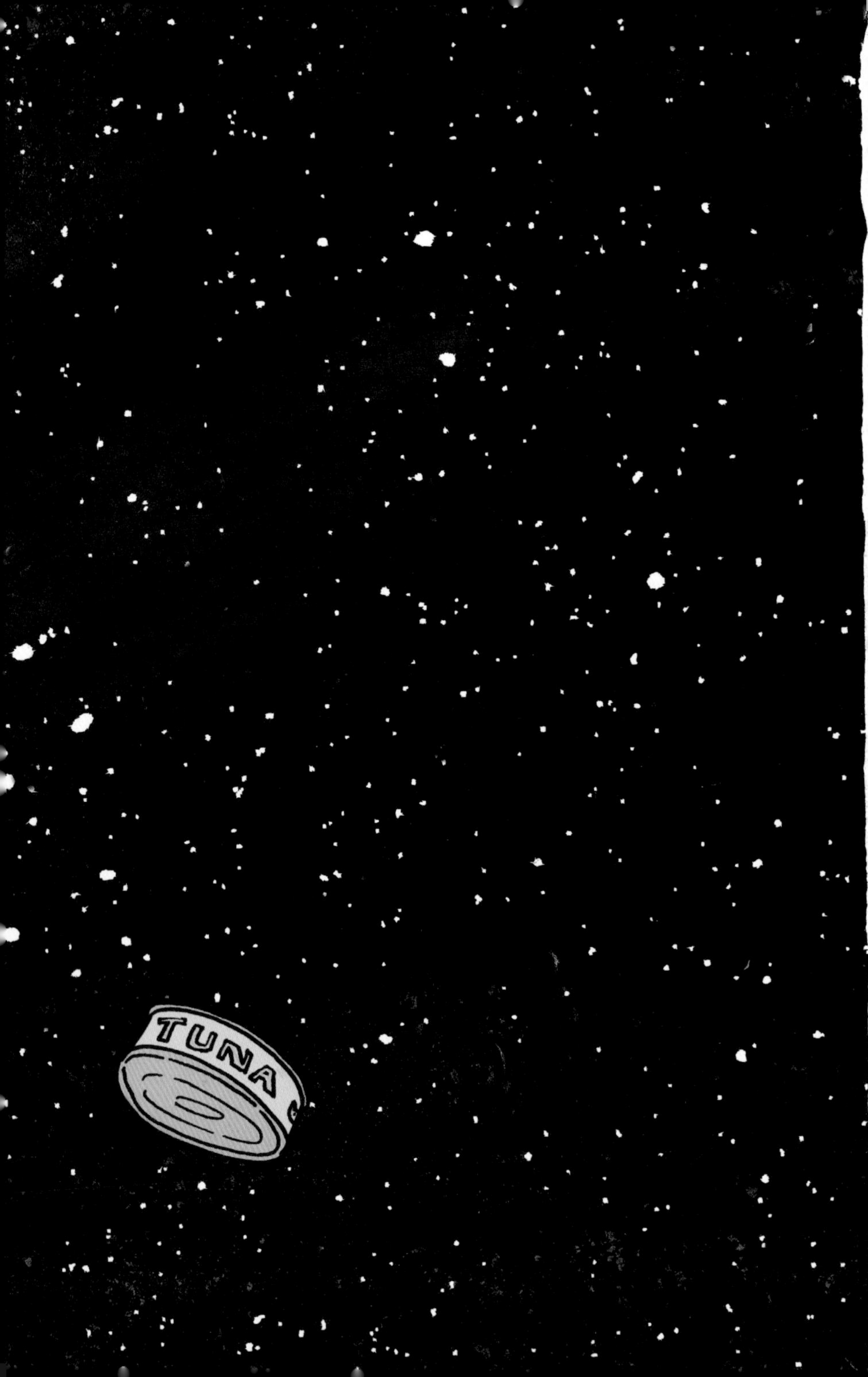
TUNA

TUNA

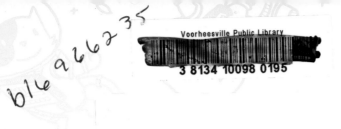